I0546098

IMMORTAL VICTORY

AN IMMORTAL STORY OF TRUE LOVE, SEX, AND DANGER

The Immortal Stories Series

Book 4

by

Linda Ashton Trott

Tagger Press

Copyright

ISBN-13: 978-1-7782949-1-4

Cover design by: 100COVERS

First Edition, August 2022

Adult Content, 18+

Dedication

I am dedicating this book to my husband, who without, it would have been impossible to complete this work.

A huge thank you to Lee Burton for being my editor. I am still learning.

Thank you as well, for purchasing this book. I hope you enjoy it! If you do, don't forget to leave a review.

Contents

What You Missed

Book 3 - Immortal Peril

- Lora went to a masquerade ball in Atlanta
- Justin and Rick had a big New Year's Eve party
- Falon starts exhibiting immortal characteristics
- Rick joins Lora in Montreal for a re-do of St. Patrick's Day
- Lora figures out Rick is supernatural
- Lora started researching at the Occult Store
- Falon started working in Kansas
- Mark gave Falon 'super' lessons
- Mark was kidnapped and interrogated by the council
- Lora's research discovers the immortals' origin
- Falon is attacked in Kansas and nearly raped
- Rick comes to Montreal to help Lora with research
- Mark escapes only to discover Falon was taken
- Falon is trapped in a building during a tornado

1- Rescued!

—Falon

I came back to consciousness like coming out of a very deep sleep. You know that point at which the dream you've been having ceases to feel like a dream and you know that you've been asleep? It feels like it should be dark but light is coming through your eyelids.

The last place I remembered flashed through my mind: hiding under an upside-down sofa, being buried alive by a building.

My eyes were closed. I didn't want to open them, so I kept them closed and took an inventory of my body, what I felt and heard.

I felt no pain. That was good, because my legs hurt like crazy before. Or maybe not good. *Am I alive?*

I didn't feel twisted in a strange position. That was also good.

I could hear voices! Lora and Mark talking quietly nearby. *I'm not buried anymore!*

Tears welled up in my eyes in gratitude for not being dead. Reflecting a moment on what happened, I realized my last week had been harrowing.

First, I got kidnapped and interrogated, then buried by a tornado. *Wait, where am I?*

I cracked my eyes open and saw I was in a hospital bed, machines and tubes all around me. *Hmmm.* This might not be a good thing either. *If I heal too quickly, that will expose my secret.*

I tried to speak but my throat was so dry that it came out as a rasp, barely loud enough for me to hear myself. I realized there was a device in my hand with a button on it. Probably a call button, but one that would call a nurse. I didn't want to do that.

While I was trying to figure out what to do, Lora popped her head around the doorjamb and looked in. When she saw my eyes were open, her face broke into a big grin. She walked toward me, pulling Mark by the sleeve behind her.

"Oh my Goddess, we were so worried!" she started. "But you're awake now, so we can get you out of here."

I tried to speak again, and Lora got the message. A straw was placed between my lips and I gratefully sucked on it until cool liquid poured into my mouth. I swirled it around some before swallowing to lubricate my tongue.

"I'm so glad to see you!" I blurted out. Tears, again welling in my eyes, spilled over and ran down my face into my ears. Lora wiped them away.

"You're all right now. We've got you."

"Mark, you escaped!" I whispered.

"Yes, and when I got back here you were missing," he said. "I called Lora, and she got on the next flight down here to help me."

"I still can't believe I survived the tornado," I said. "I absolutely thought I was going to die there, buried under ceiling tiles and concrete." I shuddered with the memory.

"The firefighters who rescued you were the heroes," said Lora. "They found you buried under an entire building. Somehow a sofa was enough to keep you alive and give you enough air that you survived until they found you."

"I know I'm immortal," I whispered. "But that's still new. I don't instinctively think that way. When concrete buildings fell down on my head and I couldn't fight my way out, it was terrifying. I really thought I was going to die.

"I remember being in so much pain," I added. "I'm so grateful to the firefighters who risked their own lives to find me and rescue me."

"You're fine now," said Lora. "In fact, you're all healed, which is the problem. Mark and I were talking about it."

"How long have I been here?" I asked.

"Two days," said Lora. "You were brought in two days ago with crush injuries. They had to reset your legs and do some surgery to repair some internal damage."

"Was that necessary?" I asked.

"No, it wasn't," answered Mark. "At least not the surgery. Resetting your legs was, or they wouldn't have healed right."

"I need to leave here, don't I?"

"Yup, sooner than later," said Mark. "The doctors make their rounds at 10:00 a.m. If they discover that the surgical site is gone and that the bones have healed, they'll be doing more tests … and we don't want that."

"What time is it?"

"It's coming on 7:30 a.m.," Lora answered. "So we have a little time to get you out of here."

"So what's the plan?" I asked.

"I'm going to insist that you be allowed to leave with me," said Mark. "I will tell them I have private nurses who can do the job better. I will get the papers for you to sign so that you can do so."

"Don't insult them, please," I said. "After all, they were the first responders who helped me."

"No, I'll be the arrogant rich prick and take the blame, don't worry."

"I've brought some clothes for you," said Lora. "You'll have to leave in a wheelchair because both your legs are in casts."

I looked down at my body and gasped at the fact that both my legs were encased in plaster.

"Geez, how did I not notice that?" I asked.

"Well, the fact that you're lying flat and not in pain would let your mind skip over that," said Mark.

"So, like I said, we take you out in a wheelchair," said Lora.

"What about my boss?"

"I've called him, and you'll be staying at the hotel and taking a few days off at least," said Mark. "I may even arrange for you to return home to Montreal to convalesce. We'll see."

"Mark, you go get those release papers and I'll get her dressed," said Lora.

"Come on, hun, I've got a dress for you to put on so we don't have to argue with the casts."

As we struggled to get me upright, at least enough to slip the dress over my head, Mark went and spoke to the woman at the nurses' station. I heard a heated argument, then calm voices. Mark returned a few minutes later.

"I had to use compulsion on her to give me the papers," said Mark. "They were not going to let me take you out of the hospital." He handed them to me. I signed them and gave them back.

"Is that going to be a problem?" I asked.

"I hope not," he said, walking away as he took the papers back to the nurses' station. By that time, Lora was back with a wheelchair. After Lora helped me out of my hospital gown and into the dress, Mark lifted me off the bed and set me down in the chair. That was easy. Lora scooped up all my tattered belongings that had been cut off me, plus the jewelry that had been removed when they brought me into Emergency, and put them all in a shopping bag.

"After you, sir," she said to Mark, with a smile.

Mark wheeled me out of the room, and the three of us moved down the corridor toward the elevator. The door opened, we got on and made it down to the hospital's main lobby. Crossing the lobby toward the main door as calmly and as quickly as we could, we were nearly clear of the sliding doors when I heard a voice yelling after us.

"Stop! You can't leave the hospital yet! You've not been cleared!" said someone.

We didn't stop or turn around but just kept going out to the parking lot. Mark lifted me into the front passenger seat that was waiting for us, while Lora dumped my shopping bag into the trunk and got into the back seat with Mark. There was a stranger, a handsome stranger, driving the car.

"Hello, I'm Falon," I introduced myself.

"Hello, Falon, I'm Robert Andrews and I'll be your driver today."

When we got back to the hotel, Mark kept up the appearance of me having two broken legs. He carried me into the hotel and up to the room. On the way through the lobby, several people stopped momentarily to give us condolences and well wishes to get better. I thanked them as Mark breezed by quickly without stopping.

When Lora opened the door to my room, I discovered it was a mess.

"Oh my God! What happened to our room?" I yelled.

"It appears that after they grabbed you, someone came back here and tore this place apart looking for something," said Mark. "We don't know what it was."

"Yeah, the kidnappers were smart enough to put a Do Not Disturb sign on the door handle, so the hotel staff wouldn't go in and discover the mess," said Lora. "That's the only reason I found the room like this."

"The first thing we did was to tell the hotel not to clean the room, and to leave it just as it is so that my security could conduct an investigation because you had been abducted from the room."

"That makes sense," I said. "But look at the mess they've left! Everything is upside down and ripped apart!"

"It's only stuff, Falon," Mark said. "You are the important one to me, and you're okay."

"I agree, it's just stuff," said Lora. "We'll get it cleared up right away."

"Actually, Lora, wait a bit. I need your help to release her from these casts."

"What does that entail?" I asked.

"Without a saw, I'll have to break them," said Mark. "Lora is going to hold you while I break the plaster."

"Oh, just that, eh?"

I lay face-down on the sofa and Lora held me while Mark applied pressure to the cast from the back of my leg. He forced it to bend at the knee until it cracked and he could peel it off in pieces. Boy, did it make a mess! There was plaster dust everywhere.

"I guess that's why they use a saw to remove them in the hospital," I noted.

He grinned at me. "I don't have a saw small enough."

Once the casts were off, they encouraged me to stand up.

"You're sure I can?" I asked. "I mean, I had compound fractures in both legs. Have they really healed?"

"Yes, mostly healed. I saw the x-rays they took this morning. You should be able to put weight on them now. It's why we had to get you out of there."

"Oh!"

Holding on to Lora and Mark, they eased me up until I was standing. There was little pain, and my legs were sort of working. *Wow!* I looked for the stitches I had in my stomach; they were gone too. So that would have been a problem.

"Well, thanks guys for getting me out of there. Now, where do we start here?"

"You look for all the valuables: laptops, phones, technology, money, et cetera. See if any of it was taken," said Mark. "Lora, you go through all her clothes to see if anything was destroyed. I'll look at all the furniture and assess the damage."

Pillows had been torn apart. Desk drawers had been pulled out and dumped on the floor. I went looking for my purse and briefcase. I last left them in the bedroom on the empty side of the bed because I had been working there. Going into the bedroom, it was clear immediately that my briefcase was gone and everything inside it as well.

"Well my laptop, phone, and other tech, as well as my files, have been taken," I reported. "Why would they take my files? I need to let my boss know."

I went to the hotel phone and dialed my boss's number in Montreal.

"Peter Prudhomme's office, how may I help you?"

"Ah, is Peter there? It's Falon."

"Oh, Falon, are you okay? We heard about the tornado and that you ended up in the hospital."

"Yeah, I'm fine, a few scratches. I was lucky. I was saved by a sofa and some firefighters."

"Good to hear. Peter is down in Kansas right now. Shall I get him to call you?"

"No, I can call his phone. Thanks."

"Bye, take care of yourself!"

"Thanks!"

Off the phone, I heard Lora telling Mark that all of the clothes she had found had been ripped apart like they were looking for something.

I called Peter's cell phone.

"Peter speaking."

"Peter, it's Falon."

"Falon, how are you doing?"

"I'm fine. I just need a few days off, I think. But that's not why I'm calling. I need to tell you that my laptop and all my tech was taken from my hotel room. In fact, while I was trapped in the tornado, someone ransacked my room. It doesn't make sense. I have filled out a police report. I'm not sure why, but they also took the files I had with me that I was working on. They also have the float of money that I had."

"So how much cash is gone?"

"About five hundred dollars."

"That's not too bad. Easily replaced. So is your tech. I'll have another laptop sent down for you today—they'll send it to the office. Anything else gone?"

"Apparently all my clothes are ripped to shreds. It seems they were looking for something, but I can't imagine what."

"Use the company card to go and replace your business wardrobe."

"Are you sure?"

"Yes, it's the least we can do."

"Thanks, Peter. That's awfully generous."

"And, Falon...?"

"Yeah?"

"Take a few weeks off. That's an order."

"Okay, boss."

I returned to the main room. It looked like a war had swept through. I stood there frozen, staring at the mess they made of our things, and I started crying my eyes out.

Mark wrapped his arms around me, comforting me.

"You should go to bed. You've been through an ordeal and you need to get your strength back. Let us take care of you."

"How are we going to explain no casts?"

"Lora has a good idea," said Mark.

"Tell them that you have stainless steel pins in your legs. It's a new procedure that allows for very fast healing."

"Oh, that is a good idea. You know what, guys, my legs are tired and starting to hurt. I think I will go back to bed now."

Mark put me to bed and I fell asleep almost immediately. My last thought was: *At least my boss won't be expecting me back to work for a while*. My legs were still unsteady—but the fractures to my bones were healing quickly. Mark figured one more day and it'd be like they'd never happened. The two of them cleaned up as much as they could, took stock of what was taken, and what needed to be replaced.

2 - Recuperate

— Falon

Day four after the tornado found me feeling right as rain. Mark woke me up with breakfast in bed.

"Good morning, sunshine. How are you feeling?" Mark asked. He brushed the hair from my eyes. I stretched and sat up and took stock of my body.

"Well, my legs don't hurt anymore," I answered. "I can move everything, and I can feel everything. So that's good, right?"

"Definitely," he said. "So you and Lora can go shopping. Peter sent you a credit card, right?"

"Yes, he did. We have his black American Express card." Peter had left the card at the front desk for me and Lora had picked it up.

"Well, here's mine, and there is no limit on this one." Mark handed me another black card that didn't have anything on it. "Use it like a debit card."

"Will stores recognize this?" I asked.

"They should, but if they question it, tell them it's a foreign debit card. When they run it through and it works, that's all they'll care about."

"Hey, Lora, are you awake?" I called into the other room.

"Yup, Mark brought me breakfast too. He's a keeper!" she answered.

"I know."

"Let's make a list of what you need before we go. It will make our shopping faster," she suggested. "If we hit the bigger department stores first, that should get us most of what you need, and then anything that is special we'll pick up later," she suggested.

"I'll have a new phone and a new laptop for you too, later today," said Mark.

"Oh, so that's one less thing I need to worry about."

"I'll leave you ladies for now, and get that organized, but I will be back later," said Mark.

"Bye, hun," I said. "Thanks for everything."

"Bye, honey," said Lora. "I'll miss you."

"Oh don't you start, Lora!" said Mark, laughing.

After breakfast, Lora and I went through what I still had and made up a list. Turned out I was going to need quite a bit. They had destroyed more than they stole. I'd need to replace most of my business wardrobe.

We went to the big stores first and managed to get all the business clothes I needed, suits with skirts and pants, shirts, jackets, a coat, a jacket, some slacks, sweaters, blouses and even a couple of dresses.

"That's the last item for here, and under $5,000. Well done!" I said. "The rest I'll put on Mark's card."

We found a nice pair of pumps in black for the office, a sexy pair of stilettos, and a pair of casual sneakers. I threw in some flip-flops for the pool too.

"Oh! The pool. I need another swimsuit," I said.

"Yeah, casual wear is next," said Lora.

We stopped at some denim stores and picked up jeans, shorts, tees, and tanks. A lingerie store supplied a two week supply of underwear and bras. I really wanted to pick up an adorable thong and bra set for my nights with Mark. *His interest will be piqued with this purchase*, I thought, grinning.

It took us about four hours of intense shopping to get everything. But it was worth it. Having Lora there made selection easy. She just kept bringing me stuff to try on. The last thing to look for was some "going-out" clothes. I let Lora lead on this one. We went to some of her favorite boutiques—same stores as Montreal, interestingly enough—and went through their selection of clothes.

She talked me into some tight-fitting dresses. One was a classic "little black dress," and I do mean little. It hugged every curve and stopped just south of my ass. *Won't be able to bend over in this.* None of the clothes Lora picked out were "conservative." From plunging necklines to tall thigh-high boots and short skirts, she was decking me out to go clubbing.

The only thing I didn't get was sexy lingerie. *Maybe I'll bring Mark shopping for the sexy stuff.* That would be fun.

We got back to the hotel room by 3:30 in the afternoon. My feet were sore, Lora was bagged and we were both starving. She grabbed a bath while I ordered room service, then stretched out on the bed. Mark wasn't back yet, and there was no note. I still didn't have a phone, and I didn't want to use the hotel phone.

Borrowing Lora's phone, I called Peter.

"Hello, Peter."

"Hi, Falon, how are you feeling?"

"Much better, thanks. Lora took me shopping and we ended up spending—about three thousand dollars."

"That's excellent. Did you get everything you needed?"

"Yes, I replaced my business wardrobe. What about the electronics, though?"

"They'll ship down a new laptop to you with all the necessary hardware and software. Luckily, you've been backing up to the cloud, so we have your latest work, and that will be on the new laptop too."

"That's great, thanks. What about a phone?"

"I presume you'll get a new personal one?"

"Yes, Mark is handling that for me."

"Good, I'll get a business one for you too. It'll come with the laptop."

"Perfect. I think that's all I can think of."

"Listen, Falon, take what time you need. Heal, both physically and emotionally. There is nothing about this project that we cannot cover."

"Thank you, Peter, I appreciate that. I may go home to convalesce. I will let you know for sure."

A few days later, Mark came back to our hotel room by five o'clock with an announcement.

"Girls, pack everything up, we're moving," he said, walking into the room.

"Why?" I asked, as I looked wearily around the room at all the shopping bags I had yet to unpack.

"Because this is the hotel that you were abducted from, so perhaps it's not a great idea to stay here."

"If they found me here, they'll find me anywhere," I reasoned.

"Perhaps, but I have a more secure hotel we can move to," he said. "These are all your shopping bags? Where are your suitcases?"

"*Muhahaha*," I said, ending with a laugh. "Wait till you see how many there are. It took the porter two trips to bring everything up."

"Wow," he winked. "Anything to model?"

"Maybe," I said. "I left the really interesting things for us to go shopping together. I just didn't want Peter to pay for them."

"Count me in!" he said. "When do you want to go shopping?"

"Lora's having a nap. I ordered room service and after we ate she went to her room. Why don't we wake her and go for dinner?"

"Did someone say dinner?" asked Lora as she came into the room.

"Yes. Mark wants to move to another hotel."

"I think that's a good idea," said Lora. "Let me go get dressed and pack my suitcase."

"Falon and I can go shopping after we move," said Mark.

"Is the hotel okay with us checking out now?" I asked.

"I've paid for the night here so they don't lose a day," said Mark.

"Do you have the new phone and laptop?" I asked.

"Yes," he said, grinning. "It's the latest available. It has been set up with our secure technology." He handed me a beautiful cherry red smartphone.

Lora came out of the bathroom dressed and ready to go. She helped me gather up the parcels and bags and the three of us took everything down to a waiting taxi.

Getting there thirty minutes later—on the other side of the border in Kansas rather than Missouri—we arrived at the Inn at Meadowbrook, a very nice-looking place. Mark had booked us a suite so Lora could stay with us.

Mark got us girls settled in and ordered dinner up to the room. We had fun chatting and telling stories. By the time dinner was finished, I was exhausted again.

Mark's phone buzzed. He picked it up and glanced at it. Looking at me, his face looked grim, but he walked out of the room to answer the call. He returned a few minutes later.

"Falon, I have to go back to the council," he said, dropping a bomb.

"What do you mean … go back? Weren't they the ones holding you against your will?"

"Yes, they were," he said with determination on his face. "This time it's on my terms. I need to challenge them on their abduction of you and make sure this won't happen again. This time I won't be alone or defenseless."

"I don't like this, so keep me posted please."

"Can Lora stay with you?" he asked.

"Yes, I can stay," said Lora. "I've arranged for my kids to stay with my cousin indefinitely. Once I realized this was an emergency, I knew I needed to be here."

"Lora, you're the best," said Mark.

"Rest now. Let your body heal." He helped me into bed and then left quietly with Lora.

I could hear them speaking softly out in the sitting room. I drifted off to sleep.

I dreamt of coming back to my hotel room, and as I walked through the door all my senses started firing on all cylinders, warning me of something. I sniffed the air because there was a strange scent—not something I recognized—a person's scent I didn't know.

Suddenly, I was right back at the moment I was abducted. There was a stranger in my room. I could taste my own fear on my tongue, like an acrid smoke, as I started to creep around. Maybe I could surprise them before they took me. I grabbed a fireplace poker and started stalking around the room, determined to get them before they got me.

I was startled by the phone ringing.

The phone was ringing! I woke up and grabbed the phone.

"Hello?"

"Very sorry to bother you, Miss Robertson, but there is a gentleman at the desk asking for you."

"I'm not expecting anyone."

"Shall I send them away?"

"Um, wait did you tell them I was here?"

"No, ma'am, we don't do that without the guest's permission."

"But he thinks you're speaking to me?"

"No, ma'am, I don't sit at the front desk. I'm in the back room. He cannot see me."

"Okay. What does he look like?"

"He claims to be a friend of Mr. Chisholm, a Franco, from Atlanta."

"Does he have proof of his identity?"

"Yes, he did, ma'am. He provided a driver's license with a photo ID."

"All right, please don't tell him I'm here. I'll come down. Give me twenty minutes."

I went out to the sitting room, where Lora was asleep.

"Lora, wake up please," I gently spoke into her ear.

"Yup, awake!" she cried out. "What's up?"

"Do you remember the maître d' from the hotel in Atlanta?"

"Sort of, why?"

"Someone claiming to be him is downstairs asking for me right now. I think it's suspicious."

"You're damned right it's suspicious," she said. "I'm coming with you."

"Thanks."

We got dressed and went down to the second floor in the elevator, and then took the stairs to the main lobby—in case he was watching the elevators, I didn't want to give him an advantage. We walked around a corner and I saw a guy sitting on a chair in an alcove by himself. It looked like Franco, but why would he be here?

"Falon, that looks like him. I'll watch while you go meet with him,"

I approached him from the side so he didn't see me coming straight toward him. When I got close, I cleared my throat noisily. The man stood up and motioned me over to a chair close to him.

"Falon, I'm glad I found you. I have some bad news."

"And just how did you find me, Franco?"

"Mark left a forwarding address," he said smoothly.

Liar. Especially since he should not have known we'd changed hotels.

"What's the news, Franco?"

"Mark has been kidnapped by the council."

"When?" I asked, trying not to panic again—*Remember, Falon, this may be a ploy.*

"About a month ago, at least," he said.

I let out a silent breath and watched him.

Why is he telling me this? Surely, he was aware I would know if Mark was missing. Franco was in Atlanta; Mark was kidnapped from Kansas. Why would Franco know? Why wouldn't he think I wouldn't know. Huh?

"Why are you just telling me this now? What does this have to do with you? Why would you not think I would know?" I fired off questions at Franco like a machine gun.

"It took me a while to track you down. I only found out about it about two weeks ago," he lied.

Liar. So now I just want to learn as much as I can and get away from him.

Feigning disinterest, I asked him, "What do you want me to do about it?"

"I thought you'd want to know seeing as—well you know, seeing as you're together and all."

"And just how did you learn about that, Franco?"

"I heard through the family. Mark left me instructions to reach out to you in the event he went missing."

That was odd—very odd. If Mark had a standing order like that, he would have told me about it, and it would not have been Franco he would have left it with. So this was a setup for something, but what?

"And what were you supposed to do?"

"I was supposed to secure you with a bodyguard."

I didn't need a bodyguard. I'd have to call Mark and ask him about this.

"Well, thank you for getting hold of me. I'm sure Mark would have told me of plans like that. I don't need a bodyguard."

I was standing there in the lobby trying to explain to Franco that I don't need or want a bodyguard, when I felt Mark's projection enter my mind. The telltale zap of electricity gives it away, as well as the sudden erotic feeling I get in my center.

"Well, one will be watching out for you now regardless."

Great, just what I don't need, a tail.

I gasped softly as I felt Mark's touch on my belly and his hand slid down to my mound. He had my attention! The warmth of his hand brought on my heat. Suddenly it felt like I was on fire. It was embarrassing to be in public. In my head, I tried to shoo Mark away.

I felt Mark leave my body when I walked away from Franco. As soon as Lora and I got to the room, I barred the door with a chair.

3 - Oregon

— Mark

I felt better settling Falon and Lora into a different hotel. Hopefully they'd be safe there until I returned.

I booked the next flight to Houston so that I could pick up an extra set of identification and credit cards. I always had extras on hand at the house.

My plan was to go to visit the council directly. This game they were playing had to be stopped. They couldn't be allowed to disrupt my life and Falon's like this. I earned enough money for the family to be left in peace.

Arriving at the residence, I ran upstairs, grabbed a shower and changed. While I was dressing, a knock on the door preceded Gwen walking into my bedroom.

"You're home," she said, without preamble.

"No thanks to you."

"You shouldn't have escaped," she said.

"No? You don't think so?" I asked. "Well, if I hadn't, Falon wouldn't know I was alive. And since we're mentioning Falon, why did the council abduct her too? What were they looking for in her things?"

"That was an unfortunate mistake," replied Gwen. "They thought to corroborate your story or not. But I don't know what you're talking about—looking for?"

"Yes, her hotel room was ransacked and many of her things were taken. What did they hope to learn from her?"

"Her room was ransacked? That wouldn't be the council. They interrogated her and got the same story you told them," she answered. "What do you plan to do now?"

"That depends on whether or not they'll see me, I guess. My intention is to confront them about these attacks and challenge them on their perceived right to do that in the first place, when there has been no evidence that either of us has compromised the family. There seems to be two parties that are attacking us then: The council and someone unknown."

"Good luck with that," said Gwen.

She walked out of my room and left me alone. Opening the safe behind the large mirror, I grabbed a duplicate of my driver's license and passport. Credit cards were easy to get, and I had a few accounts already created that I didn't use at all just for this sort of situation. I made a mental note to trace the cards to see if they could determine who stole them.

I believed that the council had removed all my ID and personal effects from me when I was being held so they weren't a risk like having them stolen. But I wanted to be careful.

Going down to the garage, I selected one of the sedans and took the keys off the rack. I was going to drive to their sanctuary. That way they would see me coming.

Sixteen hours later, I was nearly there. I stopped at a restaurant for breakfast and coffee. I filled up the tank and continued on my way. When I was half an hour away from the sanctuary, I figured they should be aware of my vehicle by now.

The sanctuary was hidden inside a mountain, but it had an office building out front for visitors who weren't family. Actual offices in the building were used by the various family members to conduct business with the mortal humans—the immortals called them "temps," as in temporarily alive.

There was a law firm, a doctor's office, a dental office, and an architectural firm. Each of those businesses was owned and operated by the family, but they worked with the human population.

I parked in the visitors' section of the parking lot outside the office building. Walking inside the lobby, I was struck by the modern security equipment all over the place. There were thick plexiglass walls around the reception desk as well, blocking off access to the elevators. The only way into the building was through a set of scanning machines that would check for weapons.

I didn't have any weapons but I still had to check in at the desk.

"Can we help you, Mr. Chisholm?" asked one of the security guards.

"Yes, please. I would like to see Councilwoman Mayer," I answered.

"Do you have an appointment?"

"Not really, but I believe she'll want to see me."

"One moment, please."

I wandered over toward the glass walls and watched the clouds go by over the mountains. It took a few minutes before the guard called me back.

"Mr. Chisholm, the councilwoman will see you. She is sending someone to take you to her."

"Thank you."

It didn't take long before a couple of thuggish-looking dudes appeared from between the banks of elevators. They walked over to the scanning machine through a doorway that was previously invisible to me.

"Come this way, Mr. Chisholm," said one of the guards.

I walked through the doorway. As I passed under the door, I felt a little zing of electricity.

So they scanned me anyway. Huh.

Once on the elevators, one of the guards pressed S5—which was a sublevel—down underground.

"Where are you taking me?"

"The council instructed me to take you to Holding."

When they got to S5, they led me to a room with a table and two chairs. It looked like an interrogation room at a police station. It even had a one-way mirror on one wall. I entered the room but didn't sit down. Instead, I paced back and forth. Eventually, the councilwoman arrived.

"Mark, I'm glad you came back on your own volition," said Mayer.

"I had to make sure Falon was all right," I answered. "But then I heard she had been abducted by you and left to die in a building that was hit by a tornado. Why would you do that?"

"We needed to corroborate your story," she said by way of explanation. "That's not much of an answer," I said, getting angry. "She could have been killed! If your intent was so benign, why did you leave her there?"

"The agents on the ground made a bad decision. They ran without thinking. I'm very sorry."

"Sorry? Sorry doesn't cut it!"

"Your girl is in danger right now. There is a faction within the family that wants to remove her and prevent you from creating another immortal," said the councilwoman.

"Is that who ransacked her room?"

"We believe so. They are looking for information about her, whether or not she was turned. The faction is against the creation of new immortals, and they are running in opposition to the current council members for the next election."

"This is not good news," I said. "What is their intent?"

"We don't know yet. We're still investigating. Unfortunately, you've begun the process of turning her, so it cannot be turned back. However, she could die from it if not given the serum to complete the process."

"What do you mean?" I asked. "She'll die because of the bite?"

"Our records show that your bite and semen may not be enough. In the past, it required multiple bites, and an added injection of a special serum to ensure the venom does not kill her."

"What is this serum?"

"It's a very well-kept secret. I do not know what its contents are, just that it must be produced and administered during the bite. To stay alive, Falon must go through the ritual again, in the presence of the council."

"You want her to have sex with me in front of the council?" I asked incredulously. "You people should get out more often. Or at least get cable TV."

"Yes, because the family doctor must be present to give her the serum," she replied, ignoring my dig.

"Well, that's rather kinky," I mumbled. "So what is next?"

"Bring her here for the ritual," said the councilwoman. "In the meantime, you'll be staying in one of the apartments on S4."

They led me to the "apartment" on S4, which turned out to be smaller than a motel room: one bed and a bathroom. I stretched out on the bed and dozed.

I got startled awake an hour later and when I opened my eyes it was dark because I hadn't turned on the lights.

I suddenly felt overcome with a need to find out if Falon was still safe and alive.

Concentrating, I sank into a deep state of meditation from which I could launch my astral self. As I separated from my body, I looked down and saw myself on the bed. I floated up and out of the building. Focussing on Falon instantly took me to where she was.

I recognized the hotel lobby they'd just checked into. She was speaking to Franco. Why was Franco there? He didn't work at that hotel. I knew he worked for the family, but he had no business in Kansas and no business visiting with Falon.

It occurred to me then that Franco might belong to the renegade faction of which the councilwoman spoke. That meant Falon was in trouble.

I felt Falon's heart beating in sync with mine. I focused on that until my projection joined with her body. As my astral self entered her, the connection was as strong as when they were connected physically. I felt the zap of energy passing between us. I touched her in her mind and slid my hand down to her belly to get her attention.

Falon shooed me away.

Falon thought I was there for pleasure. I had to get her attention.

I started drawing the word *GO* on her belly, over and over again, slowly.

I heard Falon excuse herself from Franco and return to her room. I separated from her to stay and watch Franco to see what he would do.

Franco went to a phone in the lobby of the hotel and called someone. The conversation was stilted, and Franco didn't say much. However, his intent was pretty clear. He had been instructed to take her somewhere.

I again focused on Falon and arrived in her room. I sank into her again, reveling in the feel of her. Even though I wasn't physically there, our energy passed back and forth.

I used a single finger to write on her belly. I could sense Falon concentrating on the motion, and then realizing I was writing letters—a G and an O.

"Oh! You're spelling out GO on my belly," said Falon. "Now I get it. You want me to leave?"

"Who are you talking to Falon?" asked Lora.

"Mark's projection is here," said Falon as she pulled Lora into the bathroom and pointed at the mirror.

"How do you know?" she asked.

"Because I can feel his energy, and he has a way to touch me even if it's not physical."

"Nice," she said.

"Watch my face in the mirror," said Falon, focused on the mirror.

My astral self wrapped my arms around her. I did my best to show my face in the mirror—it kind of floated over hers.

"Oh! I can see him!" yelled Lora. "Look, look at your face. His is superimposed over your face like a photograph. Wow, I can see him like a ghost over your face. I'm going to have to ask Rick if he can do this to me."

"Mark, can you hear me?" Falon asked her reflection.

I nodded and watched my reflection do the same thing.

I can speak to you in your head, but Lora won't hear me.

"Lora, did you see that?" asked Falon.

"Yes, I can."

"We both can see you in the mirror. So I can tell her what you say," Falon suggested out loud.

The distance is inhibiting some things, and I cannot hear you as well, I thought to her.

"But I can ask you questions and you can nod?" she asked.

Yes, I can do that.

I nodded my head and they both grinned as they watched.

"So I can't trust Franco?" asked Falon.

I shook my head.

"Is there someone we can trust?" asked Lora.

I nodded again. *His name is Andrews. I hired him a while back for my security company. He's the one who has been your bodyguard in Montreal.*

"He said the person to trust is Andrews. He hired him as security," said Falon.

Bellhop!

"Bellhop?" Falon asked.

I nodded my head.

There was a knock at the hotel room door. Lora went and looked through the peephole to see who it was.

"It's the cute guy who drove us from the hospital," said Lora. "Shall I open the door?"

Yes, but ask him his name first.

Lora put the chain on and then opened the door a bit after moving the chair.

"Yes?" she asked.

"Hello, my name is Andrews, I'm here for Miss Robertson," he said.

Falon, you need to leave. The council told me that there is a faction within the family that is after you. They want to capture you.

"Come on in."

Andrews walked into the room with Lora. When the door was shut behind them, he launched into an explanation of who he was. He had been hired by me to keep an eye on Falon and Lora. He'd taken a position as a bellhop so he could do that at both the previous hotel and this one. Unfortunately, someone had taken him out the day Falon had been abducted and he wasn't able to stop it. He apologized to Falon for his failure.

I listened while Andrews introduced himself and confirmed with Falon this was indeed the man hired to protect them. I told her to follow his instructions before I ran out of energy and had to leave.

Once back in my room, I hoped that Andrews would be able to get the two girls out of there and secret them to a new location. It was in his hands now.

4 - Security Move

— Andrews

I was standing there in the hotel room with Falon and Lora watching me. There was an unusual expression on Falon's face: She was scrunching up her mouth as if she was listening hard to some sound that only she could hear.

Then I saw Mark's projection on her face, like a photo being placed over double exposure. I saw him speak and nod, then fade away.

I have never gotten used to weird stuff like that happening on this job. I don't think I ever will.

"So Mark just confirmed who you are," said Falon. "He also said to follow your instructions."

The two women turned to look at me as I stood in the doorway dressed as a bellhop. I stepped fully into the room and closed the door behind me.

"Mark asked me to change your location again. Only this time we're going to use a technique designed to lose surveillance. We believe that someone has been surveilling you for a few months, and that is why they know you're here."

"Ah!"

"So what's the plan?" asked Lora.

"We're going to a safehouse first, but on the way we're going to change vehicles a few times."

"I guess we're getting packed again," said Lora.

"Nope, don't waste your time. Just put on street clothes. We have to leave now."

"I just purchased these clothes," Falon cried. "That's just not fair! Can I bring the phone at least?"

"Don't worry about your clothes, I will have one of my men grab all the bags and make sure they are clean of any bugs or tracking devices," I told them. "Then we will bring them to you. Yes, Falon, your phone is secure, so that is okay. Lora, you'll need to leave your phone behind because it's not secured."

"Rats, I like this phone," she said.

"Don't worry. I'll have the data transferred to a new secure one for you," I said. "But we need to leave now."

Once they were dressed, I led the way down, using the back service hallways. Most hotels have passages that are completely invisible and inaccessible to guests. They include secret hidden doors in the walls, back stairways, and an elevator that was outside of the hotel lobby, allowing staff to move around without the guests being aware of their presence.

Once outside, I escorted them to a nondescript black vehicle and we drove off quickly.

"How do you know Mark?" asked Falon. "Are you one of them?"

"No, I'm human. When he hired me, I insisted that he read me in on all the secrets if he wanted me to do my job properly. Sometimes I wish he hadn't, but that's the job."

"So why was it okay for you to know about the family but not me?" Falon asked.

"That's easy," I explained. "They don't know I know."

We stopped in a large shopping center parking lot next to a nondescript car.

"Okay, everyone out. We change cars here. We're going to do this one other time too," I informed them.

We all changed cars and drove to an apartment building across town. This building had an underground parking garage that we went into and again parked beside another car.

"Okay, ladies, this is the last change," I said. They both changed cars quickly for me and we were underway again in a few seconds. At the same time, I had one of my operatives take the car we just got out of and drive it in a different direction.

Forty-five minutes later, we drove into a residential neighborhood that would have looked right at home in Montreal. It was curious, really. The houses were similar: similar construction, rolling hills, and pretty landscape. Huh.

I parked in front of a simple split-level bungalow.

"Stay here for a minute while I check around the back."

I crept around the back of the house, making sure there was no ingress and that the door and windows were secure. Unlocking the front door, I entered on alert and cleared each room one at a time. When I was satisfied that the house was empty, I returned to the car.

"Okay, ladies, I'm going to drive around the back. When we're parked, please exit the vehicle and walk to the back door quickly and without talking."

As we entered, the phone in the kitchen started to ring. I went to answer it but hesitated. Only one person knew that number—Mark. As far as I was aware, Mark was still in custody at the family stronghold in Oregon.

"Falon, Lora, come here quickly, and crouch down between the counters. Don't move, don't speak. I don't want you to be seen from the windows. I don't know who the caller is."

"Hello?" I answered the phone. "The prairies are cold today."

"But the seaside is warm," came the answer. "Hello, Andrews."

"It's good to hear from you, buddy," I said. "Have you left their facility, or are you still being held?"

"I'm still here, but not in custody anymore. We've reached an agreement," explained Mark. He then went on to tell me that he needed to bring Falon to the Elders.

I listened for a while, then agreed to meet Mark in a parking garage at 1:00 a.m. with "the girls" in tow. Then I gave the phone to Falon. She spoke to him for a moment and hung up.

"Falon, Mark asked me to bring you to him so you can speak to the council together."

"So, what about me?" asked Lora.

"You can stay with me, or I can make sure you get home safely," I answered.

"Hmm, will Falon be in danger?" Lora asked me.

"Not as long as she is with Mark," I smiled.

"Can we all go together?" she asked.

"Yes."

As we waited in our car in the parking garage, another car came driving up the ramp ahead, shining its lights in our eyes. This car stopped alongside our vehicle and the passenger door opened. Mark got out and walked around the back of the car over to ours. Squealing with relief, Falon jumped out, kissing him all over his face. Mark held her in his arms while she wrapped her legs around his hips.

"I was scared I would never see you again," Mark admitted to Falon. "Thank you, Andrews. I've spent so much time over the last few days traveling, I'm not sure where I am anymore."

"Did you get to Oregon?" asked Falon.

"Yes, and I met with the council. Then I caught a flight here as soon as I could to get you."

"I'm glad you're back," said Falon.

After their reunion settled down, Mark gave me enough money to cover expenses. After hugs happened all around, Mark and Falon got into the car he had arrived in, and I transferred Lora to the front seat. We drove away in different directions.

"Lora, where do you want to go?" I asked.

"Well, I'm here in Kansas, so shall we go back to the hotel?" she asked.

"Yes, we can go back there," I answered. "If you want to help me go through all the clothes, we can make sure they're all clean. I'll stay with you until everything is clear."

"Oh, that's nice of you," she said. "Of course, I'll help in any way I can."

5 - Hanky Panky

Getting back to the second hotel, Andrews and Lora returned to the room they'd checked into earlier. Everything was still where it was. So they started to go through everything. Andrews had a scanner that he used on every piece of clothing, checking every possible seam. It was quite a thorough search. Lora folded the clothes up afterward.

"Would you like me to stay in the room with you?" asked Andrews.

"Yes, if you don't mind, please," she said. "I don't want to be alone tonight."

Andrews looked sideways at her trying to determine her exact meaning in that statement. It could mean several things. He didn't know Lora.

Lora went into the washroom and had a shower. She half-wanted that handsome Andrews to join her, but didn't expect it.

Naughty girl, Lora, what about Rick? Lora thought to herself. Well, what he didn't know wouldn't hurt him. *Besides, maybe*

Andrews was into kinky. She was in the mood for some life-affirming fun. She really needed to burn off some nervous energy and great sex was just what the doctor ordered. *Besides, even after all the sex I've had with Rick, I haven't committed to a relationship with Rick, yet,* thought Lora.

Andrews was tempted to peek into the bathroom, but decided against it. He hadn't received an open invitation, even though the woman was plenty sexy and apparently hot to handle. She had the most perfect ass, one he wanted to explore, and her curves were worth dying for. And those full breasts, he could lose his cock in between those breasts. He wanted to give her a pearl necklace.

He tried to put that out of his mind as best he could and failed. He was already hard and his jeans were uncomfortable, to say the least.

Andrews sat down in the chair by the window and crossed his legs to hide his erection. He was staring out the window when he heard the shower stop. He turned toward the room and realized it was dark. The bathroom light backlit the space.

Lora came out of the bathroom wearing a towel. She was hot and bothered. She needed release badly and there just happened to be a handsome man in the room. She was going to take advantage of that.

She saw him sitting in the chair by the window in the shadows, the light from the moon shone blue on his warm, dark chocolate-colored skin, highlighting the contours of his handsome face. The room was dark but the bathroom light was behind her, making her a silhouette. Then she had a brilliant idea.

"Andrews, remember the movie *True Lies*, the scene in the hotel room?" asked Lora.

Andrews didn't answer, but he was staring.

Stopping just outside the bathroom door, Lora turned around and looked in the mirror across from her. Dropping her towel, she turned toward Andrews and did a cat walk slowly toward him, accentuating her hip movements.

Lora stopped just before she got to the second bed. Silhouetted by the light, she started her show.

I'm going to give you a dance like never before, she thought.

Andrews was transfixed. He sucked in his breath when she dropped her towel. But the walk … the walk undid him. That ass swung from side to side and those breasts bounced to the rhythm of her steps. His jeans were about to get creamed. He hadn't been with a woman in months, almost close to a year. His cock was so hard now that, without underwear, it was straining painfully against the zipper. Crossing his legs wasn't an option anymore; that pulled the fabric too tight. So he opened his legs and tried to adjust himself.

Lora watched as his face showed alarm and lust at the same time. She saw him open his legs and adjust his pants too. How he squirmed in that chair! So Lora knew he wanted her. Good, now to see if he would play with her. She bent over at the hip and let her breasts fall straight down, displaying their beautiful fullness. Cupping her breasts with her palms, she squeezed them together and pinched her nipples.

Andrews watched as she bent over slowly and pinched her nipples, imagining himself doing that and sliding his cock between them. But her ass, oh her ass, a perfectly round heart glowing in the dark … she turned so that her ass was facing him. He watched as she took her finger and slid it in her ass and then pulled it in and out suggestively.

He couldn't hold his cream. He ejaculated in his pants. Groaning at the waste, he covered his face in shame and shook his head.

Lora heard his breath get fast and the tiny moans he was trying to keep quiet as she fingered herself. When his body climaxed in his pants, she was a tiny bit disappointed, but not too much. He was that hot and ready.

She walked over to him now and put her foot up on the chair between his legs. This displayed her pussy completely to him. She inserted two fingers in her vagina while draping her breasts on either side of her knee, moving her breasts back and forth along her knee in simulation of his cock, and then finger-fucking herself at the same time. She wanted him to be so excited he had no choice.

Andrews was almost done at that point. He was trying to keep his hands off her, but she was pushing all his buttons. The finger-fucking was special; he wanted to do that for her. She was so close, he could smell the heat coming off her. He was mesmerized by the movement of her fingers, and her breasts were ripe looking. He needed her so badly that he was aching.

Not able to take anymore, he stood up and took one step toward her, pulling her head up with his hands. He held her face and assaulted her mouth with his. His tongue took her mouth, and he sucked on her lips so hard she started to moan. He switched his attention from her lips to her breasts hanging in front of him.

He could tell that her breasts had milked before; there was a different shape and heft to them. He also knew that in some women their breasts will drip milk when stimulated enough thanks to a hormone called oxytocin.

Pulling one up, he sucked it into his mouth as far as it would go and kept sucking until a sweet liquid was coming out. They had responded to his tongue and his hands, and he kneaded her breast roughly.

Lora loved that he was sucking milk from her breast. It sent shivers through her body and made her pause in her finger-fucking. With her fingers idle, she reached for his zipper. His cock sprang out with a moan of relief from Andrews, and was standing at attention. About ten inches of pure beautiful cock. That wasn't all: he was thick, at least two inches in diameter. He would be a really tight fit. *Wonderful!*

Lora took his hands, pulled him closer, and their bodies rubbed against each other.

She stepped over to the bed and got up on her knees. She took his hand and inserted his fingers into her vagina so they would be covered in her wetness. Then she pulled them out and inserted those fingers into her ass. He obliged her by also inserting three fingers from his other hand into her vagina. Taking over from her, he finger-fucked her hard. But that wasn't enough for him. Removing his fingers, he lay her back on the bed and knelt down and licked her from stem to stern.

Rubbing his penis in her juices had him nicely lubricated. He didn't need any encouragement to impale her. Just where first? He went for her ass first. Lubing up her hole, he gently pressed inside. Her gasp was his reward. Pushing a little more, she pushed back to get him farther. He pulled out and inserted again, seeing how far he could go. Almost half of him was inside. *Not bad.* Usually the woman only took his head before crying out.

Lora was asking for more.

Lora felt him enter her ass delicately, which drove her nuts. She didn't want delicate, she needed rough. She pushed back on him. She could feel him inside and wanted another penis badly. She wanted to be double fucked so much it hurt. But for now, all she had were some toys and a cock. Well, she would get the most out of the cock. He had pulled out and was inserting again. *Enough of this tender shit.* She slammed herself against him and he sank in as far as his balls. She heard him gasp and scream quietly in pleasure. Then he started fucking her, speeding up. He released a little semen, which helped lube her up, and made him nice and slippery. He was coming faster now, and she sensed his orgasm on the horizon.

This woman is insatiable! Andrews thought as he looked down at their union. He always marveled at the contrast between black and white skin. He loved how it looked to see his cock buried deeply inside a white woman's ass.

His efforts to be gentle because he was big were wasted on this one. She wouldn't have it. She wanted it rough. As she impaled herself on his cock completely, he had the experience of a little orgasm; his cock almost let go of its payload. But not quite. The extra liquid helped him slide. She wanted it faster, so he gave it to her. He plunged himself inside her, and each time she groaned more. He watched how she had stretched around him and was squeezing him deliciously tight. And then he popped out—*Damn.*

Lora felt him pop out and took advantage. She got off the bed and grabbed her bag. She pulled out a tube of lube and some toys. One was a dildo matching the size of Andrews, another slightly bigger, and another slightly smaller. It was good to have variety.

Getting back up on the bed, she lubed up the one that was the same size as Andrews and handed it to him.

Andrews looked at the penis and then at himself. It was about the same size as him, so what did she want him to do with it?

"Double fuck me," she said.

Huh, no-nonsense woman, thought Andrews.

"Do you have a preference as to which where?" he asked.

"Yes, you in the vagina please," she said. "But first, here, please clean off your cock," she said, handing him a package of wipes.

Lora watched him as he cleaned off that beautiful black cock, which of course helped to stiffen him up again. Lora licked her lips in anticipation with lust and hunger. She got back up on her knees and presented him with her beautiful ass. He grabbed that ass and felt it all over, squeezing and massaging. She wiggled her ass.

Impatient little minx! He slowly impaled himself inside her vagina. It felt very tight and very warm, and very good. Then he slowly pushed the fake penis into her ass. That was tricky. Without the feedback his body would give him, he couldn't tell if he was pushing too much or too little. It was tough to get it inside. Lora was groaning wonderfully, and her adorable bottom was wiggling all over the place.

"Is that too hard?" Andrews asked.

"Nope. Keep going."

And so he pushed more until the dildo's head was inside her. The resistance was amazing. When he was inside her ass, it hadn't felt the same way; the resistance didn't feel as much. Then he felt the dildo against his own cock. The extra stimulation was nice. The fake cock had ridges and provided different sensations. Oh, that did things to him not done before!

Lora was squirming now, begging him to move, begging him to go faster. He was still not sure he wouldn't hurt her. He was not a small man.

Lora wanted Andrews to go! *Just fuck me already!* She could feel the two penises inside and it was heaven. To be this full, this aroused inside and out, this much sweet pain, was beyond erotic. As soon as he started moving, she nearly came right there. She had to squeeze against his cock to keep herself from orgasm. But oh, it was so worth it.

Andrews could feel her desire for him to move. The dildo was almost all the way in, and so was he. Should he move them at the same time or differently? He decided to move his own cock first. Pulling out he plunged back in with enough force to hit the end of her sheath. When he hit the cervix, his penis danced a happy tune. The added sensation of rubbing up against the ribbed dildo was stimulating him even harder. Moving faster, he built up his orgasm quickly, pumping back and forth with his cock. Once he had a rhythm with that, he used his hands to start pumping the fake one too.

Lora let out a blissful scream as she felt Andrews pumping both at different points and in different rhythms—the complete feeling of two each building up their own orgasm. Andrews was bottoming out inside and stimulating all her erogenous zones, including the one seldom touched—her cervix. She was being spoiled. As she screamed and moaned and groaned and made all manner of noises, Andrews was calling out her name and exploding inside her as he came. Her own climax happened a moment later and her own ejaculate joined his.

Andrews' legs were wobbling after that climax. He had never had one so intense before. He kept coming inside her like a hose he couldn't turn off. When his cock was finished, it slid out in a completely satiated manner. It wasn't small, but he wasn't hard anymore. It was going to take some time to get him up again. *Wow!*

He didn't know if he should remove the dildo yet too. So he left it where it was. Lora had flopped on the bed on her tummy and was stretched out with that beautiful ass facing up. Andrews couldn't resist lying down beside her, but he took off his clothes first. When he stretched out beside her, she touched his cock and a zap happened on the tip. He watched in amazement as his cock started to get hard again.

Okay, that doesn't happen, ever. His recovery time was pretty good, but after an intense orgasm, it should be twenty minutes, not thirty seconds.

Lora rolled over and faced him. Her beautiful breasts were right there, and he couldn't resist putting his hand between them and squeezing.

"I hope you don't mind me energizing your cock again," she said with a mysterious smile on her lips.

"How did you manage this?" Andrews asked, pointing to his revived cock.

"A little magic," she answered cryptically.

Lora cupped her hands on both sides of her breasts and pushed them together, trapping Andrews' hand between. She looked up at him and saw that he was smiling. He leaned over and kissed her gently at first, but she kissed back probing into his mouth. Grabbing his hair and pulling him toward her, she bruised her lips, probing him deeply with her tongue and then sucking his tongue into her mouth.

Okay, that did it, thought Andrews, his cock now fully up again and ready for more. He was pushing between her legs already. Lora chuckled, and he felt it around his tongue that she had in her mouth. He felt her lift her leg and move her hips up against his. When her leg lowered, she had trapped his penis between her legs. His cock was already hunting for her vagina; he could feel her heat again. Meanwhile, she hadn't released his tongue and he was stuck trying to breathe through his nose.

Breaking the kiss, she smiled at him.

"Want to go again?" she asked. Lora was playing with the dildo still in place in her ass.

"Are you not sore?" he asked.

"Naw, I've got more in me, easily. Ever done three?" she asked.

"Three what?"

"Three penises," she stated calmly.

"Three penises? Where would you put them?" he asked. He knew, because this was his kind of kink, but it was pretty hardcore. Usually, there were more bodies present.

"Well, I've read that some put two in the vagina, while a third is in the ass," she said. "Is that how it works?"

"Are you sure you want to go there?" he asked. "I've done this. It's pretty brutal when you're not expecting it,"

"Have you done it with dildos or men?" she asked.

"I've been part of a three on one a few times. It's sometimes tricky figuring out who goes where. I'm not sure it's fun for the lady. The guys have to be really secure in themselves too, because not everyone can share a hole."

"Well, I've only got dildos, so you won't be sharing me with anyone. Will that work?" she asked.

"Again, if you want, I'll oblige you," Andrews said.

"I know. I love that you are well endowed. I hate small men. There is nothing to feel. How would we start?" she asked, removing the dildo and cleaning it off.

"Well, let's lube you up really well. It would be easier if I came in from the back, because then I can control all the vectors, so to speak."

Lora giggled at that. "Here, choose your weapons," she said, handing him three dildos of different sizes. "I'd like to try the largest one first, if you can."

"Okay, your wish is my command."

Lora smiled widely at him and got back on her knees. He started by giving her oral to get her body excited, because her own lubricant was better. It didn't take long to get her very wet again. Then Andrews spread a generous dollop of lubricant inside her ass and vagina.

Starting with the first dildo, he inserted it into her vagina as far as he could push it. Then he started to slide himself into her vagina alongside the dildo.

Her gasps told him it hurt, so he slowed down. The first dildo was easily as large as him. So this was double overstuffing her. At least his head had some give; the fake did not. He tried again, lubricating himself more, and inserted his cock alongside the dildo. Lora sucked in her breath sharply. Andrews stopped to let her adjust to the sensation of so much inside her.

Lora made mewling sounds and wiggled her ass to get him to continue. Andrews pushed himself in a little more, again stopping to let her body adjust. He was about halfway there now. Lora made more sounds to indicate she wanted more. So he decided to finish in one stroke. Thrusting quickly until he was fully inside, she cried out in pain. He stopped and waited. Lora said she was good.

Watching her carefully, he started moving inside her. He knew that two inside the vagina was painful if not done properly. He didn't know about a dildo and a penis, because this was the first time he had done this. But Andrews wanted to make sure she had only pleasure, not pain.

The two penises moved as one, making her gasp and cry out in arousal. He stopped but she urged him on. Slowly and carefully, he pulled and pushed the two back and forth as her breathing got faster and shorter, her orgasm building. He could feel her vagina tighten up in preparation for release.

Now was the time for the third. While he was still moving in and out of her vagina, he lubricated the second dildo, slightly smaller than him, and got ready to insert it.

"Are you ready, my dear?" he asked.

"Yes! Please!" she cried out in ecstasy.

Andrews started to insert the dildo in her ass and Lora screamed his name, telling him to not stop. His hand steadily moved the dildo deeper and deeper into her while he was still pumping her vagina. He could now feel pressure from the dildo in her ass on his cock. This was a sweet spot for him. The added pressure was extremely stimulating; it squeezed him nicely. Having experienced this with other guys, the rigid dildos provided much different sensations. The smoothness of a hard penis gave you pressure, but the ridges in the dildos added a little pain. It made it rough for him, which was surprisingly arousing. He couldn't imagine what Lora was feeling though.

The third dildo was almost fully inserted. Lora suddenly started moving her hips urgently to make him move more. He used his hands and pushed and pulled both dildos in time with this cock and the wave that was building in both of them was like a tsunami. Lora was keening loudly and rocking back and forth on the triple impalement. He was feeling his cock getting so hard again that he was pushing the dildo out of the vagina and the one in her ass was coming out too. It didn't matter though, as Lora was climaxing so big she was flying.

The shudder that took her body as she released was all consuming. Andrews came with another explosion that had enough pressure to expel the dildo out on its own. He pulled out to watch Lora ejaculate on him. Removing the dildo from her ass, she sighed in contentment and collapsed on the bed.

"Oh God, I feel like a cooked spaghetti noodle. Ah fuck, that was good," she groaned out. "Thank you for giving me this experience. I had wanted to try this for a while now—ever since I heard about it. But you need the right scenario."

"I'm glad you enjoyed it," said Andrews. "You are some woman, Lora."

6 - Roadside Dining

— Mark

I glanced at my watch. Falon and I had been on the road for about nine hours now. We were traveling across the country toward Oregon and the council. It was a boring landscape—flat fields as far as the eye could see. As we passed through farmland, we started to see rough landscape and cattle.

"Mark, can we stop for food somewhere?" said Falon. "I'm really hungry. I could eat a horse!"

"Of course. I think there's a steakhouse just up ahead at the next exit."

There was still another twelve and a half hours of driving before getting to Oregon. But stopping now was a good idea. Food and rest were in order. Sure enough, a sign for a bar/steakhouse/motel appeared in the distance at the next exit. I pulled off and drove down the side road, where we found the advertised roadhouse bar and grill. I helped Falon out of the car and we went inside.

Talk about atmosphere! It felt like being transported back a hundred years to cowboy days. There was a long wooden bar that stretched from one end of the building to the other. There was a huge dance floor on one end next to a small stage where there was a band playing country music. The rest of the very large space was filled with tables and booths. Most of them looked like they were made by Amish people, all hand-turned wooden furniture. Beautiful, really. Most of the tables and booths were occupied too.

A waitress with a very low-cut blouse tied under her bust to expose her midriff came up to us and asked me what my pleasure was. The smile on her face said, "I want to blow you, but it'll have to wait for a few minutes."

"We'd like some food please," I answered smoothly. "Is there a booth open in the back, perhaps?"

"Why yes, sugar. Follow me and I'll set you right up," the waitress answered. Turning around, she walked toward the far corner, her hips sashaying gently from side to side. The short shorts exposed a little cheek as she walked, and when she bent over to put the menu on the table, she made sure Mark got an eyeful.

Falon slid in first. "Well, don't I feel distinctly invisible right now," she said.

I sat on the same side of the booth beside her.

"Don't worry darling, you're not invisible to me," I drawled, squeezing her thigh.

Bending low in front of Mark while handing me the menu, the waitress said, "There you go, sugar. You just holler when you need me, okay?" She licked her lips suggestively, turned around, and stuck out her ass again.

"Wow, talk about overt!" Falon chuckled.

"No kidding. She was hot for sex for sure. But I only have eyes for you."

"Aw, you say the nicest things," she said breathlessly. Kissing me possessively, I let my tongue enter her mouth as I took ownership of her. By the time I broke the kiss, Falon was waving her hand in front of her face as she flushed hot. My hand found its way between her thighs, and I moved it slowly up to her center. I gently rubbed my hand up against her mound through her cut-off shorts.

Falon moaned and shivered as need took over her body.

"Okay, now I'm hungry for something entirely different," she murmured into my ear.

"Let's eat first. I need to feed my girl so she has energy for later." I looked at her and saw her own hooded eyes, which were sexy deep pools again. My fangs distended just a bit, showing her how aroused I was too.

Falon kissed my fangs, licking them, which was an erogenous spot for me, and a groan escaped my own mouth. My fingers slipped inside the edge of her shorts, and I reached inside to find her wetness. There was no underwear as a barrier to her luscious petals. I gently spread her petals and caressed her nub until she was squirming in her seat.

"Well, maybe food can wait," I said, my voice slurred with desire.

My fangs had elongated a little, and they nicked her tongue as she licked their length, making me groan some more. She could smell my arousal now. She broke off her kiss to give my hardening shaft some attention.

"Would you mind dearly if I took care of this growing issue?" she asked, as she pressed one hand on my hard cock. Feeling me twitch and strain inside my jeans, she sensed the heat coming through the fabric.

"What are you going to do here?" I asked. As if I didn't know.

Falon looked around for a moment; no one was noticing us. In fact, everyone was preoccupied with the live band playing at the other end of the restaurant, so she slid off the bench seat and under the table. Undoing my belt, she let my cock peek out the top edge. A pearl of fluid was already waiting. She undid my pants and pulled my cock toward her mouth. Her tongue brushed the sensitive head and my cock surged in length.

I inhaled sharply as she slid me into her mouth. I grabbed my jacket and laid it across my lap to cover us up. We were groaning so much that I was sure someone would hear us.

"Oh fuck," I whispered. "It's been so long, Falon, I cannot hold off. If you keep doing that, I'm going to climax."

"Is that a problem?" she whispered back coquettishly. Then she paused. "I can stop if you wish, but you're so hard it would be a shame to let that go to waste."

A low growl escaped my throat and my fangs extended completely. I had to cover my mouth with my hand. Falon was now pumping my shaft with one hand while she was sucking on the end. She wasn't being gentle, and the nips and bites excited me even more. Alternating between licks and bites, then sucking and blowing, she expertly brought me to the edge. My pants were completely undone, so I picked up the menu and stood it up on the table in front of me.

The waitress was on her way back to the table. Looking at me directly, she plumped up her boobs and spread her shirt quite a bit so that her nipples were almost showing and her cleavage was popping out. She slid into the opposite side of our booth and smiled at me again. She didn't seem to notice that Falon was under the table. She only had eyes for me.

"Hey, gorgeous, what can I get for you?" she asked, in a boudoir voice. She simultaneously traced a finger down her cleavage suggestively.

I looked up from the menu, my fangs completely extended, and my eyes glowing.

"Oh my, don't you look all delicious," she continued. "Want to bite me?"

What? She can see my face and she isn't recoiling. Just my luck, I had a waitress with a vampire fetish. I will have to compel her so she doesn't make a fuss.

I looked intensely at the waitress, forcing her to look me in the eyes. As she stared back, I was able to enter her mind. *Aw God, this is not a nice place!* It was full of smut and sex and violence. *God, I hate doing this!*

I planted the idea that we were just regular customers so she wouldn't scream at my countenance. Out loud, I told her to bring us three rare steaks on one plate and a fourth on a second plate, with baked potatoes, and two large beers. My voice was very husky and full of sex, as I had to talk around my fangs. It made a slurring sound like I was drunk.

Now that she was compelled, the waitress didn't notice my fangs at all. She got up glassy-eyed, walked next to me, took my head in her hands and rubbed it between her boobs. The fangs pricked her skin, delivering a tiny drop of venom. She reached down with a finger, wiped the venom off, and sucked on her finger. Her eyes rolled back in her head as the ecstasy took her. She staggered off in a state of orgasm, not looking back.

I took a moment to look around the bar, and sure enough everyone's attention was fully on the band on the stage at the opposite end of the place. No one was noticing this table. *Good!*

I turned my attention back to what Falon was doing. She had slowed down her movements while I spoke to the waitress, but was now about to bring me to climax. As my cock got harder and longer, her head rose up and down, hitting the underside of the table occasionally. Good thing the music was very loud and most of the people were singing along. She couldn't take me all into her mouth because I was much too large, but God that would be wonderful if she could. It didn't diminish the exquisite feeling of her mouth as she worked my cock and sucked on it. I was gripping the table so hard I thought it would break.

Trying to keep my groans as quiet as possible, I was again grateful the music got louder and everyone started singing with the band. I was panting now as Falon sucked hard. It took my breath away as the wave of the climax took me. I felt her hand cup my balls and that was the trifecta to end me.

I glanced down at her and she was grinning like a cat. Her tiny fangs had extended, and I watched, fascinated, as she bit down on my cock. The pain made me scream until I managed to swallow it quickly. Then I was flooded with a euphoria I'd never felt before. My cock exploded in her mouth, shooting seed deep into her throat. Sputtering a bit, she did her best to drink it down so as not to have too much of a mess.

"Quick, hand me all the napkins!" she cried out in a loud whisper.

There was a small pile of napkins on the table for those who were eating finger foods. I grabbed the pile and passed it under the table.

"Uh oh, she's coming back, Mark," Falon said. "Cover us up again." She tossed my jacket back up and I flung it over my lap again.

As the waitress arrived again, she placed the drinks on the table. Her flaccid face showed she was still under my compulsion, and she was still horny as all get-out, showing me by standing beside the table and raising her skirt to show me her thong. Meanwhile, I was flying so high on the venom, I felt like a junkie. I almost grabbed the waitress' pussy with my hand. I'm sure she wouldn't have objected either.

Instead, I very purposely put my hands on top of the jacket to hold Falon's head down until the waitress had left. When she slithered back up onto the bench seat, she grabbed her beer and drank down deeply, washing away the cum and cleaning out her mouth. She scooched over and kissed me on the lips again. I held the back of her head as I breathed a thank-you into her mouth.

"I don't need a thank-you. It was something I wanted too," she said with a smile. "Are you coming back down to reality yet?"

"Yes, thank you. That was very, very naughty of you," I said. "I loved every risky moment."

"Good!" she grinned. "It was kinda fun doing it in a public place. The risk had been such a turn-on that I couldn't resist once I got the idea in my head."

"Unfortunately, I have to go and clean up somehow. If you'll excuse me." I grinned at her. Keeping my jacket in front of my pants, I walked toward the back and the washrooms. By the time I returned, the steak dinners were on the table.

"All better?" Falon asked.

"Well, I have a big wet spot, but it looks like I spilled something."

"You did."

"Umm, yes I did."

The steaks were not great, but we were both sufficiently hungry that it didn't really matter. They could have been charcoal and we would have eaten most of it. After eating, I called for the check. When the waitress sauntered over to get paid, she was a lusty as ever. I went into her mind again and this time compelled her to forget we were ever there. I left a payment and tip on the table and we left.

Getting to the car, I tried to decide if we should go back on the road or look for a room. I wasn't tired. In fact, I was fired up and interested in pleasing Falon until her eyes popped out.

"So shall we find a room somewhere?"

"Naturally," she answered with a foxy look on her face. "I am not finished with what I started."

"Neither am I."

Unfortunately, as soon as my head hit the pillow, the venom in her bite knocked me out.

"Ah my poor baby," crooned Falon. "So tired after a little play. I guess my venom has some punch to it after all. Turnabout is fair play."

My dreams were filled with erotic images of Falon doing things to me with her little fangs, and I thoroughly enjoyed it. At some point, I had a couple of girls biting me all over while my cock was dancing straight up. Another dream had me sandwiched between bodies and I was fucking one while one was fucking me. That one woke me up. I hadn't realized my body responded favorably to such ideas, but my cock was surely interested.

Falon was nuzzled up to my side and her hand was on top of my cock and a big smile was on her face. Even in sleep, she turned me on so much. I could tell her dreams were erotic too, because her body was aroused and she was stroking me.

Perhaps it was time to branch out and try new things?

7- Ritual Sex. Bite. Repeat.

— Falon

I woke up early, got up and had a shower. In the shower I thought about the reason we were going to Oregon. The council wanted me to go through the ritual of turning me again. After all they had done to us, I didn't trust them. They'd kidnapped and beat up Mark, kidnapped me hoping to bait Mark—it was our own wits that got us out of those binds.

Why now are we trusting them?

We didn't have much of a choice. Mark was trying to appease them so they didn't come after us again. I believed I was changing already; it just felt like I was.

By the time I got out of the shower, Mark was awake and dressed. "Falon, I need to tell you something. Get dressed and then I'll explain," he said.

"Boy, conversations that start that way don't usually go well."

"This one is to explain something that I saw, and to let you know what happened."

"Okay. Start, and I'll get dressed."

"Remember when I materialized to rescue you from that rapist in Kansas?"

"Yes, that was a shock."

"Me materializing or the rape?"

"Both."

"Yeah, well, the materializing was new for me too. I never really talked about it with you because so much has been going on. But I think you need to know before we get to the council."

"What do I need to know?"

"The man who raped you, the one I managed to pull off, I recognized him."

"You what?"

"I recognized his face. He was sent by the council. I don't believe he was sent to rape you, but I'm not sure."

"Why would they have sent someone to do that?"

"My guess is they sent him to do the sex part and bite you so that you would change."

"You mean it was an elaborate hoax to the company that they were customers and a setup to get me to have sex so that they could bite me?"

"It's only a theory. But that's all I've got. When they had me, they wanted to have the ritual performed by another male, and I got very angry and basically told them over my dead body."

"Oh."

"Yeah. So these events may have been designed with that impetus in mind."

"Where does that leave us?"

We are facing them to give them their stupid ritual and let them inject you with their serum. It won't do anything more than I have done, but it will ensure you become immortal."

"I knew I didn't trust their asses."

"Neither do I. Which is why when Lora decides to move forward with turning, we'll do it ourselves."

"You mean we'll have the ritual on our own property?"

"Or something like that, but we'll be in control of it," said Mark. "Are you okay with me telling you all this?"

"Well, I don't know about okay. I'm over the rape, mostly. It really helped that the asshole was arrested. Will the council get him out?"

"I don't know. They cannot leave an immortal in prison with humans. But they don't condone rape either, so he may be punished by them."

"What's their punishment for rape?"

"They are fitted with a special collar that will deliver an electric shock whenever their libido starts to rise."

"Castration would be better," I suggested.

"Yes, but we grow back appendages, remember?"

"Ya, but it's really painful, right? So what if they keep whacking it off?"

"Huh, I don't want to ever get in your bad books!" said Mark, shuddering at the thought of having his penis removed repeatedly. "That borders on torture."

"Serves him right!"

"Yes, it would. But at least he'll never again be able to have sex."

"That is something. Let's get going and face this music," I said.

We left the motel after breakfast. We still had a lot of road to cover, another twelve hours, but at least the scenery got more interesting.

We stopped for lunch at another roadside diner and the food was pretty good. These small places often cater to truckers, so their food isn't fancy but it's well-made.

By the time dinner came around, Mark had been driving all day. Stopping was necessary just to get the road out of his eyes. Stretching my legs, I walked around the car a few times while Mark went inside to get some takeout. He wanted to finish this journey tonight. With luck, we would get there in two to three hours.

"They didn't have much in the way of variety, but their burgers looked good. I picked up one for you and a few for me. I also got you a milkshake," said Mark, handing me the bag.

"Smells good. I'm hungry," I said, digging in. While he was pulling the car out onto the highway again, I set up a burger for him to eat.

"This is delicious!" I said. "Thanks very much for getting this."

"No problem, hon."

Handing him one of the burgers, he started scarfing it down while driving with one hand. It was starting to get dark so I was glad he was at the wheel. I hated driving in the dark. Mark didn't mind, because his vision was better than mine. Feeding him another burger, I sipped on my milkshake and stared out the window.

While we drove, he told me more about the ordeal he went through under the council. I got very angry and wanted to tear them to pieces, but he assured me they had reached a deal. On the first part of our journey to Oregon, I had asked him questions, but he remained tight-lipped and didn't want to tell me. But eventually, he gave me the highlights.

He explained to me what he learned, namely that the ritual to turn a mortal required a special serum of some kind. He hadn't known this before. He told me that the council said I was in danger now since I wasn't given this serum and that I had to go through the ritual again.

"So let me get this straight," I said. "They want us to have mind-blowing sex again in their presence so they can inject me with something?"

"Well, it's not just the sex. It is the fact that I have to drain myself into you, and then they give you the injection. But basically, yes."

"Don't you anyway?"

"No, I don't drain myself," he said. "You get a good dose of venom, but I don't drain myself."

I fell asleep dreaming about the sex I was going to have again—the draining kind. I had vague memories of that night. But they were only vague. I remembered how weak Mark was, so weak he fell asleep. The amount of venom that went into me was a lot. I fell asleep too and it took a few hours for me to come back. I remembered the euphoria that sent me out-of-body, and the waves I rode.

"Falon, we're here," said Mark gently, shaking me.

I woke up with a crick in my neck. I realized that I had been stimulating myself during my dream. I shyly looked over at Mark to see if he noticed.

"Did you have a good dream?" he asked. His grin showed me that he had enjoyed watching.

"Yes, I dreamt of you taking me, and how hot it was," I said. "I guess my body wanted to feel the stimulation my brain was telling me I was."

"You never have to be embarrassed about anything your body wants or does around me," he said, seriously. "Never. I love your body. I love how your body responds. Whether it's to me or to a dream-me, I don't care."

He took my hand and brought it up to his lips and kissed it.

"Any time you want to stimulate yourself in front of me, you go ahead. I'll watch closely to see if I can learn some new tricks to try on you."

"Great, now I'm the teacher?"

"We both are, love. We'll learn from each other," he said.

Wasn't that the perfect answer? *He always says the nicest things to me*, I thought.

Looking out the front window, what lay before me was a huge modern glass building connected to a mountain. There were lights everywhere, both decorative and floodlights, making it almost seem like daylight. A valet came and took the keys from Mark as he led us into the main lobby.

Inside, there were full glass walls surrounding the security desk and blocking off the bank of elevators. Security was apparently very strict here. I took Mark's hand to keep him close. Gwen came walking out of the elevators toward them.

"You've made it," she said.

"It was a long drive," said Mark.

"Why did you drive? Wouldn't it have been easier to fly?" asked Gwen.

"Flying would have been easier. But having a car here means we can get out of here quickly, if necessary. Besides, it gave me time to talk to Falon and bring her up to date on everything that has happened. I haven't yet had that chance."

"I've been ordered to bring you to the council," said Gwen.

We went up a few floors and walked down a hallway that was lit along the floor like running lights on a plane. Gwen showed us into a room that had six people sitting in chairs up on a dais. They were cowled and hooded, covering their faces.

"Please sit down in the chairs provided," one of the council members said. "You've been brought here to answer for your crimes."

"Crimes? What crimes? What is with you people and your fetish for self-righteous judgements?"

"Your crime to attempt turning a mortal into an immortal without the knowledge, preparation, and skill. It has opened us to exposure, and this cannot be allowed."

"No one has exposed you," I said angrily. "And wait just a minute, if I—we—are being accused of something, we have a right to see our accusers' faces!"

"Please keep your human quiet."

"I will speak for her," said Mark.

"No, you will not, Mark," I said. "I am quite capable of speaking for myself."

"You are not allowed to speak to the Immortal Council as a human," they intoned.

"So I'm supposed to just stand here while you accuse me of things I haven't done?" I challenged them.

"Quiet, you insolent child," cried an Elder. "You are speaking to an immortal Elder. You will obey our laws or be put to death."

That shut me up—*not!*

"Look, we mean you no harm. We love each other and want to marry," I said.

"Mark, is this true? Does she understand what marriage in our family means and requires?"

"I have explained to her everything I know," he answered.

"Fine! Then the human will undergo the ritual with one of our warriors."

"Over my dead body," growled Mark.

"Why do you object?"

"She is my true love, and no one else will have sex with her!" he roared.

Startled by the passion of Mark's outburst, the Elders stood up and formed a closed circle away from the table to confer among themselves. It took five minutes before they returned to the table. One spoke for the rest.

"To turn a female mortal, the immortal must temporarily give up part of their own immortality," intoned the council member, without acknowledging that Mark had coweed them into submission. "This is done by drinking a poison that alters his venom so that it kills her mortal body as it drives her into an extreme orgasm. That orgasm produces the necessary chemicals in enough quantities that react with a serum that will be injected into her. This gives her immortality. The male can only drink the poison in a state of meditation. Otherwise, his body would metabolize it too quickly."

"You both will prepare for the ritual," said another council member. "Take them both to the preparation rooms."

Two people led each of us out of the council chamber. Mark was told to bathe and then a sheer robe was given to him to wear. He then had to go into a trance-like meditative state.

I was taken to a different room. Two women there gave me a bitter tea and then they drew a bath for me. They bathed my body and washed my hair, body, and even gave me a douche. Once rinsed with sweet water they dried me and wrapped a sheer robe around my shoulders. The robe fell to my feet and opened in the front. I found a sash and tied it at my waist. When I looked in the mirror, I realized this outfit left absolutely nothing to the imagination. Mark was going to love it.

When a gong sounded, the women escorted me out to a special viewing room. It was circular, and in the middle was a very large round bed with a canopy and curtains all the way around. They instructed me to get into the middle of the bed. That was good, because I was feeling some sort of effects from the tea.

Outside the curtains were chairs in two rows all the way around. I heard people entering the area beyond the curtains and sitting down. The lights went off behind the curtains, leaving only the bed illuminated.

I was sitting there in all my glory when Mark was escorted in. The effect was instant. His cock stood up so high it pointed the direction to go. My body answered his, my nipples standing out too. All I wanted to do was grab him.

Mark was escorted to the bed. I could tell from his face that Mark was working very hard not to just jump me. They opened the curtain for him to enter and then left the room, leaving us feeling like we were alone. But I knew better.

Taking my hand, he got on the bed. He knelt before me, looking into my eyes. I suddenly felt shy. Perhaps it was the audience. Mark took my hands and lifted them to his lips and kissed their tips. Working his way down the inside of my arm, he nipped and kissed his way right to my armpit.

I couldn't believe how hot it was to be touched like this. Maybe it was the knowledge we were being watched that added something. He was touching me all over gently. It was building up such a heat inside me, I thought I would explode.

"I intend to take my time," Mark announced.

"Whatever for?" I asked.

"They want a show, they'll get a show, but at least we'll have a good time."

Mark then kissed my lips. Gently, barely any pressure. It excited me so much I took his head and smashed my mouth to his, demanding his tongue. His fangs elongated a bit, and I played with them. I had recently learned that his fangs were sensitive and licking them was like another erogenous zone. Mark was moaning as his cock pushed its way through the opening of his robe.

Flicking my tongue and sucking on his lips brought him up to the point that venom was dripping. I sucked it off and got a little high on it. My own fangs had dropped and he was having fun rubbing them with his tongue.

Mark untied the sash and let it fall off me. He took my breast in his hand and sucked on it until it was hard. Licking it and blowing on my nipple sent ripples through my body as I shuddered with desire.

Moving to the other breast, he took it in his mouth while he pinched the first one in his fingers, doubling my pleasure. Using both hands, he took over my breasts, kissed me again, and nipped at my neck. His fangs grazed the skin and raised goosebumps.

He could smell my arousal, strong and powerful. He cupped my center; the heat was coming off in waves. Caressing my nub with his fingers, he spread my petals, his fingers playing me like a musical instrument.

I was squirming now with the heat building up so intensely; I was ready to orgasm. It would not take much more at all.

Mark pushed me back onto the bed. I looked up at him with sultry eyes. He spread my legs and dove on my center with his mouth.

He lapped up the delicious juices there and licked his lips. Licking me again the whole length of my slit, I raised my hips and pushed against his face. He grabbed onto my ass and held me strongly. When he took my clit in between his teeth, I screamed out, moving my hips against him even more.

"I need you, Mark!"

"I know, love. But wait." He had to bring us both higher.

He ramped up the heat by spearing his tongue and penetrating my vagina. I was so wet it was dripping out like honey. Pushing his tongue in as deeply as he could, he repeated his penetration. My breath was coming fast now as my excitement was going even higher, but he didn't want me to climax yet.

He replaced his tongue with fingers, curling them inside to find that g-spot. Pumping his fingers brought me to the brink, but again he stopped. Then he combined sucking on my clit with three fingers in my vagina. The pressure inside me exploded with a big climax, as he had hoped.

Taking his cock, he brought it to my vagina. Spreading my wetness all over his head, he slid inside until his head was covered.

I groaned deeply, and opened my eyes.

"That's what I wanted," I said. Pushing my body against him, I impaled myself on his cock deeply. We both cried out as the pleasure got us. Mark stilled himself.

"If I move right now, I'll come," he warned.

"Then I'll hold you," I responded.

I squeezed him hard as his shaft twitched with delight inside.

Slowly, Mark pulled out almost completely. I whimpered and moaned. He pushed back in slowly but didn't stop until he was entirely inside me. I sighed with pleasure.

"Now possess me with everything you have," I commanded.

The swirling gold in Mark's eyes glowed, and his fangs elongated to their full length.

"My pleasure. You're mine."

Then he started pounding me. I lifted my legs higher and wider to give him a better angle. Each time he impaled me, he felt a little harder. Each time he touched me there, a sweet sharp sensation accompanied it. Delicious pain.

Mark had to release not only his sperm, but his essence at the same time as draining all his venom. This would render him nearly mortal and completely sap his strength. But to do so, his climax had to be hard and heavy.

He started to go faster, penetrating me deeply with every stroke, hitting deep inside me. I was grunting and moaning with pleasure and pain as he punished me with his violence.

I was riding him like a stallion. My only thought was he was possessing me; he owned me and I loved it. It was so erotic the pain was exquisite.

Just when I didn't think I could last a second, my orgasm broke like a tsunami. Wave after wave shattered me, broke me, and rendered me utterly boneless.

As my climax happened, Mark shot his seed deep into me, emptying himself. Lifting his fully extended fangs, he bit into my neck at the same time. His venom pumped into me as his seed did, draining him completely until he got dizzy. It wasn't that he stopped, he passed out still embedded inside me.

I was riding my climax when the venom hit my bloodstream and suddenly I was soaring. The euphoria was the ultimate experience. Mark had told me the effect would diminish with time, but it was still as potent as the first time, and wow, was it potent this time! My body was completely detached from my mind. All I could feel was our connection—his cock impaling me and his fangs still embedded in my neck.

It took thirty minutes or more for the two of us to come back to our bodies. When we did, we looked at each other and smiled. Mark had removed his fangs from my shoulder and the injection site had healed already.

"Wow," I mumbled. *That never gets old.*

"I love you so much, Falon," Mark purred.

I grunted. I didn't really have any speech ability right now

He chuckled.

We were lying there in each other's arms, connected, when the curtains were opened.

"It's time for the injection," said a shrouded man. He walked over and injected me with something. "This will complete the transformation process." The liquid burned as it coursed through my arm.

"You may both stay here as long as you wish," said one of the council members behind the curtain. "This chamber is not in use for any particular reason now."

With that, we listened to the council members stand up and leave the room. I wondered if any of them had the impulse to light a cigarette. The lights remained off outside the curtains, and someone turned down the intensity of the lights over the bed.

"Falon, will you marry me?" I swallowed hard and found my voice.

"Mark, I hate to say this, but I think we already are," I said, grinning.

"I know," he said. "But will you?"

"Yes, I will marry you," I answered. Perhaps that deep seeding had planted a baby for me too? *One can always hope.*

8 - Moving On Up

— Falon

After the ceremony—ritual—whatever it was called—and we were released, we went home to Montreal. It seemed like the thing to do. My project in Kansas was proceeding fine, and with Peter on site I didn't really need to be there. It hadn't been long since I had been trapped in the building during the tornado, but he understood that I had been through a few traumatic events. My boss had told me to take a few weeks off after the tornado, so I wasn't expected back yet.

When we got home, the cats were delighted to see me—and there was a pile of mundane stuff to do. I mean, what does an immortal couple do with their time when they're at home? Laundry, cooking, cleaning, that's what. Just like everyone else.

On the way home, we stopped in Kansas, picked up all the stuff from the hotel room, and checked out. Everything came home with us, including all the clothes Lora and I had purchased after the abduction and break-in. Mark brought his suitcase, but more importantly he had a lot of things shipped up from Houston. Space was getting tight in my two-bedroom apartment.

"We need to find a larger place," he announced a week after we were home.

"I agree," I said. "How large?"

"A few bedrooms?"

"Do we want to rent or buy?"

"Rent for now."

I picked up the newspaper and scanned through the listings for rentals.

"What about your place in Houston?" I asked.

"Maybe it's a good time to put it on the market," he answered.

"Here's a place, a really nice one too."

"Three bedrooms, living with fireplace, large kitchen, dining and one bath," he read out loud. "Yeah, that sounds nice. Let's go look at it."

"Well, we should look at a few," I said.

"Here's another."

"New construction! Oh, I like that. A four-bedroom town with living/dining fireplace, chef's kitchen, finished basement, and three and a half baths. Oh that's even better, Mark."

"Call them both and let's make a decision today."

Calling each of the landlords, I made appointments for each of the properties later today. This was exciting! In the meantime, we continued cleaning and putting clothes away. It's a good thing I had two bedrooms. One was Mark's closet, and the other was mine.

The second place we saw we took, the one with the fireplace. It wasn't too far away, and it had all the space we needed, all for a decent price. We were moving in three weeks—and that wasn't a lot of time to pack.

"Moving Day" in Montreal is traditionally July 1st. Everyone moves on July 1st or nearly. That causes some interesting problems like finding a company to move you, or if you're moving yourself, finding a truck. The other problem was that the week before and the week after July 1st the rates were triple! And you couldn't rent a truck for the day, only eight hours. Because everyone was on the move on the same day, landlords didn't always have the time to clear out apartments. Tenants are expected to leave their places the way they found them, and if not, you were charged heavily for repairs.

We were doubly lucky. We hired a moving company and they arrived with the truck honking its horn at 8:00 a.m. We were also moving into a new place that had not been occupied before.

It didn't take the movers very long to pack up the truck; maybe three hours. Unloading was even faster. After everything was out of the apartment, I just walked around and looked at everything. I made sure it was clean, and there was no damage on the walls. I had never painted, so I didn't have to do that. I had a few tears because I had some happy memories here.

There were a few bags of things that couldn't go in the truck, so Mark was putting them in the car—including the cats. While he was doing that, I went across the hall and knocked on Armand's door.

He answered a few moments later.

"Yeah, what's up?" he asked.

"Just wanted to let you know I'm moving out today. Mark and I are going into a townhouse not too far from here," I said. "I wanted to thank you and say goodbye."

"Okay, thanks. Have a good move. Let me know when you're settled and I'll bring over some baked goods for you," said Armand.

"I will. Bye!"

Closing the front door for the last time, I locked it and went downstairs. I needed to remember to return the keys to the landlord. Mark was in the car, waiting for me with the boys in their carriers. He had left the windows down so it didn't get too hot for them. Such a considerate guy!

"Ready?" he asked.

"Yup, next adventure!" I said.

The new place was very close—maybe five minutes away. The street was still a construction zone with mud everywhere. We had no lawn yet, or a back deck for that matter, but it was brand new; no one else had lived in it.

The movers were almost finished, and they did their best to keep the mud outside. After the last item came off, they looked around to make sure they didn't miss something, then told us goodbye. They had two more families to move that day. Hard work, but awesome money.

Mark brought the cats in, closed our new front door which had been open most of the day, and took off his muddy shoes. He set the two cat carriers down in the kitchen and opened them to let the cats go explore. They came out slowly, not sure of this place, but once they saw we were there, they both got bold and started poking their noses into every nook and cranny. I showed them where the litter box was and walked into the living room where Mark was.

I dropped down onto the sofa beside him and we just sat there in each other's arms. A big sigh escaped from my lips as I put my head on his chest and felt his arm cross my back.

"We're here!" I said.

"Yes, the move went very well. Let's hope everything made it over here in one piece!" he answered.

"Let's order dinner, 'cause I'm starved!" I suggested.

"Good idea! Pizza okay?"

"Perfect."

I heard him call in the pizza order as I went upstairs to take a look at the waterbed situation. Assembling it wasn't difficult, it just needed to be done before we could fill it. Thankfully, I had my tools taped to the pieces. I started putting the frame together and had most of it done by the time Mark found me upstairs.

"Where do you want to put the bed?" he asked. "I will move it into place for you."

"Full or empty?" I asked.

He glanced at me and grinned, remembering that night he had moved my waterbed for me when it was full. Something he shouldn't have done.

"As you wish, my lady," he bowed. "You know, I hadn't expected you to notice I did that back then. It was a surprise to me when you challenged me. I was so caught up by you that my brain had stopped working."

"Those days were indeed intense. I couldn't get enough of you, I was seriously addicted to you."

"There I was sneaking around, trying not to get caught by my family, and my sister was breathing down my neck. She knew something was different with me."

"I'm so glad I found you again," I said. "Well, you found me again."

"Let's get this filled so we can make love on it for our first night."

"Oh, let's!"

He helped me tighten the screws and move it into place on one long wall. The dressers went along the other side. Next came the footing and the heater. Finally, the bladder. I went and unwound the hose to bring the water from the bathroom to start filling the bed. Soon, it would be ready to sleep in.

"It should be ready by the time we finish dinner," said Mark.

The doorbell rang. *Yeah, food!* While Mark got the door, I made space in the kitchen; we set the pizza on the table and grabbed some chairs.

"Wait, the boys need their food too," I said as I started scrambling around looking for the right box.

"Here it is," called Mark. He brought me two dishes and a can for the boys. We all sat down and had dinner together.

Even though the big items were basically where they needed to go, there was a lot of work ahead of us. Mark was like me, he didn't want to live out of a box. So we were both very determined to unpack as quickly as possible.

After dinner, we finished the bed, getting it made and ready for tonight.

We left the rest for tomorrow and crashed on the sofa again with the cats. I managed to get the TV working, so we turned it on.

Mark, though, had other ideas. His wandering hand worked its way under my shirt to my breast and was caressing the nipple ever so gently. It responded by standing up and taking notice of the attention. My head was leaning against his chest, so I heard his heart rate elevate a touch when I placed my hand on his now swelling shaft. My hand gently caressed him up and down.

Neither of us were watching TV, so I wasn't surprised that he picked up the remote and turned it off. His arms slid under me, and he held me as he stood up. My arms went around his neck as he carried me upstairs into our new bedroom. There were no lights, but there were no curtains either. The moon was full and the light shone in brightly. He placed me gently on our bed, and carefully took off each piece of clothing, dropping them on the floor.

Once his clothes were off too, he lay down beside me, pulling me into his arms for a wonderful kiss. Skin to skin, heat to heat, we kissed. He possessed me and then took me fully in one motion. Holding still for a moment or two, our bodies were joined and speaking to each other. When he started to move, it was a slow dance that brought us both to climax in the most sensual way. It was beautiful, unhurried, and peaceful. He filled me utterly, and his bite sent me soaring.

It took a few weeks to get everything unpacked and a place found for it. The basement became Mark's office and the cats' playground. Mark made it his mission to build a wet bar downstairs so we could have an entertainment room.

Upstairs, things were going into place. The new laundry machines were off the kitchen, and they were getting lots of use.

Food stores were within walking distance. I started going shopping for things on a daily basis—so the food was the freshest.

We'd heard from the Elders since the ritual. They were clearly checking up on me to make sure I was still there. They were satisfied that I would protect their secret with my own life. So the threat from them was over—I hoped.

I was walking from the store one day when I experienced horrible pain. This was not supposed to happen anymore. I had not had my menses for months: since before the ritual, in fact. The last time was before Mark really bit me the second time, the time I'd given consent.

Yet the pain I was having felt like those only all over my body. The family had their own physician. He was an old man by their standards, even though he didn't look over forty. Mark called the family to ask their advice.

When the physician got there, he indicated that it could take six to seven months before the body had fully changed. He explained that all the cells in my body were being recreated. My blood type and bone mass would change, as well as the musculature of my frame. He explained that the change was almost equivalent to that of a butterfly in its complexity.

The doctor also explained that the few small things I had noticed to date were simply the enzymes fixing the "errors" of my mortal body, so that the process could start.

"Did anyone take blood samples from you before the ritual?" he asked.

"No."

"Did anyone measure your vision and hearing before the ritual?" he asked.

"No."

"So all we have is your eye exam from a human doctor, is that correct?" he asked.

"Yes."

"Okay, we will have to take some measurements now and see what we have. Let's check your vision first, seeing as we have historical data," replied the doctor. "I'll also do a full physical and blood work on you for our records."

The doctor finished his work-up and went on his way. An hour later, the doorbell rang. When I went to answer it, Gwen was outside. Gwen walked in like I was expecting her.

"Why are you here?" I asked.

"You need some information that a male wouldn't have, so I have volunteered to tell you," she said. "May I sit down?"

"Sure, come in. What does this pertain to?" I asked.

Gwen came in and sat on the sofa. I offered her refreshments but she declined. She seemed uncomfortable, and that had me wondering what it was she wanted to tell me.

"This is about being a female immortal. As an immortal, there are some differences. As a human, you were born with all the eggs you would ever have. As you mature, you shed those eggs in your menses. If they become fertilized, they produce a baby. It's quite a simple process.

"As an immortal, you don't have the same process. The obvious difference is your body lives much longer. However, you were still born with all the eggs you'll ever have. So our bodies don't shed them in menses. Instead, you will get pregnant when a compatible male inseminates you. In this way, your body conserves the eggs for the length of time you'll be alive."

"You mean I won't menstruate anymore?" I asked. "How does my body know what is compatible and what is not?"

"Excellent questions," said Gwen. "I'll have that water, if you don't mind."

I stood up, got her a glass of water, and sat down again.

"The intensity of the orgasm releases different hormones. I don't completely understand it because I'm not a chemist. However, I do know that there are different levels of intensity," she continued. "The highest level of intensity, experienced between true love matches, produces the most potent venom and the most hormones. These hormones are nothing more than chemicals. The chemicals unlock the sperm's ability to fertilize the egg. This ensures that only mated couples will produce children."

She added, "And no, you will no longer have monthly bleeding."

"Yahoo!" I cheered. "Mark and I are mated. Does that mean we can get pregnant?"

"Yes, in all likelihood, you will get pregnant. Pregnancy for immortals is tricky. As our body creates and builds another being, most of our strength will go into that, instead of us. This is the only time we females are easily killed. It only happens to females, so the males know that their role of protector is even more important.

"But there is another thing you need to know, and that is you won't get pregnant very often. We don't have a 'fertility range.' Our bodies have been restored to what they were when we were our healthiest. That means we forever remain fertile. There isn't a set number of years during which you can get pregnant like when you're mortal. If you are alive two thousand years, you will still be able to get pregnant. The only limiting factor is how many eggs you have."

"Whoa! That is freaky!" I said.

"Upon completing the change from mortal to immortal, your body will remain the age it is now for the rest of time. You are in your late twenties, early thirties?"

"I'll be thirty forever? What a hoot! Or twenty-nine. After all, I'll be lying about my age."

"Pregnancies can have complications," finished Gwen.

"Are you telling me this because the doctor thinks I may be pregnant?" I asked.

"What is happening to you now is that your mortal body is dying and becoming an immortal body. Those changes are painful because parts of your body are being remade."

"What other changes can I expect?" I asked.

"Your vision will improve. In fact, it will become better than the best human vision. You will also be able to see in low level light, and perhaps darkness. The males have a night vision that we don't, but we can see heat."

"You will also experience better hearing, a wider range of frequencies, as well as lower volumes," she added.

"The last major change for you will be growing fangs," said Gwen.

"Fangs, you mean like Mark's?" I asked, pretending I didn't already know.

"Yes, like Mark's but different. Your fangs will not be as pronounced and likely not useful as a weapon, except if you are pregnant. They would be your only built-in weapon. Your fangs also produce venom that enhances the sexual experience."

"So I've seen," she confirmed.

"You have fangs already?"

I opened my mouth and showed Gwen my new sharp little teeth. Thinking of Mark naked made them grow about a centimeter.

"Oh my, that was quick."

I didn't let on that the other changes she had mentioned had also started. Believing that she and Mark had already initiated her change some months ago, this was proof.

Over the weeks, I saw more changes to my strength. It may be my imagination, but the changes were happening faster now. Perhaps that injection actually did do something. I broke a jar accidentally while trying to open it. I also flipped a chair over completely when I tried to lift it. These things were startling, but I had to learn how to adapt. Pushing less, applying less pressure, all these things were not second nature to me, but slowly I learned.

One morning I woke up and my vision was even better. I could see grains of dirt on the floor, which was disturbing, but interesting.

Walking over to the window, I looked outside and saw detail I had never seen before. The veins in the leaves at the back of the yard; the feathers on a bird sitting up in a tree; even the blades of grass in the lawn were visible. What a glorious ability!

The improved vision was useful. Improved hearing? Not so much. Now I could hear people arguing across the street in their houses. And tiny noises irritated me like nothing else now. When a tap dripped, it was distracting at least, and painful at most. Being among humanity with really, really, good hearing was not a bonus. *I'll have to ask Mark about that one—maybe he has coping skills I can learn.*

Every morning after my shower, when Mark didn't distract me, that is, I went over the laundry list of scars I had on my body. All of them had disappeared, even the really deep one from the skating accident. The hole in my leg had disappeared too; and apparently the nerves had regenerated, because I could feel the bottom of my foot again.

Mark had been noticing the changes too. When I collected all my old glasses to give away to charity, he smiled. And when he couldn't sneak up on me anymore, he pouted. But he did enjoy helping me go over my body looking for blemishes that weren't there anymore.

Meanwhile, Mark relished my body becoming immortal. He could feel my strength building and that made sex exciting. I was no longer weaker than him! And my body scents had changed too. My arousal was so much more noticeable to him, just as his arousal was now noticeable to me. But his favorite change was my fangs.

He said he'd also noticed that the weakness that took hold of him right after the ritual, was gone. He'd asked the doctor about the weakness, and the answer was that the drugs he took before the ritual ensured that he passed the essence of his immortality to me. They deprived him of it, and it had to build back up. For a few days, his weakness indicated that he was, in fact, a mortal for a short while. It was the sacrifice a male must make to turn a female mortal.

Now that his essence was back, his body responded faster to me, and our lovemaking became even more intense.

9 - Retirement

— Falon

Six weeks after the tornado, I went back to Kansas to work. Things pretty much felt like they did months ago before all the trauma, but my interest in my job was waning, because it just didn't mean the same to me. I was thinking it was time to go out on my own again, build something different. Perhaps Mark and I could do something together.

The justification for this change happened the day I lifted a big box down from a shelf over my head. One of the guys in the office noticed and ran over to help me, but I managed to put him off saying it really wasn't that heavy. He looked at me sideways, but left.

It would be something tiny like that incident that would give me away. I couldn't afford to have a secret like ours get out. So it was time to leave the day-to-day world of humans, at least the mundane ones.

Walking into Peter's office, I was prepared for a bit of a fuss.

"Peter, may I have a moment?" I asked.

"Sure, kiddo," said Peter. "How are your legs feeling by the way? Six weeks isn't really enough time to heal, is it?"

"Well, with the pins my healing time was shorter. It's the reason Mark insisted on that treatment."

"Well, that is good. What can I do for you?"

"I feel that I have run to the end of what I can do here and need to spread my wings and grow on my own," I blurted out in a rush. "So I would like to give you notice of my resignation. I can stay on as long as you need to find my replacement, as long as it doesn't go past a month."

"Wow! I didn't see this coming!" said Peter. "Is there anything I can do to change your mind? Are you unhappy here with the work?"

"No, not at all, I've enjoyed the work. It's just time for a change. While I was at home working with Mark, I realized I have the opportunity to do so much more with his help. I have wanted to create my own business for years, and I feel like I'm ready to dive in."

"Okay, then, we'll be sorry to see you go. We won't need more than two weeks. There have been other plans in the works for a few months now. As you know, Norm and I have sold the company. There will be changes to the staff as they take over," he admitted.

"Huh! Well, then it seems like kismet, then. They have their own staff to do what I do. My job would become obsolete."

"I'd never let that happen to you, Falon. I personally made sure your position in the company was assured. If it looked like that would not have happened, the three of us had other plans and we would have brought you along with us."

"That's awfully nice of you. I appreciate the vote of confidence," I said. "I'm still looking forward to kick-starting my own business. But may I reserve the ability to come back to you for advice?"

"Anytime, hun, anytime!" He got up, walked around his desk, and gave me a big hug. "You've been a great employee and we—Norm and I—have always appreciated how hard you worked and that you always made it work, whatever that 'it' was."

Blushing now at the praise, I hugged him back. A tear formed in my eye unexpectedly. I had a lot of respect for this man. He was a good boss even if he was a bit of a womanizer. He was always fair, and he always spoke the truth.

"Thanks, I'll just stop in and see Norm."

Repeating the same conversation to Norm was just as difficult, but a little more stilted because I didn't work directly with him. We didn't know each other as well.

Going back to my desk, I realized that I could now think of the future. I went through all the things on my desk with the purpose of closing off all the projects I had on the go and leaving it all a clean slate. It wasn't really that important, especially if they were closing this department, but it was a matter of pride for me.

The next two weeks flew by. On my last Friday, I quietly packed up the last of my personal things. The office was basically empty as everyone had gone home. I didn't announce I was leaving to anyone on purpose. I was sitting there all finished and looking around. My keys and my pass card were in an envelope that I would leave on Elaine's desk for her. I picked up my briefcase and was walking out the door when Peter and Norm came walking down their hallway with the other two executives.

"Falon, have a drink with us before you leave," called Peter.

"Don't mind if I do," I answered.

The five of us stood around the reception desk, with a glass in our hands, and toasted to the future. These four men were about to make a bloody fortune as the new owners took over, and I was off to other pastures. It was nice to share that moment with them. I had worked intimately with each of these men over the past four years and knew them well. The sleazy VP Sales, the stalwart VP Marketing, the Exec VP Peter, and the President, Norman, we'd made some software magic together.

Now it was time for me to leave. I got hugs from all of them, and a promise that their doors were always open.

On my way home, I was both excited and sad, so driving home was cathartic. There was no one on the road as it was 7:30 p.m. on a Friday. Everyone was either already home or at a bar downtown for Friday night. I had the road to myself all the way home.

Mark was there with a glass of champagne, waiting.

"Congratulations, love," he said, taking me into his arms for a hug. "Here, put down your case, kick off your shoes, and sit down with this champagne. It's the first day of the rest of our lives together. We're going to start it off right."

I did that. I dropped my case, kicked off my shoes, and went and sat in front of the fireplace. Mark brought me my champagne. He emptied the car while I sat and mused.

Now that I was home, I could dedicate myself to developing the business that I'd wanted to do for a long time—developing education for commercial enterprises. Education, like teaching technical writers how to write a manual, or engineers how to write a report. We all knew that just because you had a degree, or a couple of degrees, didn't mean you could write clearly so that others would understand.

How many of us have tried to put an object together with a user manual written by an engineer? Too many of us.

I'd always felt that continuing learning once you got a job, especially skills necessary for the job, was the most important learning you could do. So many middle management people got to their positions because of skill, but then the skills they had were no longer used. Instead, they were expected to prepare reports, write to customers, correspond with higher-ups, and communicate to staff. Most of them don't have the writing skills for any of that. That is where I came in. Now I had to sell this idea to top corporations like banks and engineering companies.

I need a plan!

Starting fresh the next day, I set out to develop a business plan. I knew what I wanted to do, I just needed to figure out how to get there. But after working long hours, I needed a break. For some reason, it wasn't coming together for me. I was having trouble focusing on what I needed to do. I knew this business inside and out. After all, I had been doing it for about four years now.

I'm going to go have a bath. Maybe a bottle of wine and some bubbles would help me think my way through this apparent block.

I stepped into the hot water and eased myself into the bubbles. I had a bottle of white wine and some crackers and cheese to go along with it. The tub had this nifty tray across the tub to put my glass and bottle on. I put on some music and let myself sink into the water up to my chin. As my mind emptied, I drifted between memories.

"Falon, I'm going out for a while. Do you need anything?"

"No, I'm good, thanks."

I went back to my musings. *My God, the past six years have been tumultuous!* I'd been kidnapped, raped, tortured, caught in a tornado and a hurricane, lost a love, discovered an old dead love is my new love, learned about supernatural beings, and now I was one myself. *No wonder my mind is chaotic! No wonder I can't think of anything! Yikes.*

Okay, Falon. What's wrong with your business model?
Nothing really, except, except that it was a human's aspiration to
achieve. *I'm immortal now. Does that change things?* Yes, it did.
How? Well, building a small business seems so minor in
comparison to living forever. So insignificant. So needless. The
world didn't need another small business fighting for their share
of the pot. Does it? *No.*

So what does the world need?

It needs solutions to some pretty big problems, that's what.
Can I do that? Could I find solutions to big problems? *Maybe.*
Maybe I just needed to solve one. Maybe I needed something
that I could sink my teeth into. Okay, it wasn't going to be a
writing business, nor was it going to be an education business. It
needed to be something different. *But what?*

Could I get involved with emergent technologies to help
solve pollution? What about the alternative energies industry?
Either of those had a huge learning curve though, and by the time
I was knowledgeable about those subjects, they'd already be past
me.

My stomach growled, telling me I was hungry. The cheese
and crackers I was nibbling weren't doing it for me. Besides, my
head was starting to feel a little light from the heat of the water
and the wine. I'd better get out and get dressed again. I decided
to go out for a bite to eat while Mark was out.

Dressed, I grabbed my sweater and purse, left the
townhouse and started walking down the street. There was a
coffee shop not too far away from where I was aiming for. About
halfway there, I got that creepy feeling on the back of my neck.
You know the one that tells you someone is following or
watching. Yeah, that one. I stopped and listened with my new
and improved hearing. Other than the scuttling of small rodents,
I heard nothing out of the ordinary. My sense of smell didn't
pick up anything either.

I stopped at a corner and slowly looked 360 degrees around me. I didn't see anyone, so I shadow walked to the coffee shop. When I got there, the restaurant was busy. That was good, because I suddenly didn't want to be alone. I got a table by the window in the corner. I could see the whole restaurant from there. I ordered a sandwich, coffee, and a donut.

I pulled out my book—I took one everywhere—to read until the food arrived. Thanking the server, I started eating my food when that feeling returned. Carefully, I looked around the coffee shop. Everyone was minding their own business or talking to someone they were with. So it wasn't coming from here. I looked out the window beside me. The parking lot wasn't well lit, but my vision let me see into the shadows. There was no one there. I tried to find someone who might be staring at or tailing me.

It didn't make sense. Why would someone be watching me? I mused.

Still not clearly seeing anyone, I went back to my meal and book. Mark called me during my meal to let me know that he was on his way home.

"I should be home in about half an hour," he said.

"That's nice," I told him. "I am grabbing a bite at the coffee shop."

"Well, why don't I meet you there instead?" he suggested. "Then I can drive you home."

I finished my meal before Mark arrived, so I decided to order a dozen donuts to take home. My favorite ones were the maple glazed custard-filled ones. I got a couple of those and ate one while I was sitting there. Yes, a second donut. *I don't have to watch what I eat anymore! Yeah!*

Out of the corner of my eye, I swear I saw someone sneak up behind a car parked outside. I actually looked straight at the spot and didn't see anything. *I think I'm going crazy.* There have been too many creepy things that have happened, for me to completely relax anymore. I kept jumping at shadows. A minute later, my peripheral vision caught movement again, and this time when I looked, I thought I saw Brandon ducking behind a car. *Brandon? Why would he be here in Montreal? It must be some look-alike.*

Mark finally arrived, and when he walked in the door, all the female eyes snapped to him. Clear disappointment showed on their faces as he whizzed by them and sat down with me.

I could swear there were some sighs or growls—maybe both. *Too bad, ladies, he's mine!*

"Hi, love," he said after kissing me hard and then sitting down.

"That was quite the entrance," I said.

"Oh, how so?" he asked, grinning.

"Well, when you walked in all eyes swiveled to you, mister. You should have seen the hearts breaking as you walked past," I sighed.

"Your gain!" he said cheerfully.

"You're in a good mood," I said. "What's up?"

"The new deal I've been working on went through," Mark said excitedly. "That's the new technology company I was talking about last month. They are investing heavily into artificial intelligence for the future and we'll be on the ground floor."

"Oh, that does sound exciting," I said enthusiastically. "What field are they in?"

"Developing autonomous operating platforms that can be used in a variety of different machines."

"Tell me more," I said, offering him a donut.

As he was telling me all about the deal, what the company did, and why it was good for us, I kept one eye on the parking lot outside. I was still hoping to see the stalker I felt earlier.

"Falon," said Mark. "Are you in there?"

"Oh!" I said, shaking my head back to reality. "Sorry. I was listening to the noises outside to see if I could detect my stalker out there."

"Stalker?" growled Mark.

"Well, I don't know if it's a stalker. I thought I felt someone following me on the way here."

My phone rang. I startled and then laughed as I answered it and there was silence on the other end. Then Mark's phone did the same thing.

"How often has this happened?" he asked.

"A few times on the hang-ups. I haven't thought much about it."

"Our numbers are not available to the main system. No one should be calling them that aren't known to us."

"Even a lucky telemarketer with an auto dial?" I asked.

"Not even them," he insists. "I am going to look into this. I don't like these calls. In the meantime, let's go home and devour those donuts."

"Fine by me," I said.

Another stalker incident occurred when Mark arranged for me to meet a colleague who could use my business services. It was a law firm downtown. The meeting went very well. In fact, they purchased my services to develop language education for their interns and residents. The lawyers themselves didn't do any writing anymore. It was all done by underlings.

Coming home from that meeting, my spirits were soaring. This was a good break. I took the train into the city because it was just smarter, but I parked at the train station. When I got to the station, it was quite dark outside. That in itself no longer bothered me because I could see in the dark now, but it was a long way to walk across empty space. With my history of being followed, it freaked me out. I wasn't looking forward to this.

Walking across the empty parking lot, I went from light to light. It was pitch black in between them and they were far enough apart that the pools of light didn't overlap. For absolutely no reason, I started to feel panic rising in me. There was no one there. I pulled out my phone and called Mark. He was at home. I felt stupid for being nervous. He stayed on the phone with me until I was inside my car and driving away. I still didn't think like an immortal.

A third incident happened a week later when I was walking through the pedestrian tunnel. It went over the road so you could get to the other parking lot. The tunnel's lights were out. I freaked myself out again. By the time I got to my car I was shaking like a leaf.

Finally, a fourth incident happened, and Mark came to my rescue outside a building downtown. I was on my way to the train, and there were a lot of dark streets to walk. I was certain someone was behind me. This time, I decided to use the shadow walking skill Mark had taught me. I hid in the shadows of a building to wait for my assailant.

"Falon, where are you?" asked Mark as he approached the corner where I was waiting.

"I can see you. Can't you see me? You're right in front of me," I answered.

"Not yet," he said. As he walked closer, his eyes widened. "Well done!" Mark exclaimed. "You figured that out all on your own!"

"Figured out what?"

"You're wrapped in shadow. That's a skill that is related to the shadow walking I taught you," he explained. Mark finally was beside me and he folded me into his arms. "You're trembling."

"I think I'm becoming afraid of my own shadow!" I said disgustedly. "Now, what do you mean?"

"Don't be so hard on yourself," he said. "You've had some nasty experiences recently. I expect you've got a little PTSD. Let's go to the car and I'll explain on the way home. I'm calling Andrews too. This has happened too often."

We thought we spotted a person behind us once or twice. The face was a flash of familiarity, but it was never clear.

"Mark, could it be someone we know already?"

"Yes, it could. Are you thinking of anyone in particular?"

"Yes. While I was at the coffee shop, I could swear I saw someone who looked like Brandon."

"Brandon?"

"Yeah, the guy from Atlanta."

"Hmm. Well I'm hearing rumours that there is a hunter around again. So it could be them. We'll just have to stay alert."

10 - Be Ready!

— Falon

Mark was right. I've been through some nasty experiences recently. I needed to be better prepared for the complications that seemed to be constantly thrown our way. I needed to learn how to take care of myself. In short, I needed to take an inventory of my new "powers" and learn how to use them.

First was learning how to fight. I didn't know the first thing about throwing a punch or defending myself. This had to change.

I asked Andrews what he recommended I learn. He told me Krav Maga, which was an Israeli martial art taught to the military and adapted for civilians. It was one of the most effective forms of self defense, because it used real street-fighting techniques. So I signed up with a private instructor that Andrews recommended.

My new immortal body was made for this. It was fast, strong, and well balanced. The forms came naturally to me. It was like I knew it all along, I just had to be reminded. The movements were lightning-fast and deadly with a weapon in hand. The form taught you to use what was at hand too, not to rely on specific objects. "Anything can be turned into a weapon, even a slipper," said my trainer.

While I doubted the generalization, I accepted the philosophy. Learning to grab what was at hand in an emergency and use it in self-defense was a truly useful skill. I thought back to when I had escaped that room, and while I didn't run into people, I left behind a valuable resource: the chair.

Using Krav Maga, I could have turned that chair into a number of weapons; even the ties that were on me would have been useful. So already I could see ways to help myself better.

Another thing I needed to do was to learn from Mark about the special skills I had. One evening, I decided to corner him and get him to teach me.

"Mark, I want more lessons on immortal powers. What kinds of things can you do?" I asked.

"Well, I've shown you shadow walking," he answered. "How is that going?"

To answer him I shadow-walked upstairs to the kitchen and back in a second, bringing him a glass of water.

"Very good! You've been practicing," he said proudly. "You have figured out how to get to a location that you cannot immediately see, so how did you do that?"

"I know the location, so I just pictured myself in front of the sink and took a step and I was there."

"Exactly, and that is how we move greater distances. As long as you know where you are going, you can use that technique. When you don't know where you are going, you need to use sightlines to move in stages. Think of it as point-to-point walking."

"So let's go somewhere together," I suggested.

"All right, how about a restaurant down the street? We know where they are but not the exact look of it. So this time we're going to go in increments as far as we can see."

"From where do we start?"

"Let's go to the balcony and spot a point," he said. "How about the telephone booth on the adjacent corner down there?" he asked.

"Okay, so we move to the outside of the box?"

"Yup. On three: one, two, three." He disappeared.

I focused on the box and concentrated hard seeing myself just outside the door. Taking a step, everything blurred, and a second later I was standing on the corner outside the telephone booth.

"Wow! What would the humans see?" I asked.

"They would see a blur that was beyond their ability to decode. Then they would just see us here. Most will not realize we 'appeared' suddenly, and think we were simply out of sight."

"Cool! What next?"

"Well, look down the road. What's the furthest point you can see?"

"Um, the Red Lobster sign."

"Meet you there."

And he was gone. So I quickly focused and shadow walked there too. He was standing in the shadow of the sign and was barely visible.

"How did you do that?" I asked.

"This is shadow wrapping. It's very useful when you don't want to be seen. Remember that night you were scared when someone was following you?" he asked. "While you were standing on the corner, you instinctively wrapped shadow around yourself. So we're going to try to do that now. Come stand here in the shade. See the shade as an object extending from the sign. Make the shadow have a body and then take hold of the sides of it," he instructed.

I tried it. It was difficult! As I concentrated on the shade, it gradually started to see the edges of it as if it were an object separate from the sign. However, when I tried to grab the edges, it all disappeared like steam.

"This will take lots of practice. We should work on it at night, when the shadows are darker and easier to work with. For now, let's return home. Do you think you can do it in one step?" he asked.

"Hmm, let's try!" I closed my eyes, picturing my balcony and me standing on it waiting for Mark. Then I took a step.

And like magic, a few seconds later I was there. That was amazing. Well, it's not *like* magic. It *is* magic. *Who knew I could do magic?*

"That will never get old," I said to Mark as he came through the door.

"You learn fast!" he said, hugging me.

"So what else can I do?" I asked, eager to learn.

"You have fangs," he said.

"How can I use them?"

"You should be able to incapacitate an enemy with the venom. They are not as large as mine, so they won't get so long they come out of your mouth. But they are long enough that if you bite someone, they will receive a dose of venom."

"Will it matter where I bite the person?" I asked.

"I don't think so, they'll receive a dose no matter what. However, the closer you are to the heart, the faster it will take effect."

"So don't bite their ankles," I grinned.

"Only if you want to be an ankle-biter!" he laughed.

"Ha ha," I said.

"Neck is the fastest, but a wrist would work too," he said. "Now, it's the duration that is key: longer than a count of five and you're getting into killing doses, so avoid that. You want a bite that is three counts to incapacitate. That will make them unconscious. That's a 'one Mississippi, two Mississippi' count."

"Okay, what's that do to an immortal?" I asked.

"You know the answer to that one. You experience it when I bite you," he responded, stepping a little closer and dropping his voice.

"The longer I bite?"

"The more venom is pumped into the person, the higher he gets to the point of overdose."

"Could I accidentally overdose you?" I asked, suddenly fearful.

"It's possible, yes. It would take a lot of venom though."

"What about strength?"

"Let's do a fun test. Arm wrestle me," he said.

I would never have done this before because it was a lost cause, but now I was curious to see how I measured up to his strength. Setting up on the kitchen table, we did a classic arm-wrestling scenario. He didn't try to take me down, but let me push myself and judged how strong I was against him. Then he pushed me over.

"That's not bad, Falon. Pretty good in fact. I'd say you're easily as strong as the average human male now. The Krav Maga will improve that too as your muscles become more accustomed to the exertion."

"My hand strength is what I have noticed the most. I can squish and crush things much easier than I used to," I said.

"We should get a device to measure grip strength. We can monitor it over time to see where it improves."

"Busting out of that building, I was able to twist the locks on the doors until they broke."

"Useful skills," he said. "Next, vision: you could see quite far during the day. Let's test darkness."

He brought me into the bathroom and closed the door. While it was dark there, it was far from total darkness. I felt my human eyes could still see once adjusted.

"This isn't difficult enough. I can still see in here," I said.

"Can you read? Can you see the colors?" he asked.

Now, that I hadn't thought of.

"No, but I can see your face pretty clearly, and the details of the bathroom."

"Close your eyes for a few moments, then open them again. Like human eyes, ours need a few moments to adjust."

I did that, closed my eyes and counted to ten. When I opened up my eyes I gasped. I could see colors in the dark. Where once it was shades of gray, I could see the slightest blush of color.

"How is that possible? I thought our eyes need light to see colors."

"Look into the mirror."

I turned to the mirror and gasped again. My eyes were glowing purple! *How cool is that!* A gentle light was emitting from them—enough to give me color on the objects I was looking at. Truly amazing.

"Why are my eyes purple? Your eyes are gold. What does purple mean?"

"I'm not sure, I haven't seen purple before. Usually it's gold, so this may signify something special."

When I looked back at Mark's face, his eyes were glowing now too, but not the swirls I usually saw, but a gentle light.

"So the swirling means...?" I asked.

"Aggression or arousal," he answered.

"And when they're red?" I asked.

"This indicates an increase in blood flow to our eyes for hunting. The blood flow helps us see heat signatures—sort of like infrared."

"You have heat vision!" I said excitedly. "Can you see through walls?"

"No, that's not in our repertoire. You should be able to access heat vision yourself. I don't know what would trigger it, or if you can just make your eyes do it."

Staring at myself in the mirror, I focused on my eyes being red. I tried really hard to "make myself do it" but it didn't work. Then I thought of the night I was raped and suddenly my eyes were glowing red.

"Ooooh! That is scary looking!" I said.

"Your other senses, hearing and smelling, do not have offensive uses, but they are very useful in defensive maneuvers. You will hear someone much sooner than they will hear you.

You'll be able to smell emotions too, like lust, guilt, anger. These will give you an advantage and let you 'read the room'."

"Anything else?" I asked. "Like what did you do to Brandon in the bar?"

"I compelled him to answer me," said Mark. "It's a technique that has many uses. It's where the myth that vampires thrall their victims comes from. We can manipulate human minds. Some of us can do much more than others. For example, there are those who can remove memories, or make a human follow a complex set of instructions. Hearing thoughts is another, and so is reading emotions."

"Can these be taught to me?" I asked.

"You will develop your own special power. Not every immortal has all abilities. When you discover something is different, let me know and perhaps I can help you learn how to harness it. Have you noticed anything different?"

Hmm, had I? I hadn't noticed anything, but then I didn't know what was possible.

"Not yet—I don't think so anyway," I answered.

"Oh, the last skill I know of is the least common, and that is shape shifting. A very few of us can change our forms completely. That is not the same thing as a glamor to disguise our faces. It involves completely changing your body shape. The restriction is, you cannot change your mass. So whatever you change into must have the same mass and weight."

"So like a person into a wolf?" I asked.

"Yes, as long as the wolf has the same mass as the person. It usually ends up being a very large wolf."

"But not a bat?"

"No, not a bat," he burst out laughing. "Only in the movies will you see a vampire change into a bat. Maybe a small dragon, though."

"How about a cat?" I asked. "Familiars are part of the mythology, aren't they?"

"Again, it would have to be the same mass—so the cat would be a panther, not a house cat."

"How do you know if you have these abilities?" I asked.

"It usually happens by accident the first time," he answered. "It's not uncommon for a partial change to happen, signifying the ability is latent. Like a hand becoming a claw, or part of your face changing texture or shape."

"Can you fly?" I asked. "Can we fly?"

"Not without a plane," he chuckled. "That would be a very useful power to have. The fastest we can go is shadow walking."

I was thinking through my memories of books and movies I had read to come up with other tropes and myths about vampires. Drinking blood was the only other obvious one, but Mark had already disqualified that nonsense. *Oh!* I thought of one.

"What about the thing of having to be invited into a person's house in order to be able to go in?"

"That's pure myth. We have no restrictions at all where we can go," he answered.

"Oh last one, what about sunshine?" I asked. "Does it affect you?"

"You know the answer to that one. It does not. We can walk around in daylight as much as humans. However, our eyes are sensitive, so we need good sunglasses."

I decided that on a daily basis I was going to start practicing as much as I could. I wanted to find whatever latent abilities I had.

11 - Declarations

— Lora

Life seemed to be moving slowly for me. I didn't know why. Rick and I were getting along well. The kids were doing well. Heck, even their father had been cooperating recently. Yet I seemed to be in a funk.

Falon and Mark were back in Montreal after their ritual in Oregon. They had moved to a new home too. Falon had quit her job and had a brand-new life ahead of her. Her life was changing quickly. Maybe that was why I was antsy for change.

I think I was a little jealous. I'd never been jealous before. It was a strange, unsettling feeling.

The excitement of meeting Rick had dispelled a bit, as we had several weekends together now. *I need to start something new.*

But what?

I got the kinky sex thing out of my system. At least for now. I was looking forward to being with Rick again. I'm not sure why I had to experience triple penetration, but ever since I heard a friend talking about it, I was curious. For me, curiosity is sometimes a dangerous thing.

But I'd done it. It was a lot of fun, and the feeling of having been penetrated by three at once—well, that was spectacular. It had hurt like a bitch though, even with lube and being over-excited. It was the kind of pain you can get over, a pain that was pleasurable, but I didn't want pain with lovemaking all the time.

Not everyone can do kinky. There were so many different types of kink too, it was astounding. But perhaps Rick would explore some with me. It wasn't that I was bored with traditional sex, just that I liked pushing boundaries. I believed he did too.

It had been a while since Rick and I were together. Two months. Well, at least we had been talking on the phone. Rick and Justin had a big party for July 4th, and they were really busy, but Rick said it was extremely successful. He believed that he and Justin could actually start to take their hands off the day-to-day management. They had hired new chefs, and the manager was working out really well.

Of course, Rick says Justin was bored. He liked building things, and with nothing to build he was twiddling his thumbs. I kind of made the suggestion of opening a restaurant in Montreal. After all, our city had a reputation of having some of the finest dining anywhere. Rick loved that idea, and said he wanted to talk to Justin about it.

My phone rang. It was Rick calling.

"Lora! How are you, beautiful?" he asked.

"I'm doing well, you? I asked.

"We have some great news!" he cried. "Justin loves the idea of opening another restaurant in Montreal!"

"Oh wow! That's amazing!"

"We're coming up to scope out locations and venues," said Rick.

"When?"

"In a couple of days!"

"Oh, it will be so nice to see you again!" I cried. "I miss you so much, and so does my body."

"I know what you mean," he said, his voice suddenly dropping an octave. "I've been having wet dreams about you for weeks. It's like I'm a teenager all over again."

"Anything specific we can make real?" I asked suggestively.

"Hmm, yes. I've got a new fantasy," he divulged.

"Oh?"

"I don't want to tell you on the phone," he said shyly.

"That sounds good and deliciously bad," I said. "Now I'm all excited!"

A groan comes through the phone as Rick sucked in his breath.

"Lora, you always know just what to say to get me hard," he said.

"I love you too," I said.

Ooops, that popped out! Did I love him? I believed I was falling in love with him. But allowing that to happen would be life-changing. My kids would need to know. *Do I want them to know?* If they were now coming to Montreal, this might be the opportunity to introduce them formally -- not just as mommy's friend, but as mommy's boyfriend or more. *Am I ready for that?*

Did he notice me saying that? Yup, he did. Oh boy!

Rick gasped on the phone line and fell silent for a moment.

"Did you mean that?" he asked. "Did you mean that, really?"

"I think I do," I admitted. "I think I'm falling in love with you. I felt this way the last time we were together, but wasn't really certain. But if you're coming here, maybe we have a chance?"

"Oh, babe, my heart just grew ten sizes," he cried. "I fell for you a long time ago. I know that leaving you was the most difficult thing I've ever done. We need to talk more about this. Oh my God, I so want this, I so want you. I want you in my life, forever."

"Forever has a different meaning for you than it does for me," I said quietly.

"Yes, it does," he agreed. "But maybe, just maybe, we can change that?"

My own heart took flight. I knew now with certainty that was what I wanted. It was just a matter of figuring it out.

"You think so?" I asked. "I dare not think that we can do this. I'm just hoping."

"Lora, ever since I met you, I knew you were the one for me. I tried so hard not to apply pressure, go too fast, say the wrong thing. Over and over, I've wanted to tell you how I feel. Every time you were in my house, I knew you belonged there, that you were supposed to be in my life. But I knew that you needed to make that decision. You needed to be the driver in this couple. I had to wait for you to arrive at the same place as me, even if you never did. I knew I would be heartbroken if you never got there, but I hoped," he admitted.

"I didn't know what I was, or even if you would ever accept me. Now that we've discovered who and what I am, my only thought has been to make you like me so that we can have forever together. I want to be happily-ever-after with you.

"Am I saying too much?" he asked.

"No, I don't think so," I said, my voice hitching on my words. Tears were flowing down my face hearing his speech. "Normally, I think I would dismiss a speech like that. But from you, no, I can't because, frankly, I've been thinking about the same things. I never believed in 'happily-ever-after," I admitted. "After all, I've had a lot of screwed-up relationships and three kids to prove it. But you, you're different. Not in the obvious way. I mean, we relate to each other differently. We seem to be in sync with each other. It really helps that the sex is outstanding —I gotta say that. I've never had sex that was so, so, so … perfect. That is the only word I can use to describe it. Perfect. And I've had a lot of sex."

"You've mentioned that," said Rick. "I feel the same way about you, even though my experience pales in comparison, I'm sure,"

"Now you're just making fun of me," I said.

"Not really," he said. "But I know what you mean. We fit like a hand in glove. That, I've never experienced before. Usually, I'm much too large for the lady. It's a problem that guys rarely have apparently, and it's a problem because if it doesn't fit there is no sex. I gave up trying."

"Rick, I want you in my life. I want you to meet my kids for real, not just as a friend and I want you in my life. I don't know how. It's crazy, but I don't think I'll be happy without you."

"Well, we are coming up in a few days. Let's see what happens."

12 - Location, Location

— Lora

Justin and Rick arrived in Montreal. Justin booked a hotel room downtown, while Rick came to stay with me. After our long conversation on the phone, I was more anxious than usual to see him again. We had said some pretty big things to each other.

He decided to be casual, which I appreciated. I introduced him to the kids; they were non-committal. *Figures.* He didn't sleep with me in my room either, but chose to stay on the couch. What a sweetheart! My oldest kind of thought he was cool; my youngest loved him instantly, and the middle child—well, was my middle child: difficult. But they'd come around. Pascal considered himself non-binary.

Justin wanted a few days to acclimatize to Montreal. I told him about the different neighborhoods and gave him a map. I think he spent the time going to those places to get a feeling of them. Justin is an emotional guy, and things need to speak to him.

Three days later, Rick and I met Justin downtown for brunch near his hotel.

"Lora, it's so good to see you again, girl!" he cried as he ran to hug me.

"Justin, welcome to Montreal," I said. "I hope you've enjoyed tooting around town and seeing things."

"Oh *oui, ma cherie*, I have indeed!" he replied. "I love this restaurant!"

"This is one of my favorite places, Eggspectations," I informed him.

"I just love the decor," gushed Justin. "It's so urban and funky."

"The menu is very good too," I said.

We ordered coffee and juice first. Once that was brought to the table, we ordered food: I ordered pancakes with blueberries, Justin ordered eggs benedict, and Rick ordered crepes.

After coffee, toast, bacon, juice, and our meals, we were all very stuffed!

A boy came, bussed our table and gave us coffee refills. When the dishes were cleared away, Justin grabbed his bag and pulled out some notes and a couple of newspapers.

"Okay, kids, this is what we're looking for." He showed us his criteria for what would constitute an ideal location for Escalata II. I picked up one of the newspapers he had and looked at the date.

"Oh, we can get a better one than this," I said, and went and got the *Saturday Gazette*. It had an entire section on industrial, commercial, and residential rentals.

"Oooh, look at this, Rick," Justin said excitedly, as he peered over my shoulder. "This is a warehouse property with seventeen-foot ceilings and no walls. Where is this, hun?" he asked me.

I looked at the address and realized it was Old Montreal, which was an ideal place for tourists and locals alike.

"That is right down in Old Montreal, by the Old Port. Very trendy, and a perfect spot for tourist traffic," I said. "Old Montreal is where the city was founded. Most of the buildings are at least 375 years old. There are some really cool buildings down there, and the streets are still cobblestoned.

"Rick, let's go take a look!" said Justin excitedly.

The three of us left the restaurant, and I took them to Old Montreal via the Metro. They were amazed at how clean the subway cars were— just like everyone who visits Montreal.

Exiting the Metro at Place St. Jacques, we came up into bright sunshine. You could tell the buildings were very old here. The stone walls looked hand hewn and were uneven. The buildings were all very close to the street. The streets were cobblestone and so pretty to look at, but they were rough on the cars. I could not imagine driving a horse and carriage through these streets all day long like the calêche drivers.

"Wow, I love the ambience here!" said Justin. He was practically jumping up and down, he was so excited.

"Come this way, gentlemen, it's a bit of a hike. We're going down to St. Paul Street."

We wound our way through the buildings, which took more time than necessary because the two of them were sightseeing as we went. They both loved the old buildings and the cobblestones, and the feeling of the old city. So did I; it was another of my favorite places.

I gave them the history as we walked, pointing out old jails, stables, and armories. Most of the streets along here used to be old warehouses that served the port. The buildings had mostly been converted into condos, but there were a lot of street-level businesses, and many restaurants. You could throw a stone and hit three or four four-star restaurants in any direction.

We finally reached the address in question, and Justin was squealing in delight. Jumping up and down, he screamed, "I'm in love! Oh, Rick, this is the place. We have to have it!"

It was a corner building that had a facade that wrapped around two streets with large windows on the street level. The street widened a bit here, and it was sort of a square of four streets. The building was very old, and the architectural detail was beautiful.

"Well," I said. "Let's go in and see if we can afford it."

"May I help you?," asked a very well dressed woman.

"We are here about the building," said Justin. "I'm interested in purchasing the building for a new restaurant."

"The building is for rent, and only the main floor," said the woman. "The owners want to retain ownership because they have apartments on the top floor."

"Oh, that is perfect!" squealed Justin.

"Justin, it's not for sale," I said.

"Oh honey, that's realtor-speak for 'not enough money on the table'," he said. "Isn't it?"

"Let's go to my office and chat, shall we?" she asked, smiling from ear to ear.

The nice thing was the building had four floors in total. The ground floor would be the restaurant. The second floor they were thinking of a lounge of some kind. The third floor was apartments that were rented out. And the top floor was a penthouse suite which would give Justin and Rick somewhere to stay while they were in town.

I walked around the ground floor space while I waited for Justin and Rick to finish negotiating. Because the building was on a corner, the floor-to-ceiling windows wrapped around two sides. The ceilings were nearly two floors tall, with the interior walls made from the original old brick. Hardwood flooring that looked original was throughout the first floor, giving it lots of character. There was an elegant circular staircase about halfway to the back on the inside that went to a second-floor mezzanine. In the back on the ground floor was a large back room that could be converted into a commercial kitchen quite nicely. There was already a kitchen on the second floor, and they could connect the two with a dumb waiter.

At the very back of the building there was a private elevator that went to the third and fourth floors. Justin was saying that they should create a foyer to separate the elevator from the restaurant and add an exterior door for the tenants and the private residence. That way they wouldn't have to go through the restaurant to get upstairs. There was a fire escape on the back of the building leading to a courtyard that had a street entrance. The courtyard also provided private parking for the residences.

It truly was an amazing building. No wonder Justin wanted to purchase it.

Once the deal had been struck, the boys walked around. They made plans for what would go where, and what kind of decor they would use. They didn't want a carbon copy of the one in Atlanta, because the environment here was so specific. They decided that the new restaurant was going to have Old World charm and romance. I thought the idea was amazing.

Four hours later, we left with a new contract of purchase and a set of keys. Rick and Justin were now the proud owners of the building whose first floor would soon be transformed into Escalata II. The owner had only wanted to rent initially, but Justin made him an offer he couldn't refuse. Justin, it turned out, was filthy rich. He was right, it was just a matter of price.

"Now we have to find an architect, a builder, and a lawyer! Oh my!" said Rick. "We better get cracking!"

"But first, let's celebrate!" said Justin.

"What would you like to do?" I asked them.

"I am going to find someone to celebrate with, a gorgeous, hunky piece of man-meat. You two can go and do your own thing," said Justin. "Ta-ta for now."

"Well, where does that leave us?" asked Rick.

"Let's go home. We can celebrate there," I suggested.

13 - Parenting

— Rick

When we walked through the door to Lora's house, her eldest accosted us with a request immediately.

"Mom, can I go to Ashley's for a sleepover tonight, please?"

"Yes, call me when you get there," said Lora. "I want to speak to Ashley's parents."

"Mooommmm!"

"It's that or no sleepover."

"All right," she answered, storming out the door.

"Is that usual?" I asked.

"Nah, but she's at that age where she's going to try to sneak things," said Lora. "So my philosophy is to give her enough rope, but keep holding on to the other end and making sure it's tethered with another parent. Too many kids get into trouble when they sneak, so the only way to combat that is to make sure all parties know what's happening."

"How long will it take her to get to her friends?"

"It's five minutes down the street," answered Lora. "If she hasn't called in six minutes, I'll call Ashley's parents."

A call came in precisely five minutes after her daughter had left.

"Good girl," murmured Lora as she picked up the phone and put it on speaker. "Hello?" I was listening in.

"Lora, it's Marion, Ashley's mom. How are you?"

"I'm fine. I understand the girls are sleeping at your place tonight, so I just wanted to make sure they didn't have plans to go out, and that they would be monitored all night."

"Yes, the girls are here. They told me that you said they could go to the park, so that's not correct?" asked Marion.

"No, it is not," said Lora. Chuckling, she added, "I've tried every trick in the book already. I know this one, which is why I wanted to speak directly to you."

"I'm okay with them going to the park, though," said Marion.

"So am I, if that's where they are going," said Lora. "Unfortunately, I don't trust that's all they want to do."

"What shall we do about it?"

"Well, watch what they take with them. If it's their purses and phones and they're dressed nicely, stop them because they're on their way to some party we don't know about. I'd rather not have to pick my daughter up drunk somewhere."

"I hear you," said Marion. Marion dropped her voice. "I have a small tracker I can put in Ashley's purse. My husband brought it home from the station months ago in case we felt we needed to track our daughter. Shall I deploy that?"

"That would be perfect. Trust, but verify. That's my motto," said Lora.

"Okay, I will slip that into her bag before they leave." said Marion. "And I'll keep you closely updated. This will be the first big test of the girls and whether they are lying to us or not."

"Yes, it is. And I want to trust them, but I remember what it's like to want to go somewhere you know your parents won't like," said Lora.

"Speak to you later. Bye."

I got up and poured us some drinks. "That sounded intense."

"It was," said Lora. "But luckily it seems Marion is onside with us. You heard she has a tracker she can slip into Ashley's bag. Her husband is a cop."

"You know you can track their phones, right?"

"Yes, but I haven't set it up on Minni's phone yet," Lora said. "I will be doing that tomorrow now. This is the first time this has happened. In the past, the girls made plans with us and we knew about it from the get-go. This is the first time they've made plans and surprised us with them at the very last minute. Something is fishy."

"Hence the 'trust, but verify?'"

"Yup. I'll extend trust to her, but I always want to be able to verify she's telling me the truth," said Lora. "Now, what about us?"

"Where are the other two children?"

"They got picked up by their dad. My eldest is old enough to decide where she wants to be, so she doesn't always follow their schedule. And that's another reason to trust but verify."

"We have the house to ourselves?" I asked, winking at her.

"Why, yes, Mr. Benal," said Lora in her best Irish accent. "We do indeed have the whole house to ourselves tonight."

I pulled her into an embrace and kissed her lips gently. The hunger behind them gave way, and our kiss grew deeper and more urgent.

"I've got an idea."

"Ya, hon?" Lora asked.

"Let's get a little kinky."

"Ooo, a man after my own heart," she cooed. "Follow me, big boy."

Lora took me into a room in the back that was closed and quiet. She sat down on a daybed and pulled out a bag. She reached inside and brought out some toys.

"What's your pleasure?" I asked.

"Let's start with one the same size as you," she said. I knelt on the bed beside her and laid my hands on her ass.

"Ah, you have a gorgeous ass. I just want to possess it."

Lora turned around and lifted her beautiful bottom up to me.

"Please do." She handed me a tube of lubrication.

After much exploring, I first removed her pants and thong. With her heart-shaped ass filling my vision, I inhaled her scent deeply. Licking her entire length, Lora quivered in response.

Pulling my pants off quickly, I slathered lube all over my cock, and then lubed her up too. When I pressed myself up against her, she wriggled her bottom in delight, encouraging me.

"I'm still new at this," I said. "You'll need to guide me so I don't hurt you."

"I will widen to fit you, you don't have to worry. Push gently," she said.

So I pushed gently, and the muscles around her ass opened to admit me. I felt her relax a little as my head started to enter. It was very erotic to watch as my cock slowly made its way into her body that way. It was almost like being a voyeur. I paused for a moment, letting her body adapt to my size. After all, the ass was not as flexible as the vagina. She nodded to proceed.

"How does that feel?"

"Mmm, that's lovely. Move a little."

So I moved my penis with my hand, up and down and in and out. Her ass let go a little, and I wasn't being so tightly held.

"Good, now push a little more."

I stroked my penis to keep it nice and hard and pushed inside some more. Lora gasped as I slid inside about half my length. My penis hit a curve and bent slightly, giving me a small jolt of pain. Stroking my penis again and adding some lube, I pushed past the resistance and slid home all the way. My cock was being forced into a curve inside her that added an interesting sensation.

Lora was humming and wriggling again as she moved on my cock, causing me to rub up against different points along the channel. Her gasps and moans were delightful to hear.

"How does that feel?" I asked her.

"Delicious. Now move, please."

I started to move inside her in and out, each time pulling out until my head was the only thing inside and pushing past the curve. The movement through the tight channel was almost overstimulating as my cock showed its pleasure by getting longer and harder. Soon, I was gasping with Lora as the wave of an orgasm built higher.

"I'm going to climax," I gasped.

"Hold still for a second."

I stopped my movement as she asked, and watched her as she pulled herself off my cock. She pushed me down on my back and straddled me with her back to me.

"Now push into me again," she said.

As I found her ass and pushed inside, it was tight but slippery, so I slid in nicely. I was about halfway in when Lora sat up, fully straddling me. That pushed me even further inside her as her weight settled on top of me.

"Oh! Oh my, oh God. Lora, I am very deep inside now. Are you okay?"

"I can feel you, I'm fine. In fact ... never better."

She lifted her body up off my cock a little and started to move her hips in circles. That drove me mad.

"Oh fuck, oh fuck, fuck, fuck, ah my God, oh fuck, Lora!"

"Yes," she smiled. "Do you have a problem?"

"I'm going to come! Oh God."

I was starting to ejaculate when she forcibly sat down on my cock, fully impaling herself as I managed to slow my ejaculate.

She cried out in pain that wasn't pain.

"Ah! Oh! Oh my Goddess. Blessed pain, you are delicious," she yelled.

Lora then started pumping on me faster and harder. With each pounding she screamed out with pain, and I was screaming with her because my cock was so hard, I was about to explode. I reached around her body to find her nub and used fingers to rub her, bringing her to a climax with me at the same time. I exploded inside her as her body shuddered from her own orgasm.

She relaxed down on me, hands resting on my legs, while she held her upper body vertical.

"I can feel your cock flexing and squirming inside me," she said, as she pushed her hips into mine, shoving my cock as deep inside her as possible. Rick, I'm going to turn around so you have complete frontal access."

She turned sideways and stopped for a moment.

"Oh, this is an interesting position! Wow! What a different sensation this is."

Lora continued until she was facing me. In response, my cock basically corkscrewed itself out and ended up on my stomach, in front of her. Lora picked up a wet towel and cleaned me off from tip to balls, which got me hard again.

"Let's start over." She again presented her ass to me. I took it and caressed her cheeks and licked her slit.

"Ah, your ass is raw from me filling it," I growled. "Perfect round cheeks that fit my hands. This is the biggest turn-on ever."

I stood on the floor and pulled her back to the edge of the bed. In this position, I could apply maximum force. I moved closer to her and watched while my cock penetrated her ass again. Adding lube again, I pushed into her. She felt me shudder with arousal as she groaned in pleasure.

"You like watching too?" she asked.

"It adds dimension to watch myself enter you, yes. But nothing is better than feeling it."

"Fuck me hard, please," she groaned out.

I pulled out again and drove into her like a piledriver.

"Ah!" she yelped. "Yes, again!"

I pulled out again slowly, until my cock was almost out, waited a moment, then drove it into her right up to my balls, feeling that curve again.

"Eeeek, ow, ah, oh, yes! Again! Keep going!"

So I did, starting a rhythm that was slow out and fast and hard in, it didn't take more than five or six strokes before she screamed in ecstasy and I was about to erupt.

She met my strokes with her own movements as I slammed into her the last time and erupted inside her. Her screams trailed off as her body shuddered from the release of another orgasm.

Nuzzling her down on the bed with me behind her, she crooned small purrs and mews as I took her in my arms and gave her a bite on the muscle of her neck.

"Ah! Oh my Goddess!" cried Lora as she had yet another orgasm because of the venom.

"That was amazing," I said.

"That was fun," she said ten minutes later. "Ready for more?" She slid herself off my cock.

I reached for the wipes and cleaned myself off. I then cleaned Lora before lying down beside her. I couldn't resist gently playing with her lady parts.

"What would you like, my love?" I asked.

Lora was getting very wet again. The anal sex hadn't compelled me to bite the same way, but I did nonetheless. Lora reached under her pillow and brought out a dildo.

I looked at her quizzically. "Are you replacing me with this?" I asked.

"No, it's in addition to."

"Mmm, how does this work exactly?" I asked. "Like this?" I took the dildo from her and started stimulating her clit with it, before pushing it into her vagina.

"That's good, yes," said Lora. "Now use this in one and you take the other," she whispered. Lifting her butt off the bed, she moved herself into a downward dog position, giving me full access. I growled low and grabbed her hips.

I stood behind her and removed the dildo before I took her fully again. As I impaled myself deeply in her vagina, we both sighed.

"There is nothing more perfect than you inside me," she said.

She took the dildo, and reached around herself and started to push it into her ass. That visual set me off like nothing had before. Watching her impale herself with a second penis caused my own to elongate and harden.

"I did not expect that!" I said.

"What?"

"That I would discover watching another penis penetrate you would be erotic and arousing to me," I said.

I took over the dildo and pushed it in as deep as it would go for her. She squirmed and rolled her hips as the two penetrations moved inside her.

"Oh wow, I can feel that."

"Yup, stimulates both of us."

She couldn't help herself, she started pushing against me to bring me farther into her. Her wave was growing fast as the climax built to a peak.

"Ah, ah, ow, ah, oh God, ow, oh, OH, oh just fuck! Oh my God," was the gibberish coming out of her mouth.

"Fuck me!" she screamed.

I joined her in thrusting hard, using my length to reach her very core while stimulating her with the dildo too.

It took no time at all for both of us to climax again. This time Lora was raw because the dildo doesn't lube itself. My climax brought another bite for us to ride another orgasm.

"Again, new experiences for me," I said. "I can't wait to try more with you, but you look sore." By then, I had pulled the dildo out of her ass and her body was raw and red. I was surprised at how dilated her ass had become. I was still deeply inside her. My cock wiggled to make its presence known. Then I pulled myself out and lay down beside her on my back.

"Apparently he's not finished," she said. She was looking at my body, which was relaxed and languid. All except for my cock, which was still interested in the conversation we were having.

"Let's leave some for later. Right now, I want to make love to you," I said.

"How is that different?" Lora asked, knowing the answer.

"I want to completely own you so that our bodies are one soul," I said. "But first, let me bathe you."

I got up and disappeared for a minute and returned with a bowl and some towels. I delicately bathed her lady parts, gently washing away the lube and semen, kissing away the hurt and bruised sensitive areas. Then I continued to sponge bath her all the way up to her breasts. I got sidetracked there. But the love and care I took made her cry. When she was clean, I washed myself, making sure that my cock was clean, pulling the foreskin down and getting into all the creases. My cock danced a little with the attention.

"You know, I don't hurt anywhere."

"No?"

"It's the venom. Falon says the venom removes all the pain."

"Good to know," I said. "Are you hungry?"

"A little," she admitted. So I went into the kitchen and found cheese, bread, meats and a bottle of wine and brought back a platter. We sat contentedly, her cuddled up against me munching quietly. Occasionally, I would feed her a piece of food with my mouth and bend to kiss her and pass it to her.

"Let's go upstairs," she said.

"Is it better?"

"It's more romantic."

She led me to her sanctuary and closed the door against interruptions. Lora lit some of the candles in the room, giving it a warm glow and a sensual feeling. She also went and put on some Goddess Oil. I caught the scent and came up behind her and took her wrist and sniffed. My fangs elongated quickly. Licking my lips, I gently licked the spot where she had put the oil, and bit down with just enough force to give her some venom.

I felt, heard, and scented, all the changes in Lora's body as I bit her. She watched me in the mirror right in front of us, and when I licked her wrist I smelled the change in her own arousal. When I bit her, the arousal became more intense. I felt her body against mine, my erection pushing between us. I felt her heart quicken. The venom had ignited her arousal, and mine too. I hadn't expected her perfume to have the same effect on me as my venom had on her.

"What is your perfume?" I murmured in her ear.

"It's not perfume, it's Goddess Oil," she groaned back. Her back arched, pushing her bottom against my erection, and her back against my nipples.

I brought her wrists up behind my neck and reached around her and started gently rubbing her nipples. She held onto my head and rolled her head against my chest. She was grinding herself on my erection now, and her arousal was blooming across her body.

I cupped my hand under her breast, holding it with great care while flicking my thumb across the nipple and exciting it. Then I cupped both, and they were large enough that it was more than a handful. I played with her nipples until they stood out and demanded my attention.

I turned her around and sank to my knees, taking one of her breasts in my mouth, nipping and licking alternatively. I pushed them together and buried my face in her cleavage, inhaling deeply of her intoxicating scent that was mingled with the Goddess Oil. I gave her a long lick up her breastbone. The oil hit my tongue and immediately gave me an orgasm-like trip, but it didn't make me ejaculate. Thankfully.

"Oh God, I want you so much," I murmured in between her breasts.

"How do you like the Goddess Oil?" she asked.

"It's an aphrodisiac, I think," I said.

"Yes, a powerful one," she said. "I've got it applied in many spots."

I looked up at her and smiled.

"I'll have to go on a hunt, then." Since I was at eye level with her bellybutton, I worked my way down from her breasts to her innie, and discovered another drop of oil. Licking it up zinged me again, ramping up my arousal.

I slowly kissed my way down to her mound. My nose could detect some more of the oil, but I wasn't there yet. I leaned back and gazed at her. I took in all her curves, the wide hips, the full breasts, the somewhat flat tummy, the adorable bottom, and I couldn't get enough of her. My hands were traveling everywhere, touching everything. She was mine.

I lifted one of her legs so I could get my nose in her mound and took a deep breath. I loved her scent; it was earthy and green. It smelled like a woman and life and energy. I also scented more Goddess Oil, but it wasn't on her mound, it was deeper.

I picked her up, and reverently placed her down on her back. Lora spread her legs in invitation and I didn't hesitate a second. I didn't know whether I wanted to use my tongue or my hands more. So I decided on both. While my fingers opened her flower and delicately caressed her nub, my tongue explored her vagina. Her sweet juices were flowing abundantly, and I finally found the spot where the Goddess Oil had been applied. Licking her thoroughly, I took up her juice and the oil at the same time, and my head nearly exploded—not the one on my shoulders. My cock, now so engorged, almost released its payload from the startling wave of euphoria from the oil.

"I need to make love to you," I said.

"I need you too," she answered. "But first…"

She sat up and let her fingers play over every inch of my skin, teasing ripples of energy from me and watching them move over my muscles. She slid to her knees on the floor and licked my nipples and excited them until they were as erect as my cock.

She followed the "map," as she called the line of hair pointing down my belly to my cock. Slowing down at my belly button, she licked and sucked there for a minute. Continuing on down, she could see the V-shaped muscles of my torso, right down to the top of my cock.

My cock was standing erect waiting for some attention. She sat back on her heels and took it in her mouth, gently wrapping her lips around my soft head. The steel in my shaft was a contrast to the softness of my head. As she grasped the shaft, my cock danced in her hands and gave her some pre-cum.

"Ah, mmm, that's so good," I groaned.

Lora let her tongue move wherever it wanted, licking me down the hole, around the edges, across the top, as she brought more into her mouth.

"Oh God, that's exquisite … ah, mmm."

Lora applied her teeth to the underside of my head, taking the whole head inside her mouth and biting down gently.

"Oh! Ah! Oh…" I gasped with a sudden breath. "God help me."

Lora giggled and the vibrations traveled through her teeth into my cock, where they caused me to release a little.

"No! No, no, no, no, no, ah, oh my, oh, calm yourself," I groaned.

Lora started to rub my shaft, making it longer and harder while she was sucking on the tip. She suddenly released my cock and blew tiny puffs on the head, causing me to shiver.

"God help me, woman, I won't be able to stand much more of this."

So she stood up and sat back on the bed, and pulled me with her until we were lying together with me on top, her legs wrapped around my hips. My cock was perfectly aimed for her, and I pushed into her gently just a little.

"Ah, ah, ah, oh, more," she gasped. "I want more."

"Patience, my little vixen. If I go too fast, it will be over too soon."

"Nonsense, he's never exhausted."

So I pushed in quickly, impaling her with my cock.

"Yes! Ah, oh, my sweet Goddess, yes. You fill me perfectly, Rick Benal. I just never want to be disconnected from you. You're like the key to my inner self."

My cock was quivering from the strain of being so excited. It was throbbing with life; it wanted to share. I exercised extreme will to bring it back down a notch or two, because I was feeling the intensity of our connection too.

"I feel this too, my love. Oh, Goddess, you gave me this amazing woman. Let me be worthy," I prayed quietly.

"You prayed to my Goddess?" asked Lora.

"I'm only thanking her for giving you to me." I felt a little more in control now, so I leaned down and kissed her deeply. She opened up to me and gave herself, and I took everything. I started moving my hips, our bodies moving together in their life-affirming dance. They were one, completely connected and whole.

My gentle pumping became hungrier, and her hips started to push back more as their rhythm got faster. Soon there was nothing but the connection as I pounded into her, and she responded by equal force pounding back. Each time I reached her innermost pleasure point, she screamed in ecstasy and I moaned with deep pleasure.

"I'm not going to last long now," I admitted.

"Neither am I, so let's go together."

The last few strokes, we put everything into it until the last stroke I was buried deep inside her and exploded. Her orgasm took flight. I bit down on her flesh, releasing venom which made her orgasm turn into four. As the waves crashed over her one after the other, her body shuddered in rhythm with my venom and seed being pumped into her. The two of us, spent, collapsed in a sweaty heap.

I took the wrist I hadn't licked before and gave it one big lick, removing the Goddess Oil and giving me an additional kick into euphoria.

It was thirty minutes before either of us could speak, let alone move. And another thirty minutes before I could move off of her. I was indeed limp. I'd emptied everything into her, my very life essence.

"Mmmm, love, you conscious?" I inquired quietly.

"Define conscious."

"Able to move, or speak, or think?"

"Sort of. I'm still floating on pink clouds somewhere," she said. "Oh Goddess, that took everything out of me. I feel like I haven't a bone in my body."

"I've pulled out."

"Ha ha. Not what I meant," she laughed.

"I know what you mean. He's actually limp."

"Oh, so no more?"

"Talk dirty to him. I'm sure he'll perk up."

"That would mean moving and thinking. I'm not sure I can get that far just yet."

"Lora, I've never expelled so much. Not ever."

"I noticed that you released a lot. Venom too, I think."

"According to Mark, this is what is necessary for turning someone. An extra-large dose of both."

"Mmm."

"Do you want to be like me?" I asked. "We haven't really talked about it."

"Rick, I want to be with you. I love you. I cannot see the future, but I want you in mine, and if I have to be like you to make sure we are together, then that's what I'll do."

"I feel the same way, Lora," I said. "I've been in love with you from the moment I first saw you. I just don't want to rush things, or put you in a position you don't want to be in."

"Hon, there is no position you could put me in that I wouldn't want to be in," said Lora with a seductive smile. "In fact, I've got some new positions we could try if you're up for it."

"Let's just lie here for now, please. I feel like I'm empty of semen and venom."

Sure enough. My energy was down for a couple of days after that epic sex. I didn't say anything, but I watched Lora carefully for signs of change.

Justin and I took turns running back and forth between Atlanta and Montreal. We decided that we wanted our grand opening to be in December. That gave us four months to make our goal to celebrate New Year's in Montreal like we did at the end of our first year in Atlanta.

It's amazing what money can accomplish.

14 - Vampires?

— Falon

Mark got home, went down to the office, and made a call to someone in his family. He was speaking to them for thirty minutes or so before he came back upstairs.

"Well, we may have a problem," Mark announced.

"What kind of a problem?" I asked, not being able to think of one.

"There is a vampire hunter in town," he said without preamble.

"A what now?" I asked, stunned. "Did you say 'vampire hunter?' For real? Like I thought vampires don't exist."

"They don't. Vampires are completely fictitious and made up by humans. However, their origin is not—that's us."

"You've said the origin story for vampires was the Olde Ones." I said.

"Yes, Vlad the Impaler was one of us," said Mark. "Unfortunately, he was a very sick man, suffering from a number of very serious mental issues. He impaled people he didn't like and hoisted them up on posts outside the village. He also had a disease which is now referred to as Renfield's syndrome. It's an obsession with drinking blood. People afflicted with this disease think they are vampires. It didn't help that he also suffered from xeroderma pigmentosum—a rare disease where the skin has an extreme sensitivity to sunlight. Put those two problems together, and you get a blood-sucking man who only goes out at night."

"So that's why people thought he was a vampire?"

"No, they thought he was evil-incarnate. Bram Stoker turned him into a vampire. In those days people were extremely superstitious. When villagers disappear while someone is sneaking around at night, people talk. Enough incidents and a mythology sprouts up like beans.

"But that's only the beginning of the crazy. Then you get people who want to 'be' a vampire and seek out people like Vlad. Because he's an Olde One, he's still alive. The villagers knew he never died at a normal age, so they attributed demons and hell and the devil to his affliction. Not a medical problem."

"Okay, I get it, and that creates hunters going after people who want to be vampires. But there are no vampires."

"No, vampire wannabes are just killing people and draining their blood because they think it will keep their 'lord' Vlad alive. Frankly, he won't die regardless, but they don't know that, or won't believe that. It's all very twisted."

"So now who are these hunters, and what are they doing in Montreal?" I asked.

"Our family Elders' network has been tracking a group that have called themselves vampire hunters for centuries. The group dates back to the same time period, the mid-1400s. A fraternal order of monks took it upon themselves to put Vlad out of his misery and end his reign as a vampire. Except, they didn't know how to kill an Olde One. Everything they tried only injured him and he came back."

"This has been going on for like five hundred years?"

"Yes, this stupid war between our family and the monks," he said. "Before that, many cultures had myths similar to vampires that were based on their people seeing us with our fangs out. Vampire myths go back to Mesopotamia and the Ancient Greeks. Our species pre-dates all of them."

"And you've always hidden in plain sight?" I asked.

"We have to. As humans developed new technology, each improvement changed the way we had to hide. If we just separated ourselves from society, that wouldn't work either, because they would eventually find us. So instead we tried to be like them in the open. It's more difficult these days, especially now that facial recognition is being employed. It's another reason we have to change who we are about every ten to twenty years and stage our own deaths."

"Back to the vampire hunters. What does this mean to us?" I asked.

"There are indications the group is now operating in Montreal. It means that for some reason they detected me in this city, and they are looking for me."

"But why you?"

"They know about me because of some mistakes I made many years ago, long before I knew you."

"But how are they tracking you?"

"I don't know. I have to find out. That's what the call was about earlier. I've contacted my security guy, Andrews. He's going to look into it for us."

"So where does this leave us? Could that be who has been 'stalking' me?"

"The Elders have started an investigation and have enlisted some of the Elder Sentinels to help."

"Is Andrews a sentinel? He does your security."

"No he isn't, but that's a good idea," said Mark. "The Sentinels have been around for hundreds of years. They don't have any humans, but if Andrews was to become immortal, I would recommend him to the group. They have policed and safeguarded our family for generations. Andrews was telling me that they have found the Fraternal Order in North America—New Orleans, Louisiana, through a connection in Savannah, Georgia. You'll never guess who that connection was?" Mark asked.

"Who?"

"That Derek creep who got in your face in Atlanta. You told me about him: He kept bothering you at the hotel for a date, but you got a really bad vibe from him. Apparently, he's been tailing members of our family for years. He found me in Georgia keeping company with you, so he decided to go after you. I'm sorry about that. You wouldn't be on his radar if it weren't for me."

"Well, at least the Elders no longer think I'm the leak!" I said.

"The Elders will be assisting us now," he reassured me.

"And the Fraternal Order is after us…" I concluded. "That just sucks."

15 - Ch-Ch-Changes

— Lora

Awesome, incredible, marvelous, unbelievable, wonderful. I needed to look up in a thesaurus to describe the sex Rick and I had a few nights ago. *OMG!* It wasn't the playing, it was the lovemaking. I felt a connection like I never had before, and that was saying something after nearly a year of amazing sex with Rick.

What was different?

The build-up was higher, the wave was bigger, the climax was huge, and he literally drained himself until he was finished. He even went soft. That had never happened before.

I started feeling different almost immediately. Like a low-grade fever had hit me. You know, when you feel something has hitched a ride on you and is working on making you sick. Sort of like that, but not sick.

The first change I noticed was my hearing. I was down in the living room doing some research and I started hearing my kids talking upstairs in their room. They weren't speaking loudly, but I heard them clearly. That hadn't happened before.

This morning I had no problem doing things that would have required an effort, like moving the sofa and pulling out the fridge. Something was happening.

For me, the ultimate test would be if it had affected my magic. So I went into my study room where I kept all my magical materials. I had a simple spell to perform that would tell me if my magic was still there and if it had changed. It was creating a ball of light.

I spoke the incantation and snapped my fingers. A ball about the size of a snowball appeared floating over my palm, glowing with a greenish-white light.

"Perfect! It worked just as it should," I said out loud. Focusing on the light, I pushed energy into it to make it larger, and it jumped in size to a beach ball.

"Whoa! That is different!" It startled me because the increase in size was sudden. Before, it would increase in size slowly. So my magical abilities seemed to have been augmented too.

"I can't wait to tell Rick. He'll be excited that I'm changing." But I had to call Falon first.

"Falon speaking."

"It's me!"

"Lora, nice to hear from you. What's up?"

"Rick and I had transition-type sex a few days ago."

"You mean…?"

"Yes! That's what I mean, and I'm experiencing little differences already."

"I started with small changes quickly too, but the final change didn't happen until, you know…"

"I hear you. We need to meet to compare notes confidentially."

"Yes, not over the phone. What are you doing tonight?"

"Nothing in particular. The kids are with me, Rick is busy with the new restaurant, so it's a home night for me."

"Okay, I'll come over to your place after dinner. We can go over all the things I was told to expect and track them."

"Sounds like a plan. See you then. And thanks."

"My pleasure."

16 - Charity Starts at Home

— Falon

I was walking down Ste-Catherine Street the other day, when I noticed just how many homeless people there were on the streets. Rather than being annoyed, I felt desperately sad about that. It was a travesty these people were not being helped, and that they had nowhere to call home.

I suddenly needed to do something about that. My brain popped a memory of me in the bath trying to figure out what to do with my immortal life. *Could this be it? Could this be the problem to solve?*

How, I had no idea. It's not like I had money of my own to make a difference. I wondered if Mark would support something for me.

At dinner I brought it up with Mark.

"Mark, I have this idea. I cannot do it by myself, but it would be very expensive…"

"Go on."

"I want to do something to help about homelessness in Montreal."

"That's a big undertaking," he advised. "What do you want to do?"

"I don't know exactly, but would you be willing to help me raise money for it?"

"Of course, that would be a fine idea," he said. "But my experience has taught me you just cannot raise money. You have to raise awareness for the problem, and you have to have something to put the money into."

"What do you mean?"

"If you just raise the money, who do you give it to? Do you trust them to do something constructive with it? You see? You need to have a purpose."

"I get it," I said. "Well, maybe Lora can help me with a purpose. I'm meeting her tomorrow."

The next morning, I called Lora. She had been busy with Rick and Justin as they worked on opening a new restaurant in Montreal. But maybe she had a few minutes for me.

"Falon, are we still getting together?" asked Lora.

"Yes, absolutely. I also want to talk to you about an idea I have."

"Yes, come on by this afternoon."

I picked up some pastries on the way to Lora's, figuring showing up empty-handed was not fair. We both loved milles feuilles. Rick answered the door, which was a surprise.

"Falon, how nice to see you," he said, and hugged me. "What are those?"

"Mille feuilles," I said guiltily.

"Let me look at them. Hmm, I can do better," Rick said with a smile. "Look, the crust is tough, and the flaky pastry isn't. The custard looks good, though."

After critiquing my pastries, he carried them into the kitchen. Lora came downstairs and gave me a hug. We made a pot of coffee, and when it was ready sat around the kitchen table with our pastries and coffee.

"This was a nice indulgence," Lora said. "Thank you for bringing them."

"No problem."

"So let's swap stories!" she said.

"You and Rick had transitional sex?"

"Yes we did, and I'm already seeing differences in my hearing and vision."

"Those were the first things that changed for me too. At the same time, my scars started disappearing."

"Oh, I hadn't checked that."

I went on to relay to her what Gwen told me about being female and immortal.

"Cool. No more cycles! Yeah!" Rick had been listening to this without comment.

"You can still have children?" he asked.

"Gwen said as long as we have eggs, we can get pregnant. Our bodies will determine the timing somehow."

"Do you want kids?" asked Lora.

"I do. I want children with Mark. What about you?"

Lora looked at Rick and they smiled. "I think we want a child too. Even though we already have families, we want one that is us," answered Lora. Rick nodded. "What did you want to talk about?"

"I want to start a charity for the homeless—actually, I want to solve the problem somehow. Can I brainstorm with you?

"Good cause," said Lora.

"I walk by so many homeless people now, it saddens me every day. I want to do something. What can we do?"

"Let me get a laptop and we can do some research."

We started researching. Why do people become homeless? There was a scary answer—it was really easy. In some cases, it only took one crisis in a family's life to lose everything. Most people were only one paycheck away from homelessness. The more we learned, the more I cried. It seemed hopeless. The city didn't have the resources to do anything constructive, and the police were left trying to evacuate people from where they were trying to exist. This problem was huge.

"Okay, let's step back," said Rick. "This is a way bigger problem than we figured. So what can we do?"

"One of the problems we read about was that homeless people cannot get social assistance because they don't have an address. What if we gave them an address?" Lora suggested.

"How? What kind of an address?" I asked.

"A tiny house," cried Lora.

"Tiny house? What is that?"

"It's a new fad actually, they started hitting mainstream in the late 90s, but they are now not just a fad. It's a real alternative to apartment living. They have a small footprint, as little as four hundred square feet, usually mobile, often custom-made, that are complete homes. The best ones are completely four seasons. I was reading up on them because I was interested in shucking the weight of renting and buying myself a house once the kids are grown-up."

"This is definitely the place to start," I said. "Giving them an address. Wow! Thanks, Lora, you're brilliant."

"That's going to need capital," said Rick.

"A lot of capital," said Lora.

"Well, we will have to get rich people involved. Rich people donate to all kinds of charities. We just have to make them care about this one," said Falon.

"How are we—two young women who are not rich, who don't know rich people, don't walk in their circles—ever going to convince rich people to part with their money for this cause?" asked Lora.

"Wait, but you do know wealthy people," said Rick, smiling. "Justin and I are wealthy, so is Mark. And I'm sure his whole family is. We can get you into their circles."

"You're a good man, Rick," said Lora.

"Yes, Mark will help. But he said we have to have a place to put the money," I said.

"How will we get money?" asked Lora.

"Hmm, how about a fundraiser event?" I suggested.

"What do rich people like to go to?" asked Lora.

"Galleries? Parties? Symphonies?" Rick suggested. "They spend a lot of time trying to look like they're interested in helping, but all they're doing is throwing their money around. The actual people running those events are the ones who are charitable. But you can always count on the 1% to show up for a good party."

"A party? How about a Gala, not just a party?" asked Lora.

"Okay, a Gala to raise money to build tiny homes, but where?"

"That's the hard part. I expect we'll need to come up with an entire plan, location, budget, with contractors. Not to mention, how will we choose the residents?" I said.

"There's our charity," said Lora. "So what next?"

"Setting it up and staffing it I can only assume. You in?"

"Absolutely. I've been dying to quit my job for something more meaningful. You're going to pay us, right?"

"Yes, name your salary."

17 - Out of the Blue

— Falon

Now that we knew someone was hunting us, Mark and I took extra precautions when going out among the humans. We could not afford to let our guard down for a second. We always had to appear mundane.

We were sitting on a patio having lunch one fine bright day when out of the blue Brandon walked up the sidewalk across the street and stopped and stared at me sitting there.

It took me a second to recognize him because his hair was a bit different. I saw it was him after he started walking across the street right at me.

I was surprised. "Brandon? Is that you?"

"Falon, wow, what are you doing here?" asked Brandon.

"I'm here with my husband, Mark. Mark, this is Brandon—oh, I never got your last name! Anyway, he's a member of the band I told you was playing at the hotel in Atlanta."

Mark stood up to reach across the fence to shake his hand.

"Would you like to join us, Brandon?" invited Mark.

"That would be nice, thank you," he answered in his melodious Southern voice.

"Garçon, please set another place at our table for our friend?" Mark said as he flagged down a server.

The hostess brought Brandon around the entrance of the patio and to our table. The third place setting was made closer to Mark than me, which was just fine. *Let him play footsie with Mark.*

"Brandon, why are you in Montreal?" I asked once he was seated.

"We've got a gig here. First time in Canada, actually. Playing at a neighborhood bar called Cheers. I heard it was named for the TV program."

"Oh, that's exciting! How long is the gig?"

"We have two weeks here downtown, then two weeks in Pointe Claire. But I don't know where that is yet. Is it far from here? We hate having to travel in the middle of a gig."

"That's wonderful. Pointe Claire is still on the island of Montreal, just twenty minutes west of here."

"Cool! That is much better. Are there hotels nearby so we don't have to travel back and forth to the one we're in now? It's convenient here, it's only a block from the bar."

"Yes, there are a few hotels close by now," I answered.

"How do you like Montreal so far, Brandon?" asked Mark.

"Sir, you have a bit of a Texan accent there. Are you a recent import to this city?" asked Brandon.

"Actually, no, I used to live here many, many, years ago and moved to Houston with my family. Now I'm back setting up a business. So for me it's like coming home—especially since I married a local girl," he said as he smiled at me.

Mark's nerves went through the roof as he talked with Brandon. Something had set him off. I could smell the suspicion coming off him in waves. Maybe he had picked up on something. I listened closer and took a good long whiff as delicately as I could.

"What's that you're sniffing?" asked Brandon.

"Oh, I thought I smelled cigar smoke and was trying to detect where it was coming from," I countered. "I just hate getting smoked on during a meal, don't you?"

I couldn't detect anything at all. My senses weren't as acute as Mark's yet. So I was going to rely on his instincts.

Once the food arrived, the three of us were content to just eat quietly. Mark was used to the high-quality food here in Montreal, but Brandon wasn't. The beer he ordered was going to his head because it was stronger than American beer. He was about to order a third, when I tipped him off.

"Brandon, that brand of beer is six percent alcohol. So go easy on it," I advised.

"So that's why I already have a buzz?" he asked. "Huh!"

Mark picked up the tab, for which Brandon was very grateful. We said our goodbyes, wishing him good luck with the gig. We told him that we would try to stop by the bar one night to cheer them on.

When our day was finished, we made our way home. On the way in the car, Mark started thinking out loud about our lunch.

"So how do you think he found us there?" asked Mark.

"I dunno. It looked like he had been casually walking down the street, but who knows? We didn't get the hotel he was staying at. He said it was a block away from the bar, and if so it's likely on Sherbrooke Street, but not necessarily. He could have just been walking by. But it was strange."

"I'm not sure we should trust him," said Mark. "Something doesn't feel right. I was getting some strange scents off of him. Something like guilt, but also like deception or hiding. Not clear anyway. I'm going to get Andrews to look into him."

"I felt your tension. I didn't detect anything myself but I'm new to this," I said. "I think it's a good idea to investigate, but let's not hang someone for smelling bad. He may have just been surprised. Remember, I thought I saw him that night tailing me to the coffee shop. I could never confirm it, but he's actually here in Montreal."

"Yes you did. I am going to call Andrews. Perhaps he can find a connection between Brandon and Derek."

Andrews had Grisham do a deep dive on Brandon and his band. Turns out, they, not too recently, got an angel investor. Someone was paying for their hotel and travel expenses so they could go to more distant locales. Further digging produced a name for the angel investor: Derek Staung. If Brandon was being helped by Staung, was there a connection back to Derek's club of hunters?

The plan became Andrews and his team keeping an eye on Brandon and the band to see if it would lead back to the hunters. They knew there was a connection but didn't know exactly what it was.

Andrews caught up with Brandon at the bar downtown and sat watching for a few hours. He paid attention to the members of the band, what they were doing, who they were talking to. They seemed like normal musicians doing a gig. Brandon sat with girls all over the bar, charming them with his Southern accent. But nothing seemed out of the ordinary the first night.

A few nights later, after the band had packed up, Grisham and Parsons came in dressed like police and pulled Brandon aside. Their job was to scare Brandon and see what happened.

"Hello there, we're doing a random check for drugs and firearms. We understand you have recently arrived from the United States."

"Yes, myself and my band are from Georgia. What does that have to do with anything?"

"Well, your passport was flagged upon your entrance into our country for follow-up," said Grisham.

"What sort of follow-up?" asked Brandon.

"Please state your full name for the record," said Parsons.

"Brandon Wallace."

"Mr. Wallace, how long will you be in Canada?"

"About five weeks, I expect."

"Did you bring any drugs or firearms into the country with you?"

"Um, no."

"Are you sure, sir? We have someone searching your hotel room right now. It would be better if you admitted that you brought something, rather than us just finding it."

"Okay, yes, I brought some recreational weed for me and the guys."

"Did you bring any firearms?"

"Why the questions about guns? I'm allowed to carry, I have a permit."

"Not in Canada, sir. We do not have carry permits for citizens unless they have a special permit. Handguns may be kept at the residence, but there are no 'carry' laws like in the U.S."

"Oh, I didn't know that," lied Brandon. "Yes, I have a handgun with me. It's in my equipment case. I keep it with us in the event that someone tries to steal from us."

"You'll need to hand that over now, sir."

"And then what? How do I get it back when I return home?"

"That's not our problem, sir. It is illegal to bring firearms into Canada," said Grisham. "Now how much weed did you bring?"

"Uh, a few ounces, I guess. Enough for a bunch of hits."

"Is it more than three kilos?"

"I don't know what a kilo is. It's a small baggie about yay big," said Brandon, showing about the size of a Post-it Note with his hands.

"That too may be illegal, sir. They will weigh the marijuana when they find it."

"I thought weed was legal in Canada now."

"Yes, but if you have enough to distribute, you need a licence," said Parsons. "You can purchase what you need from dispensaries all over town now. They're almost more popular than McDs."

"But I'm not distributing it!" Brandon said exasperatedly. "It's just for the band—you know, on off hours. Are you going to arrest me?" For the first time he'd lost his smug face and looked nervous.

"If you surrender the weapon and the drugs voluntarily, we'll let you go this time. However, if we find you with either of these again while you're still in Canada, then you will be arrested. Am I clear, son?"

"Yes, Officer, you're crystal clear. I'll get the gun." Brandon walked to the back of the stage, opened one of the large travel cases. He pulled out the gun he owned and walked back to the "police" and handed it over.

"Thank you, son. Have a good stay in Canada."

Grisham and Parsons then walked out of the bar. Andrews left the bar by a side door after listening to the interview and met them around the corner. By that time, they had lost their police uniforms and identification, and looked like ordinary people. There were always a lot of people on the streets of downtown Montreal—so it was easy to blend in.

"What do you think?" asked Andrews.

"He was startled about the interview and was shocked about possibly being arrested," said Parsonst. "He said he didn't know the laws here about guns or drugs. I think this shook him up enough that he'll be careful."

"Do you think we should toss his room?"

"Well, considering we said we were going to, yes. Let's toss his room, find the drugs and ammo, and confiscate them. That will reinforce that he's under watch."

"Who knows, perhaps we'll find a connection in the room," said Grisham.

"Keep digging. The Elders think there is a connection somewhere. We need to find it," replied Andrews.

The agents went to the hotel room and searched it thoroughly, finding a plastic bread bag filled loosely with weed and a box of ammo for Brandon's handgun. They didn't find any paperwork for the weapon, whose absence would have been an arresting offense had they been real cops. Going through his suitcase, they found a laptop, which one of them took to the next room while the other continued searching.

The laptop yielded a number of communications between Brandon and Derek Staung, the leader of the Fraternal Order in New Orleans. They definitely established a connection. The question was to what extent? The agent forwarded the message threads to his own system, then slipped the laptop back into Brandon's room before they left.

18 - Fraternal Order

— Derek

Derek sat there tenting his fingers like a low budget villain in a bad movie. He was watching CCTV video of a woman drugged and tied up in the basement of the building he was renting.

Derek Staung had been a member of the Fraternal Order since his induction at the age of sixteen. His father and grandfather before him were members. It was a family thing. In fact, all the males in his direct lineage had been Fraternal Order.

The Fraternal Order was a cult of assassins trained to remove supernatural beings from the world. The order had no documents telling of the origin of supernatural beings, but they believed it was as many as 10-15,000 years ago. These supernaturals had always been there, it seemed, lurking in the dark, waiting to strike. They stayed hidden from human life.

The Order came into being around the 900s with the mission of ridding the world of supernatural beings. Since their quarry was generally hidden from humans, they too stayed out of view, waiting to strike when needed. You never saw the Order's assassins coming, and they were only identified by a mark on their left palm: the three blades tattoo.

Derek no longer followed the Fraternal Order's leadership. Some years ago, they demonstrated to him that they had gone soft. After millennia of existence, he believed they had become lazy and unfocused. They were unwilling to hunt anymore, and much more willing to let supernaturals live in peace.

This was unacceptable to Derek.

So three years ago, Derek Staung had started his own Order. Its adherents identified each other by a tattoo on the inside wrist of their left hand of a holy sword with a snake coiled along the length, but the sword had cut its head off and it was bleeding. There were some other members of the Fraternity in the Texas chapter that were as disillusioned with the Order as Derek and agreed to leave together and join him in his own holy war against this evil. Roughly seven had become ordained in the new group and received their tattoo.

Derek had been brought up to believe that failure wasn't an option. But at the moment he felt like a failure. His father would never have let the immortal get away, much less turn an innocent.

Derek had been tracking Mark Chisholm since 1988 after he suddenly showed up in Houston as the leader of a large company that was under suspicion of being owned by immortals.

He was certain Chisholm was an immortal, which is why he had to be eliminated. His mentor in the order had taught Derek that immortals cannot be left alive. As soon as one is discovered, all efforts must be made to kill it.

However, in spite of the information Derek had provided to the order, they'd refused to make a move on the company or its new CEO, Chisholm. They told Derek that he didn't have enough proof.

Proof? Well, *crap!*

So Derek had made his own plans. First, he was going to eliminate Chisholm. He had a plan to use Falon as bait to get the immortal. Early that morning his men had picked her up, drugged her, and brought her to the holding cell—the very holding cell he was watching now on CCTV.

However, he had just discovered something sinister. It appeared that the immortal had turned the lovely girl into one of the vampiric monsters. His people told him that when they went to catch her, she fought them like crazy and almost got away. It was only the tranquilizer gun that stopped her, and they had to give her a triple dose. Derek had been watching the unconscious woman for the past hour, trying to catch her using immortal powers to escape. He needed to know more about her—much more.

If Chisholm is spreading their disease, then we have to find the nest! I'll let her escape and she'll lead me back to them.

Derek had been on Chisholm's trail so long, he had been a voyeur in many of the dramas that happened in his life. Once he discovered the girl's existence, he'd place a watch on her too. They'd been on her ever since New York. It was pure luck that they found Brandon, a young member of the order.

Derek's operative in Atlanta had been Franco. Franco was employed by the immortal family, and they were as yet unaware that he had turned against them. Franco said it would be easy to get Brandon to be their patsy. He was young and in love with Falon. *Perfect!*

The original plan had been to arrange for Brandon and his band to be in Montreal to distract Falon. He would seduce her away from the immortal, allowing Derek to make his move.

Now that might not be possible. If she had been turned, then they had already consummated their relationship with sex and a bite. It would be impossible to seduce her away from her immortal.

Plan B was to get Brandon to cause a scene in front of the immortal in a public place—hence the crowded bar—so that Chisholm would lose control and reveal himself.

The cunning part of the plan was to get Brandon to "rescue" Falon from the clutches of an abductor and return her to the immortal. Brandon would ask her out for lunch and the immortal would follow, walking into the hunters' trap.

Chisholm didn't know yet that Derek had Falon. Derek was waiting for a day before calling with his threat.

But now, he wasn't sure it would work. Derek had let his attention drift.

From the corner of his vision, Derek saw movement on the screen. Snapping his attention back to the CCTV monitor, he only just saw the door closing after Falon as she left. The room was now empty.

Derek had been sure the locked room would hold her. So now he must think of another way to destroy Chisholm. Fine: he would manipulate Brandon without him knowing it to achieve his ends. Derek continued staring at the CCTV in fascination for a minute before remembering to sound the alarm.

"Hit the alarm! Our prisoner has escaped!" he screamed into his phone at the security desk guards.

Immediately, he went and pulled the security alarm so that security would search the building for her. Their security alarm was a blue switch on the wall, not unlike a fire alarm. He wanted them to discover how she got out so easily without anyone noticing.

Derek went down to the main lobby to question the guards on duty at the desk.

"Who was on duty here for the past thirty minutes?" hHe demanded.

"We both were," said one of the guards. "We are always paired, even on walkabouts."

"Did you see anyone in this lobby at that time?"

"Only the people who came in the front door, sir."

"We saw someone exit through a door on the back side of the lobby about five minutes ago. It was a woman. But she came out of the elevators, so we didn't think anything of it."

Derek charged out the doors, and looked frantically up and down the street. He called four of his security staff down to the sidewalk and instructed them to search in all directions for her.

They returned some fifteen minutes later to report that she wasn't found. Derek was staring out the window, when a limo pulled up to the curb across the street. A red-haired woman exited the building, got into the limo and they drove off. Before she got into the car, she looked directly at him and taunted him with a cute wave.

"Fuck!" yelled Derek. "That proves the girl has been turned and now has immortal strength. She is no longer a rescue, but a target."

"We will need a new plan to get them to reveal themselves. The boy Brandon Wallace may still be a good dupe, if we play him right," said one of Derek's men.

"Boss, what if we play him against the girl?" came a suggestion.

"That won't likely work anymore, anymore. She is now in thrall to the immortal, Chisholm. The bond between them will be extremely difficult, if not impossible, to break.," answered Derek.

Of course, Derek didn't tell his people the truth of what they were up against. Most only thought the two of them were immortals, creatures of myth that don't go out in daylight. These would-be hunters were enamored of the lifestyle of hunting creatures of the night. They were zealots and easily led, which was why Derek kept them around. He could get them to do anything if they thought they would actually get to kill a vampire.

Derek, on the other hand, knew what he was up against. An immortal Olde One, who had a vast network behind him: a real true-to-life evil. And unlike storybook vampires, phantoms and immortal demons, Chisholm would be difficult to capture—at least by humans.

19 - Escape!

— Falon

Falon woke up tied to a chair again. She was much stronger than a human and her new physiology let her burn off drugs faster than people.

Aw, come on! Really? Abducted again? This is getting old!

As Falon tested the restraints for weaknesses, she thought of the things Mark had taught her. She knew she was by herself because she couldn't hear anyone else. She had no clue what this was about, only that she was sick and tired of these games! So she tried to see what other information her new senses could give her.

She couldn't hear anyone else. What could she smell? Inhaling deeply, Falon tried to get information from her environment. It still smelled like the city, so she hadn't moved out to the country. She smelled damp, so she might be underground. She smelled oil or something oily.

Next, she tested her bindings. There was only a little wiggle room in them. Not enough to slip out of. But could she break them? She never could have as a human, but now she had immortal strength.

It was an awkward position to get any kind of leverage. She tried twisting and that didn't work. So she tried pulling. She pulled with all her might, and just when she felt like her shoulders were going to dislocate, the bindings tore and her hands were free.

Ripping the blindfold off her face, Falon got her first good look around where she was. She noticed the CCTV high in the corner and the one-way glass on one wall.

Definitely in some kind of underground holding cell. No windows and only one door.

Removing the ties from her ankles, Falon got up and walked over to the door. It was locked of course. Grasping it with both hands, she started to twist the knob. With a groan of failing metal, the knob came off the door in her hands. Saluting the camera with her middle finger, she opened the door and looked out into a hallway.

No one was watching when Falon freed herself. Because if they were, they'd be in the room now.

In the hall, Falon didn't see any visible exit marked, so it was a 50/50 guess. Going to her right, she passed other doors but didn't bother looking in the rooms. When she got to the end of the hall, there was a set of stairs with an Exit sign on her left. *Yeah!*

Going up the stairs carefully, listening for people as she went, Falon reached the top landing, and another door. It was locked too. This one was a lever, not a knob—easier to pry open.

Again, the metal in the lock squealed as it failed. She froze in place, listening for someone coming.

After thirty seconds, Falon decided that no one had heard, and slowly opened the door. She was in the lobby of an office building. In front of her was a two-story glass wall and a bank of elevators. A security desk was over to the right in front of the street-facing doors. Did the security desk know she was downstairs? She was about to find out.

Walking with as much purpose as she could muster, Falon strode directly past the security desk and straight out the front door. Not a single person stopped her. That meant the person who took her didn't know she was free yet. So she might have a few minutes ahead.

Once she left the building, she walked quickly across the street and into another building and up to the front desk.

"Excuse me, is there a courtesy phone I can use please?" Falon asked them in her sweetest voice.

"Yes, ma'am, there is one on the wall over on the east side of the building," replied the desk clerk.

Walking over there, Falon noticed that there were very few people in this lobby, so it should be easy to spot a tail. She got to the phone and immediately called Mark.

"Mark, it's Falon. I was taken this morning but I've got myself free. Can someone pick me up?"

"What? What do you mean 'taken this morning?' Where are you?" demanded Mark. She could hear the panic in his voice.

"Calm down. I'm okay. In fact, I'm pretty proud of myself. I used my new superpowers to escape."

"Start from the beginning, please," said Mark.

"This morning, someone grabbed me off the elevator on my way up to the office. They were two very strong men. One of them put a bag over my head and then I got injected with some drug that knocked me out. I fought like a she-demon before that though. I even think I got one of them with my fingernails."

"Okay, then what happened?"

"Well, I woke up in a windowless room in a basement somewhere. I remembered your lessons. I listened really hard. I sniffed the air for smells. I couldn't look because there was still a bag over my head. But my hearing told me I was alone, and my nose told me I was in a basement."

"Good! What happened next?"

"I analyzed—look, why don't I tell you all this when I get home?"

"Yes, love, I'll send Andrews. You're sure you're okay? Where are you?"

"Oh, I forgot to ask the address of the building. One minute, let me go ask the front desk."

She put the phone receiver down and ran back to the desk to ask them the address and ran back to the phone.

"Mark?"

"Still here."

"The building is at 1001 Metcalfe Street," I said.

"Okay, love, we'll be there shortly," said Mark. Hanging up, he took three deep breaths. Then he called Andrews.

"Andrews, Falon was kidnapped," said Mark.

"Oh my God. I'll be right there."

"No! Wait! She managed to free herself and get to an adjacent building."

"Oh, good girl!"

"Go pick her up directly. She's at 1001 Metcalfe."

"Right away, boss."

Andrews arrived about ten minutes later in the limo. As Falon ran out, she spotted Derek staring out of the windows across the street in the building she had been held in. Taunting him with a wave, she jumped in the car and drove away. When they arrived home, Mark was waiting at the door.

"So you got out by yourself?" he asked. He hugged her hard and walked her inside.

"Yes, I decided to stop being a weak human and rescue myself," she said, grinning.

"Good!" he said. "But don't scare me like that!"

"You didn't even know I had been taken. You can't now say you were worried after the fact."

"No, you're right. But when you told me, it felt like you were giving me heart failure," he grinned. "I'm going to make sure these holes in our security are closed. Right, Andrews?"

"Right, boss."

20 - The Devil in the Details

— Falon

Mark wrapped his arms around me and asked again if I was okay.

"I'm fine, not a scratch. And I know who did this," I said. "I saw him watching me in the building I was held in. He looked really steamed when I was leaving."

"Did you recognize him?"

"Yes I did. It was that creepy guy from Atlanta that tried several times to get me to go out with him."

"Derek?" asked Mark.

"Yes, that's the one. Why is he in Montreal kidnapping me?" I asked.

"I believe Andrews has some information for us, right?" he said, looking at Andrews.

"Yes, I do. Derek is the Hunter," said Andrews.

Upon hearing this, Mark instantly became aggressive, his teeth elongating and his eyes getting dark and red.

"Calm down, love! Let's listen to Andrews," I said soothingly.

"The Hunters are part of a group called the Fraternal Order," said Andrews. "They are ancient. They have been chasing immortals since their inception."

"Why?" I asked.

"It used to be that they believed they were vampires. Now they know they are immortal and supernatural, which is close enough to vampires as far as they are concerned.. They still think it's their duty to 'cull the herd' and protect humanity, so-to-speak."

"But that's ridiculous!" I laughed.

"Well, we'll leave that 'til later," said Andrews. "Right now, we need to focus on the Hunter."

"Come, let's sit down and talk. We have to figure out what to do," I said quietly.

I stepped up to Mark, tucked myself under his arm and placed the palm of my hand on his chest. In spite of himself, I could feel Mark calm down as he breathed in my scent.

The three of us then went into the living room. Andrews called his team over to the house. In the meantime, Mark poured drinks for us and sat down. Turning on the fireplace, we watched it together.

A little while later there was a knock on the door. Andrews went and let in his crew.

"Mark, Falon, may I introduce you to two of my guys, Grisham and Parsons?" said Andrews.

"Good evening, gentlemen. Won't you come in by the fire? Can I get you a beverage?" asked Mark.

"Wouldn't mind a scotch, please," said Grisham.

"Me too," said Parsons simultaneously.

"I'll get it," I said as I jumped up to get two more glasses and a bottle of Macallan.

Once the drinks were distributed, I sat back down beside Mark and the agents sat across the room on the sofa.

"What do we know?" asked Mark.

"May I?" asked Grisham.

"Go ahead," said Andrews.

"We know that Derek Staung was the North American leader of the Fraternal Order," said Grisham. "He worked out of New Orleans. He had a situation office in Houston and, as near as we can tell, that is where he picked up your trail, Mark.

"Some background: he was recruited about thirty years ago as a teen. His father was a member as well, which follows for most of the membership. Derek was operating in New Orleans for most of that time, until he somehow got wind of something in Houston. Some sort of break happened between him and the Order, and Derek broke away to start his own neo-Nazi group."

"Around the time you were in Atlanta, Falon, he got wind of something and went there. We are still not sure on that detail. It could be a leak from the family, but that's unlikely. My thinking is there is a mole somewhere—but that's just a feeling," explained Grisham.

"Franco," I said. "It's Franco. He's the mole."

"What makes you so certain?" asked Andrews.

"Because he showed up unannounced in Kansas with an old story of Mark being kidnapped," I said. "At the time, it was weird, disconnected, and out of place. Now it makes sense."

"I see your point," said Andrews. "I'll put someone on that. I think you're correct. Please continue, Grisham."

"Staung is crazy," Grisham continued. "Certifiably so, in fact. His mother tried to have him committed when he was eighteen after he came home from a trip with his father talking about vampires and vampire hunting. The couple were divorced many years before, and had not shared a home for ten years. Unfortunately, the father stepped in and took the boy away from his mother and the proper treatment. His father died about seven years ago, leaving his son running the chapter in New Orleans. Eventually Staung realized that vampires weren't real. But his need to have an evil enemy to brutalize—so that he could believe himself to be a hero—led him to turn his molten hatred towards the Olde Ones instead. For him, they're as bad as vampires, but with the added bonus of being real."

"Staung recruited Brandon Wallace for his order when he was in Atlanta but has not divulged just what the group does. He's alluded to saving women who are being tortured or abused. This fits in with the self-image of who Brandon thinks he is, and what he considers to be right. Unfortunately, Brandon is easily manipulated, so he has no idea what's in store for him," noted Grisham.

"Staung took Brandon and his band under his wing to manage them and find them gigs. So far, he's used their group as a cover to go to about twenty different cities. It's a good cover, because the boys don't realize they're being used. Brandon has a tiny inkling that something is not right, but doesn't know what to do about it," he continued. "Emails we were able to get off his laptop showed that Brandon is asking questions that Staung isn't answering."

"Right now," said Andrews, "we are waiting for Staung to make a move. We know that the abduction and rescue was part of a plan, but we're not sure what that plan is. It's rather radical and odd."

"We're expecting that the next play will be something that Brandon has been instructed to do," said Parsons. "He may be under the impression that Mark is an abusive husband and is keeping Falon locked away and is beating her. That would fit the profile that Staung likes to create. If that is the case, expect Brandon to try to make a date or something."

"Like, he'll try to get a date with my wife?" asked Mark.

"Yes, we didn't say he was smart, but he may use his gig in town to suggest they have a meeting of some kind. We expect that will be the moment that they will snatch her again."

"This abduction stuff is getting old," I said. "Fortunately, I don't think that will happen. He saw me leave. Staung knows I freed myself. If anything, his plan won't be to abduct me again, but to catch me off guard somehow."

"The Hunter wants both of you to reveal yourselves so he can justify killing you," said Andrews. "He needs to, in order to maintain his fantasy that he is a hero rather than a washout. For that reason, Derek's play will be different, but the same. He still needs you to lose it in public. Which means he needs to put Falon's life at risk somehow. He will believe that is the only way to get to you."

"He would be right on that too," stated Mark.

"We can't let that happen."

"And you cannot react either, my love," said Mark.

"So what do we do?" I asked.

"Unfortunately, we must wait," explained Grisham. "We will continue to gather more information and try to figure out his play. We have his base of operations under surveillance. Most of the people he's recruited are human with a 'hunter complex' and just want to see a living vampire. They have no idea what they are up against, or who Staung actually is. And he doesn't care. If his henchmen are willing to die for their delusions in his service, it's no skin off his nose."

21 - Brandon, the Patsy

— Derek

"Brandon, it's Derek."

"Hey, Derek, good to hear from you! Look, I want to thank you for setting up this gig in Montreal. It's sweet. I've already run into Falon, if you can imagine! So thanks for the tip! Will you be coming to Montreal yourself?"

"No problem, my boy, no problem," said Derek smoothly. "I fear for her safety though."

"What do you mean?" asked Brandon. "You fear for Falon's life?"

He's so gullible! thought Derek.

"I don't like that fellow she's hanging out with. He looks mean. I noticed him manhandling her and pulling her along by her arm today," lied Derek. "I think she's in danger."

"I could visit them and see if there is anything there," suggested Brandon.

"Would you?" asked Derek. "That may help. But you know, if he is a brutal man it's not likely he'll be that way in front of you."

Derek was carefully tugging on Brandon's heartstrings by reminding him about his own childhood. Brandon's mother was abused by his father, so he knew the pattern, and he knew it rarely came out in front of strangers.

"If that's the situation, I know what to do," said Brandon. Derek could hear the anger building in his voice. "I'm not a helpless nine-year-old anymore."

After a pause, Brandon continued. "Give me a day or two, I'll come up with something," he said.

Excellent! Brandon will instigate something of his own free will without any prompting. All I have to do is be there to make sure the shit hits the fan and then put the two immortals out of their misery.

"I'll let you know when I am going to make a move, okay?" asked Brandon.

"Of course, take your time," answered Derek.

"Oh, by the way, the cops took my gun."

"How? Why? When did that happen?"

"Long story short, I was flagged or something coming into the country. Two cops showed up and were asking questions and searched my hotel room. They found my stash of weed and ammo, and took my gun from me."

"Oh, that's too bad. Well I can get you another if needed," said Derek.

"Good, thanks. I hate being without it. I feel naked."

22 - The Setup

A few days later, an opportunity came up that Derek hadn't expected. Brandon got notified that the TomCats were coming to Montreal and were going to play at another club in the West Island. It was the perfect chance to get Falon away from Mark. The guy couldn't begrudge them a night out together for old times' sake, could he?

Brandon cleared it with Derek, then went and picked up tickets. He had received a "change of address" notice for her and Mark a while ago. He didn't know why he got one, but it was nice to have heard from her. This would make it easy for him to get her out of the house.

Not wanting to "run into her" again so soon, Brandon watched Falon's house for a few days. He decided to make his move at the train station as she was getting off. Lining himself up to bump into her, he faked having his nose in a book while walking down the platform. He ran right into her, causing her to be knocked down.

"Oh, I'm very sorry, miss," said Brandon, as he looked up to see who he walked into. "Falon! Oh, it's you. Here, let me help you up. I'm so sorry about this. I was in a good part of the book."

"No problem, Brandon. How are you?" said Falon.

"I'm fine. I decided to take a trip out here to see the end of the island."

"Good. How are you getting around?" she asked.

"Hmm, I didn't think of that," he said, blushing. "I guess I'll have to get a ride share."

"Where were you going?" she asked.

"To a bar called McKibbins. They have live bands, so I was hoping to see if I could book a gig."

"Oh, that's a fun Irish Pub not too far away. I would have gotten off at the last stop though. Still, it's not difficult to get there. Do you want a lift?" she asked.

"If it's not too much trouble," he grinned. "We can catch up with just the two of us."

"My car is over this way," she pointed.

They walked over to her car while she called Mark to let him know she was driving Brandon to a bar for him to speak to the manager.

"Do you want me to meet you there?" asked Mark.

"No, it's all good," said Falon. Then she hung up, and rejoined Brandon to drive to the pub.

"It's only about fifteen minutes from here," she said.

"That close?" asked Brandon.

"Well, it's not a big city geographically. We're confined to an island after all."

Fifteen minutes later, they pulled into a parking spot at the pub.

"Are you coming in?" asked Brandon.

"I think I will. You talked about catching up, so why don't we grab a pint and do that?" Falon said.

"I'd love to," said Brandon.

The two of them walked in. The first thing Brandon did was ask for the manager. He was escorted back to the office by the hostess. Another hostess seated Falon in a booth by the window.

"What can I get you?" asked the server.

"I'll have a pint of Guinness, please," she answered.

"And for your friend?"

"I don't know what he's drinking."

"I'll come back for his order, then."

Falon was sitting there with her foot tapping to the music being played by the band in the back. It was lively Irish music. Watching out the window at the people that went by, she spotted Andrews in the parking lot. Mark must have sent him to watch out for her anyway. When Andrews realized she spotted him, he saluted and faded back into the shadows. Nice trick.

While driving over, Falon realized that she had an opportunity to find out what Derek and Brandon were cooking up. She might be able to get him a little drunk and get him talking. Her new immortal body didn't get drunk easily, so she should be able to drink him under the table.

"Come to think of it, I could do that when I was mortal," mumbled Falon, under her breath.

Another server came by with menus. Falon ordered some appetizers to go with the beer. Guinness was a sipping beer, so it was not going to go down fast.

Both the appetizers and the beer arrived before Brandon left the back office and found Falon at the table.

"Well, did you get a gig?" she asked.

"Yes, he's hired me for a week following the last week we have booked downtown. So we'll be in town for another three weeks. That's exciting!"

"Did he just hire you guys without knowing what you sound like?" asked Falon.

"No, of course not. No one does. I carry a demo tape with me of some of our live performances," he explained.

"That's a good idea!"

"So what have you been up to? It's been almost a year since we were last together," he asked. "That was the night I proposed to you, if I recall."

Falon blushed because that was the last time she'd seen him, except for bumping into him just a couple of days ago.

"Let me see, I've been buried by a building, caught in a tornado, driven to Oregon and back, become engaged, and moved houses!"

"Wow! You've been a busy woman," he said. "Tell me about being in a tornado."

As she related the story of the tornado, the server brought drinks for him and another round for Falon. She also returned with a tray of shooters. Alabama Slammers. So he remembered what got her drunk.

By the time she finished that story, they had polished off the appetizers and one round of beers and half of the shooters.

Falon was careful to sound a little drunk with that much alcohol going down. She didn't want to give away that she was an immortal.

"Excuse me!" Brandon called a server over. "Can we please see the menu again and bring another round please."

"Yes, sir."

Brandon ordered a burger platter and Falon ordered the Irish Stew. More drinks and shooters arrived.

"Go on and continue with your stories," said Brandon. "They're fascinating."

She finished up describing the move and turned it around on him, asking him what he had been doing the past year.

"Oh, you know, a little of this, a little of that," he said evasively. "Mostly the band and I have been touring Mississippi, and we've been pretty busy with bookings from Georgia to Texas. It was in Texas I met a guy who wanted to manage us, and became our booking agent."

"You didn't have one before?" she asked.

"We did, but he wasn't doing us any favors, if you know what I mean," he answered. "The gigs were always low-pay and local. We were tired of locals and wanted to expand our horizons. Derek said he could do that for us."

Bingo! The connection to Derek.

"That's great!" Falon said. "So is that how you ended up coming to Montreal?"

"Yup, he got the first gig for us in Kingston?" he said. "Is that right?"

"Kingston, Ontario?"

"Yes. We had a week there just before this one," he said. "Then two weeks here—one downtown and one out here. So it was kind of natural to see if I could find more live band venues here before we leave."

"Well, good work," she said.

"Hey, the manager gave me two tickets to their show tomorrow night. It's the TomCats. Would you come with me?" asked Brandon.

"The TomCats are playing here?" she asked.

"Yeah, one night only," said Brandon. "Apparently, it's between two big gigs so they agreed while they were in town. It's quite the coup for a small place like this."

"I'll say," she said. "I'd love to. It will be fun. I'll get Mark to come too."

"Can we not?" he asked. "I'd rather it be just us."

Now this is tricky, Falon thought to herself. I don't want to go on a date with Brandon. But we need to know what he's up to. What am I going to say?

"You know, I really have to go to the ladies' room. Will you excuse me for a minute?" She got up and quickly made her way to the restrooms.

Once inside, she called Mark.

"Mark, I have another opportunity to get him to talk. He's asked me to go to the show here tomorrow night. Maybe you and Andrews can be here too?"

"We'll figure that out. You say yes, and I'll let you know what the plan is when you get home," he answered.

"Okay, got it."

Getting back to the table, Falon found that Brandon had gone. "Perhaps he went to the Men's Room," she murmured out loud. She waited a few minutes and then heard a familiar voice on the house speakers.

"I'd like to dedicate this song to the only woman I've ever loved! Falon, come on up here, love."

Crap! I don't need this! said Falon to herself. Nevertheless, she made her way toward the stage and found Brandon in the middle, ready to sing.

"Five, six, seven, and..." said Brandon. The group launched into a rendition of her favourite song. Everyone got up to dance too, starting off a party.

When the song was done, Brandon thanked the band for letting him jam with them and jumped off the stage right in front of her. He scooped her up in his arms and whispered into her ear that he hadn't been joking.

Walking back to the table, his hand was on her back and he was behaving like the Brandon she knew in Atlanta. She wasn't interested. But she was stuck playing this game as long as something was going on.

Checking her watch, it was after midnight, and she wanted to go home. Falon called the server over and paid for her portion of the night. She asked Brandon how he was going to get home, and he told her not to worry. She said good night and started walking for the door.

Brandon came after her and caught up just before she got to the car.

"Wait! Falon, where do I pick you up?" he called out.

"I'll meet you here. What time?"

"I'd rather pick you up like a lady," he said as he caught up to her.

"It's not a date, Brandon," she said firmly. "I'm engaged to be married. We're just two friends having a night out. I'll make my own way here, thank you." She couldn't let this get too far away from reality.

"Nine o'clock, then? Out front?"

"Yes. See you tomorrow."

23 - Shake Down

— Mark

When Falon got home, I was waiting up.

"That was a long night!" I said.

"Jealous?" she asked.

"I am. Another man was spending time with my woman," I said as my fangs protruded a little. "But not seriously."

"Good. I love you," she said. "He's trying to make it like Atlanta again. He wanted to pick me up like a date tomorrow. I put my foot down, though, and told him I would meet him outside."

"That's good."

I got closer. She caught the scent of my arousal and suddenly she was there with me. My hand caressed her back up and down then took hold of her neck. She bent her head back to look up into my face. My fangs were elongated now. She reached up and kissed me gently. They were in the way, so she licked my fangs and I felt shivers go through me. I pressed another hand into the small of her back, bringing our bodies together, grinding our hips. She could feel my arousal too.

"I like you a little jealous," she said. "It brings out the animal in you. Shall I be the animal trainer?" she asked coquettishly.

A deep rumble came out of my throat and I knew my eyes were glowing. Oh yeah, this is going to be a fun night.

She took my hand and led me upstairs to our room. We didn't play master/slave, but she liked taking control of our lovemaking and making me lose control. I controlled myself so much to pleasure her and she didn't get a lot of opportunities to give back. The last time was in a restaurant.

Upstairs, she ordered me to strip. I did so, slowly, teasing her with glimpses. I peeled off my shirt and she walked up to me and laid her hands on my torso. She inhaled deeply against my skin, drinking in my male musk. She moved her hands all over me, feeling my muscles lying under my skin. Sliding her hands down my waist and then my hips, where my trousers were hanging barely, Falon traced the V of my abdomen cut into my body, down to where it was joined with a fine line of hair pointing like an arrow down into my pants. She licked her lips as if a tasty morsel was in front of her.

Falon returned her eyes to my chest, where she licked one nipple, and brought it out like a little soldier. Both my nipples reacted. I started to caress her nipples through her blouse; they were reacting like mine. She was biting and licking them one after the other, until I was groaning with desire. Her own nipples were straining inside her shirt. I stopped touching her.

"I never said to stop," she commanded.

She loosened my belt as I caressed her nipples, making them pucker and poke through her blouse. My belt had been pulled out of the loops and was hanging in a loop in her hands. I wanted her to use the belt. I was eager for it.

"Have you been naughty?" she asked.

I growled through my fangs.

"Continue stripping, I want skin," she demanded.

I undid my top button, slid down the zipper, and my trousers fell off my hips without any help. I usually wore underwear, but I had a surprise for her tonight. I was going "commando". Falon walked around me as if she was appraising a prize stallion.

Falon made a comment under her breath about my beautiful buttocks as she grabbed them and dug her fingers in. She slipped a finger between my cheeks and rubbed my slit, causing me to gasp and groan.

When she walked around to my front, she pressed her body up against mine and ground her hips into my hard shaft. My breath hitched at the skin contact. She reached around and grabbed my butt again and pulled me harder against her as she kissed and licked her way down the middle of my chest, following the line of hair all the way to my toys.

My cock was waving at her, vying for attention. She ignored him and instead focused on my balls. Gently cupping them, she played with them for a few minutes. She was causing sensations all over my body, and they all came together to harden my cock. When she leaned in to kiss my groin and lick the crease between my leg and my body, I was compelled to separate my feet.

Her hands slid up my inner thighs to cup my balls again, and one took hold of my cock. While she stroked my cock, she started kissing, nipping, and licking her way all around my balls and the base of my cock. She was using her newly finished fangs to deliver small doses of venom to me.

This started to make me dizzy. I was gasping and breathing very heavily as my hips developed a mind of their own and started to rock. She finally took my cock in both hands and a deep sigh escaped me. She was gentle at first but increased the pressure of her hands as she stroked my entire length slowly. Her lips pursed, she kissed the tip of my shaft, and the softness in contrast to the hard grip she had with her hands caused me to jerk and nearly come.

My body needed her, needed to be connected to her, to be inside of her. The not being there was torture. My moans accompanied my body's gyrating. Standing, there wasn't much I could do. I reached for her head to move it.

"Na ah-ah," she said. "Keep your hands at your sides. I will tell you when you can do something different."

Another growl escaped from my chest as my hands dropped back down to my sides. My calm, such as it was, was trashed when she wrapped her lips around my cock and swallowed me as far as she could go. I felt her teeth gently scrape along as she pulled me back out. My cock jumped and danced in her hand. She kissed the tip of it and was rewarded with a little pearl drop. I was watching her as she stretched her lips over it and enveloped my head in her mouth. I was watching her as she tongued me all around and then sucked hard on me until I nearly came again.

She pulled away and looked at me. Her eyes were glowing purple. I briefly wondered what that signified before my attention was drawn back as she caressed her own fangs with her tongue. Opening her mouth wide, she showed me her fangs with a hiss. The anticipation of her bite had me panting. She buried her face on my inner thigh and bit down. I felt her fangs pierce my skin, and I cried out, and then the sensation of something flowing into me was remarkable.

I started gasping and making all kinds of new noises.

After that, my erection was the longest I'd ever seen. Interestingly, the bite didn't make me ejaculate.

"Lie down," she ordered. My belt had materialized in her hand somehow. She held it in a loop threateningly.

I basically collapsed to the floor. She straddled me and lined up my cock with her opening and impaled herself. As she came down on me hard, my cock rammed into the end of her vagina, lighting up the nerve endings in my head and the end of her channel.

She lashed me with the belt across my chest as I gasped at the pain. My gasp became a deep groan of pleasure as she moved in a circular pattern. Another lash across my chest had me gasping again and my cock was pushing against the end of her with force. I had completely filled her. I felt her entire channel along my cock, especially as she squeezed with her muscles. I could tell when her body adjusted to my size. There was a relaxation of the exterior muscles around the base of my cock.

Another lash made me jerk and my cock was rammed again against the end of her channel. Then she wrapped the belt around my neck and lid it through the buckle and tightened. For a second I thought she was going to choke me, but she didn't tighten it that much, just enough for me to feel it. Then she bit me again, this time on my nipple. My body's nerves lit up with the venom this time, and everything became hypersensitive.

She sat there, in control, for a minute, relishing in the feel of being connected again. I looked up at her feeling the bliss too. She squeezed me again and I danced in joy.

"I'm tipping you," I said.

"I know, and you're pushed to the very end. How does it feel? Hmm?"

She slowly raised her hips until I was completely out but nestled in the opening. Then she forcefully impaled herself again, sinking as far as possible.

"Ah, fuck!" I cried out

She smiled. Repeating the slow withdrawal and the fast sheathing cycle brought us both very close to climax. But it wasn't enough. I needed to be driving, to take possession of her.

"Take over!" she yelled. She held onto the leash around my neck, as I flipped her over.

"With pleasure, my lady," I growled. I rolled her over onto her stomach, and while she held onto the leash, I pushed her neck down until her shoulders were on the floor and her ass was up in the air. I took hold of her ass.

"Oh, woman, you have a wonderful ass. I love your ass but now I'm going to abuse it."

She yanked on the leash to draw me closer. I licked a finger to wet it and pushed it into her ass at the same time as I drove my cock into her vagina. The double penetration caused her to squeal. And she yanked on the impromptu leash again, holding me down. I pulled out and pounded into her and repeated. She was no longer my wife, she was the mate to my animal, and we were performing the long-tested ritual of mating violently. She matched each stroke with her own and each one brought us closer to the edge of the abyss.

She shuddered each time my cock reached the end of her channel. The sweet pain of the pressure told me I had completely filled her. I kept up the pace and pounded her over and over again, while one of the hands not occupied with her ass reached around to her clit and touched her there too. It didn't take long for her to climax; it exploded out of her.

Because she held the leash, my body was leaning over her back so I could reach her front, and my fangs were right over her neck. I delivered her a second orgasm with my bite as my seed shot into her. When the orgasm finished, we were both panting and shuddering from the pleasure, and fell over sideways and lay there on the floor for a few minutes. We were still connected, spent and out of breath.

When I came to, Falon was lying there with my belt in her hand and a devilish grin on her face. Someone had enjoyed her kinky idea.

She snapped the belt. "I don't think we got around to the punishment."

I made a noise deep in my throat and my cock danced beside her.

Pulling away from me, she got up on her knees and faced me. Snapping the leather again, Falon licked her lips.

"Mark, on your knees."

"I'm spent, can we wait a few minutes?"

Falon slapped the leather against my ass with a resounding smack. The slight sting sent a zap to my libido. I shivered a little as a caress covered the sting of the slap, and groaned in pleasure.

"You dare speak back to me?" she spoke haughtily.

"I'm a very naughty boy," I said with a rough voice. "Please."

She spanked the other side and repeated her follow-up, getting another groan from me.

Then she got a little rougher, and I gasped when the leather stung my skin, and groaned deeper when it was covered with a caress.

I wanted to take her in my arms, but she stopped me.

"No, don't move. Stay right where you are until your punishment is finished."

I growled; I couldn't help myself. Falon stood this time and straddled my hips, spanking my ass with both her hands and the belt.

That got me really excited; my cock told the story. My breathing was ragged as I fought to keep in control of myself.

Falon started caressing my balls, and every time I tried to move she spanked me. She gave me venom nips on my ass and watched my flesh flick and respond.

"Okay, you've been punished. Now it's time for a reward," said Falon. "What do you choose?"

"He wants to get bitten again," I said quietly. "He quite enjoyed that experience."

"Well, let it never be said, I do not satisfy my man."

24 - TomCats

— Falon

I love the TomCats—one of my very favorite bands. And I wasn't one to miss a concert opportunity to see them, but this one was a bit strange.

Mark, Andrews, and company were going to the bar too. They already left earlier so they could get tables spaced out to watch. Their covers would be just picking up girls, like that wasn't going to be difficult.

I arrived just before 9:00. I didn't want to wait outside, so I sat in the car until I saw Brandon walk up to the door.

Locking up the car, I approached him at the door. He wanted to give me a big hug and kiss before going in, but I resisted.

It seemed he had a table reserved right near the dance floor. He was trying to recreate that night we ended up having sex in the hot tub.

When I looked around, I was able to spot all four guys, and that made me feel better. Mark was at the bar, so he had a clear view of me.

The bar owner announced the band, and they came on the stage. When Bobby saw me in the front row, he made a thing out of it.

"Gosh, folks, my biggest fan is here tonight! Give it up for Falon! She has been to our shows in Florida, Atlanta, and now here!"

"Gee, thanks, Bobby—now I sound like a groupie!" I shouted, laughing.

And with that, the TomCats started playing my favorite song. I forgot all about the subterfuge under way and just enjoyed myself. Brandon was dancing with me most of the night, but I got asked by a few other guys too.

"May I cut in?" asked Andrews.

"Oh, I guess," said Brandon. He reluctantly went and sat at the table, leaving me with Andrews. Brandon was definitely steamed about a big handsome black man dancing with me. We were dancing to a slow song too, so he had me in a pretty tight grip, pretending to grind our hips together.

"How are you doing, Falon?" asked Andrews.

"Good, nothing has happened so far, and he hasn't said anything yet."

"Okay, well, we can make contact all night long like this. I may get a little more, shall we say, handsy, to see if we can incite him."

"Thanks for the warning. Does Mark know?"

"Yup, his idea."

"Well, thank you, Robert," I said loudly as I broke the dance and started back to the table. Before I reached it, another man asked me to dance. I didn't know this one though. The rest of the set, I was dancing with all kinds of guys, and Brandon was getting hammered and annoyed.

At the break, I excused myself and went to the ladies' room. When I got back, Brandon had ordered more drinks and shooters.

"Brandon, don't you think you should ease up on the booze?" I asked.

"Why?" he answered. "I am n-not d-drunk y-yet."

"You're pretty close to it, then."

"N-nah, I-I'm f-fine."

During the second set, Brandon started getting handsy. His hands were all over my back, but when he openly cupped my boob on the dance floor, I pushed his hands away.

"H-hey, w-why w-won't y-you l-let m-me t-touch y-you?"

"I don't want you to touch me, Brandon," I said. "That's why. Now stop that."

"Y-you're m-mine," he said, and forcefully grabbed me tightly, wrapping one arm all the way around my waist and then shoved the other hand inside my shirt and grabbed my boob.

"Take your hands off me, Brandon, right now. If you don't, you're going to get hurt."

"W-who? B-by y-you?"

That was a mistake. Two seconds later, Andrews was there twisting his arm around the back of his body at a frightful angle.

"The lady said to take your hands off her, man," said Andrews quietly. "Let's not make a scene here on the dance floor."

I thought Andrews had him securely, but Brandon had one hand open and grabbed for me again, taking my wrist. That was enough to activate my Krav Maga training.

I don't know what I did exactly, but I reacted violently. The next thing I know I had him on the floor and the offending appendage was behind his head. The wrong way.

Brandon was screaming and the other dancers on the floor had formed a small circle around us. Mark jumped into the circle and pulled me off Brandon, and Andrews picked Brandon off the floor. Grisham and Parsons grabbed girls, got up, and started dancing to get things back to normal.

The four of us went to a booth in the back. Andrews fixed Brandon's dislocated arm, and shoved him into the booth and sat next to him. Mark slid in opposite him.

"Brandon, you're going to tell me what this was all about, and you'll tell me now," commanded Mark as he was staring intently into his face.

Brandon's face went slack; his eyes went dull as he spoke.

"I was supposed to distract Falon away from you and make you jealous to the point you would attack me," answered Brandon. "I swear that's all. Something I was happy to do. Derek told me you were an abusive man, and she's had enough of that crap in her life. She deserves better!" He was yelling at the end, indicating he really believed what he was saying.

"Do you know any of Derek's other plans?"

"No, he just told me about you being an abuser and I made the plan to try to get her away from you," answered Brandon.

Mark got up from the booth with Andrews, leaving me sitting there with Brandon. They went and stood outside to have a quiet conversation.

"What do you think?" asked Mark. They were standing by the window where I was sitting so I could hear them speaking with my immortal hearing.

"I think he's a dupe and he doesn't know anything. He's telling the truth," replied Andrews.

"So keep him here for an hour or so, then let him go," said Mark.

"Will do. Now what do we do next?"

"If he wants me to lose control, maybe that's just what I'll do," said Mark.

"That will have repercussions, both with the family and in the human world."

"I'm aware. But what do we do? Run?" asked Mark.

"If it were me, I'd avoid him and draw him out somewhere I controlled."

"Let's make a plan, then," said Mark.

The two of them came back inside and motioned to me to follow them.

"What about Brandon?" I asked. "You can't leave him there like that!"

"My compulsion will wear off in a few minutes," assured Mark. "He's drunk enough that he should stay here and sober up. Then he'll be all hell-bent on killing me again."

Creepy.

25 - Talking Money

— Falon

Luckily, things calmed down for a while. How strange. After Brandon was questioned, he quietly went about his business and left Montreal without another peep. It was suspicious to say the least. But you cannot look a gift horse in the mouth.

It had been weeks since I had worked on my business plan for the tiny home project. I really haven't done anything recently. Mark's businesses were flying as always, so money wasn't an issue at all. I learned that in some circles he was considered a billionaire. A billionaire! Oh. My. God. No wonder he spent money like water.

There is a good reason for the Olde Ones' wealth. They have been accumulating it for millennia. Time to give back!

It had been a couple of weeks since my mind-opening bubble bath and the meeting where Lora had come up with the idea of tiny houses for the homeless. Now I needed to figure out how to do that.

We could get the very rich to pay for it. It was just a matter of separating them from their money.

We had decided a charity ball would be a good way. One of my pet peeves was that obscenely rich people don't often pitch in to solve problems like hunger and homelessness. I was now in a position that I could actually do something about that. I wasn't going to squander the opportunity.

Of course, I had to tell Mark I was planning on spending a whole whack of his money. I mean a whole whack. He had offered, but I'm not sure he'd offer as much as I thought I would need. This would be tricky, considering I didn't really feel I had a right to his money. I was just presuming, big-time.

So I did the classic bribe set up. I made a really special dinner, complete with candles and soft music, put on my sexiest outfit, and planned a seduction for money.

Mark came home that afternoon around 4:00—perfect timing.

"Wow! What's the occasion for this special setting?" he asked when he walked through the door.

"I have to ask you a favor, a really big favor, so I'm buttering you up," I said while twisting some hair around my finger.

"You know, if you're trying to seduce me out of my money, you're not supposed to tell me first what your plan is," he said, smiling.

"Oh, I guess I blew it, then."

"Not at all, seduce away. Please," he said. "Just as long as you'll know I'm going to say yes no matter what you do."

"Oh, that's not fun. You have to resist a bit or all this planning is for nothing," I pouted.

"Don't use that pout on me, woman, you know what it does to me," he growled as his eyes hooded over.

"Fine, then I'll just serve dinner," I huffed, spinning around and displaying my bottom, which was currently being hugged ever so perfectly by my stretchy red dress.

I heard Mark groan and sigh behind me, then his hands grabbed my ass.

"Oh, what a perfect ass. I love your ass, woman. Come here and give me your ass. I'll give you anything." He growled some more.

He dragged me backward a little until I was leaning up against him and I could feel his hands roaming all over my ass. One managed to sneak under my dress and reached my slit. His fingers were pushing their way between my legs to find my vagina. His face was up against my ass and inhaling my scent.

Groaning, I let him thoroughly feel me. I was getting wet with his fingers probing me. A little shiver took me as his finger lightly pierced the entrance to my vagina. He pulled me closer and turned me so that his other hand could reach me from the front. Now I had his fingers gently parting my petals and rubbing my clit.

So much for me seducing him! He was taking over. I could smell his desire as I sat on his knee. One of his hands was still rubbing my clit, but the other had wrapped itself around my body and was diving into the top of my dress and pulling it down. Its destination was my breast, whose nipple was already hardening in anticipation of being touched and pinched by his fingers.

It's a good thing I'm not wearing underwear, I smiled to myself. He bit into my exposed shoulder gently with his fangs, releasing a little venom, and then licked the wound to heal it. The venom coursing through my blood, of course, brought on an orgasm. I turned and faced him to kiss him, and he released his hand from my clit, taking hold of my naked breast. His kiss was hot and demanding as his tongue took my mouth.

I pushed my tongue into his mouth and caressed his fangs. Ever since I discovered that they were sensitive, I loved touching them with my tongue. It always made him shudder with desire. This was no different. As the desire swept through his body, I nuzzled my face into his neck and licked a spot on the soft muscle. My bite wasn't as deep, but it delivered my own brand of venom. I felt the moment it flushed through his system, because it was like lightning had struck. His back arched and a long loud groan—between a groan and a scream—escaped his lips as his eyes rolled back in his head.

A moment later, his eyes were glowing like they were on fire and his fangs were primed as he sank them into my shoulder. The duet of screams that came from us as we both blasted into orbit must have been something to see. And we weren't even undressed yet.

The high was immeasurable. I'd felt nothing like it before. Perhaps, because I was able to deliver as well as receive, it became something else. It took a while before Mark could speak—me a little longer.

"Falon, your venom is potent," was the first thing out of his mouth.

"Was it good for you?" I asked.

"Oh geez, I don't know how it keeps getting better. No one told me females had venom and what it could do. I don't know if anyone in my family knows."

"How is that possible? Didn't Gwen tell you I'd be getting fangs?" I asked.

"Yes, that's true. But she didn't say they'd have venom, did she?"

"Well, shall we have dinner now, or more sex?" Glancing at his pants, he was still in a state of readiness. I reached for him and stroked him through the fabric and was rewarded with a subtle twitch. Clearly, the orgasm that the venom brought didn't stop his erection. That was nice; he could now have intermediate orgasms like me.

"Considering that I'm now completely aroused, I vote for more sex," he said. "I'm going to be busy for a while."

With that, he picked me up and carried me upstairs to our bedroom to ravage me thoroughly. Our clothes got strewn all over the room as he rushed to get us both naked. Once inside me, he sighed with contentment, and I smiled.

"Now I'm home," he said. Kissing me deeply again brought out my fangs as well, and I broke the kiss to grin at him.

"Nice hardware," he said. "Show me what you've got."

Licking and nipping his neck, I chose a spot and bit him. Feeling the venom flowing through my teeth and into him was a strange experience. But the result was epic. Mark's eyes rolled back into his head as his body shuddered. It was a good thing he was inside me, because he very nearly erupted.

"Oh, woman, I don't know how, but I love you even more," he whispered as he was coming back into his head. He kissed me deeply again, driving me hotter and wetter.

He made love to me then with the sweetest reverence, bringing me to an explosive orgasm that lifted me off and had me soaring.

Coupled together, I marveled at just how perfectly he filled me. Time and again, our union was so complete it was hard to believe it was possible.

I didn't want to come down, but it happened anyway. At least reality was good right now.

Mark was lying beside me, caressing my face and brushing back the hair. The tingles on my scalp felt lovely as he ran his fingers through my hair.

"Welcome back, love. You went sailing for a while," he smiled.

"Well, that was some amazing send-off. It would be an insult not to take advantage when it's given," I said.

"Dinner, all the effort you went to, let's not waste it," he said. "Come on, I am intrigued to hear your idea."

He pulled me up and I realized he'd already cleaned us both up. The little things he did like that were so considerate. We got dressed—I pulled the red dress back over my naked body. As he watched, his fangs extended again.

"You know, it's going to be near impossible to focus on food knowing you're not wearing underwear."

"Tough it out, big boy," I smirked.

Leaving my shoes off, I padded back downstairs to the kitchen to check on the food. Everything was still fine. Thankfully, I had left everything on warming. Bending over to pull things out of the oven, Mark's cock snuck up behind me and under my dress. I glanced over my shoulder to see that he hadn't bothered to put clothes on. *Okay, that's fair.* I was wearing a dress commando, and he was naked. All was hanging out. *Fun.*

His cock was just nudging against my vagina, so I rubbed up against him, and he slipped inside when I tried to stand up.

"I cannot help it if I desire my wife more than food," he said.

"Okay, Romeo, I'm bending over a hot oven. At least let me stand so I can have some fun too," I said.

"Falon, sometimes I'm afraid of how much desire I feel for you. It's like I've got no control anymore," he said. He disengaged and stepped back, letting me stand up.

"It's okay, big guy, I feel the same. We'll learn together."

I went and made up plates and I asked him to light the candles on the table. He was walking around doing things with an erection. It was a hoot.

Sitting down to dinner, we were watching each other and making eyes at each other. It was quite entertaining.

"Okay, so what's this idea you have?" Mark asked, trying to get down to business.

"Go put some pants on, will you? I can't talk business with your cock dancing around in front of me," I said. Laughing, Mark got up, pulled a pair of pants over his naked butt, and came back to the table. His torso was still naked. Sigh!

"I want to do some good in the world. I want to start a charity that will help solve homelessness. You have lots of money, much more than we'll ever need, so I think we should give back to the world for the good luck we've had," I blurted out in a rush.

There was silence for a few minutes. *Hmm.* I waited. I didn't want to interrupt whatever he was thinking. Finally, he spoke.

"Okay, and what would this entail, in your mind?"

Good! I haven't been shut down completely. Yet.

"I don't want to use your money entirely, so don't worry that I want to bankrupt you. I want to raise money. You know, there are lots of rich people, and I think we could raise enough to make a difference. We could have one of those big fancy balls for the rich, and raise money that way. We could say that we can match everyone's donation, to a point, and use that money to build shelters for the homeless. I don't know how to solve it yet, I just want to. We'd need to hire the right people to help organize and work on everything."

"Having a party to raise money is a good idea. But you need an organization to administrate the money, and decide where it goes, and how to spend it. It's actually quite a big deal, not just one party. Unless you plan on giving the money to an already existing charity," he explained.

I hadn't thought of that.

"That's an interesting idea. I would go along with that if we could find the right charity. I am going to research this. But in the meantime, are you opposed to us doing something?"

"No, not at all. In fact, I think it's the perfect thing for you to focus on. It will give you a purpose, better than a business. You can make the charity your business. We can use our own money to get it off the ground. This will become a yearly event, because the money needs to be replenished every year. So this will become a long term, permanent vocation."

"I kind of like that."

"So do I. I think you'd be very good at it. And you're right, we have been very lucky, it's time to give back. I will confirm with our accountants, but I expect you can have at least a hundred million to start."

"A hundred million to start?" I choked on the words. "Really? Wow, that's a lot of money."

"It's a drop in the bucket really. Barely .001% of my net assets."

"Now you're just bragging," I said.

"A little, yes. But it's worth knowing. You don't know how much I'm worth. You've never asked. Which is one of the things I love about you. It's not the money. It never was."

"Were you rich when I met you as Zisis?" I asked.

"Yes, even then our family was worth billions."

"Billions, plural?"

"Yes. Plural. Don't forget we have been investing money for over six thousand years. In those days it was just accumulating gold and precious stones. Now it's stocks and bonds, ownership in companies, and such. But money is money."

"Wow, we could really do some good. I mean, really solve problems," I said, dreaming. "I need to look into this for real. It was just a 'what if' before, but now it's real we can actually do something for good!" I said excitedly. "I love you so much. Thank you for supporting me." I hugged him.

"No problem. This is worthwhile," he agreed.

26 - The Tiny House Project

— Falon

"A Tiny House For Everyone Who Has Nowhere to Call Home."

That was my new slogan. Having decided on creating a charity to tackle homelessness, we needed to start with a plan on fixing the problem. Then we needed to look at how to prevent it, and that was a huge topic. But first how do we get people off the street?

Lora's answer was a good one—tiny houses.

A town in Alberta, Canada, built tiny homes for every homeless individual and gave them all an address. Once they had an address, they had self-respect, they could get a job, they could get assistance from the government. The skies opened up for them!

So that's where I wanted to start—with tiny houses.

It took a month of reading, research, and asking lots of questions, but I had a direction. Now I needed a staff to help me accomplish my goal.

We set up offices in one of Mark's buildings downtown. I had a suite of six offices, a reception area, and a conference room on the sixth floor. Now, I needed staff. An assistant first, someone who would handle the day-to-day things. I also needed a lawyer to handle things like contracts.

Gwen was willing to help out but wouldn't be at our disposal all the time. I understood that. At least she would be another pair of eyes.

Andrews thought his security company could play a role in the new endeavor. He saw a security role as well as a research role. His group could provide background checks about people getting involved.

I set it up that Gwen and Andrews could share one of the offices, since they were both part time.

I wanted to work with Lora. I wanted her expertise on the Gala. She'd been there from the start; she was interested in the charity part: organizing events and making sure the money got to where it was supposed to go.

But I really needed an assistant. So I started interviewing people. Both men and women applied for the "Person Friday" job as I called it. It wouldn't have a real definition. It was going to be whatever I needed the person to be. I described it as everything from answering phones to zookeeping.

I settled on a shy yet well-spoken young man named Gregory—not Greg, Gregory—who was well-organized, and I think that skill alone would go far. His first task was to speak to the city administration and get some hard data about the homeless in Montreal. We needed to know how big the problem was before we came up with the answer.

When Lora came to the office the first day, she was truly impressed.

"You can pick your office," I said to her.

"Oh, really?" she said. "Okay, may I have the one next to you?"

"Certainly, consider it yours. Now let's have our first meeting."

"Fun!"

"Gregory, will you join us in Lora's new office?" Thankfully the office space came with furniture, so we already had desks and chairs. The only thing we needed to purchase was equipment.

"Lora, can I make your first task the Gala? I would like you to come up with a theme for our first charity ball and a name."

"I'd love to do that. It's like planning a huge party. I'm good at that."

"Excellent. Coordinate with Gregory for whatever you need. As soon as you have some numbers, we can set a budget."

"How big are we talking?"

"Hundreds. Expensive, elite, and exclusive," said Gregory.

"Oh, I like his style!" said Lora.

Gregory grinned. "Falon, Lora and I can get some ideas put together in a couple of days."

"Good," I said. "I like the idea of calling our initiative Project Tiny House."

"I like that," said Lora. "It is a simple name that speaks to the heart of the solution."

"Gregory, we'll need to get computers, printers, maybe a fax machine, phones, all that good stuff. Can you coordinate with Andrews for security as well?"

"Yes, Miss Falon."

"Enough of the miss … just Falon is good."

"Yes Mi—I mean Falon," said Gregory.

While they were off doing their thing, I started working on a press release, and registering the business name and getting the incorporation of the charity set up. Gwen was essential in making sure that all our I's were dotted and T's were crossed.

Gwen was in town reading over some of the documents to sign for the incorporation of the business when Andrews came in.

"Oh, Andrews, I'm glad you're here. There was something I wanted to go over with you," I called out to the hall.

Gwen looked up from her papers.

"Who is that?" she asked.

"I thought you had met Andrews before," I said.

"Perhaps, he looks familiar, but I don't remember being introduced."

"Andrews, come in please. Andrews, this is Gwen, Mark's sister. Gwen, this is Andrews, Mark's security guy," I said. "You two will be sharing this office because you both are here occasionally."

"Pleased to meet you," they both started at the same moment.

"Gwen, pleased to meet you," Andrews offered his hand.

"Me too, glad to meet you that is." Gwen shook it. She was blushing! *That's unusual.*

"Andrews, Gwen is handling all the corporate, legal, and financial papers for how, until we can hire someone," I said.

Andrews was staring a little at her, and she was returning the stare. *This is cute!*

At that moment, Lora walked in talking a blue streak about an idea for the caterer. She stopped cold when she saw Andrews.

"Um, hi, Andrews," Lora mumbled. "It's been a while since we last saw each other." I detected a lustful scent coming off Lora and Andrews. However, the one on Andrews happened before Lora walked in.

"Hello, Lora," he said, trying to sound nonchalant. "Nice to see you again." He seemed to be staring at her like he could see through her clothes.

Meanwhile, Gwen was looking at Lora like she wanted to kill her. Something was going on under all this, and I needed to get to the bottom of it.

"Lora, with me a moment please," I said, pulling her down the hall to my office.

"We'll be just a minute, if you could wait for me, please?" I asked as I left Gwen and Andrews.

Closing my office door, I rounded on Lora. "Okay, what happened? What is between you and Andrews?"

"Oh, well, um, I wasn't going to say anything," said Lora.

"Clearly, but now it's an issue. So spill," I said, a little miffed.

"Remember that day Andrews and I drove you to meet Mark in the parking garage?"

I nodded.

"Well, he drove me back to the hotel. He offered to stay in the room to protect me. I was so tense, so stressed, I needed some really rough sex to relax," she admitted.

"You didn't?"

"We did. I took a shower and when I came out, he was sitting there in the dark. The sexy striptease in the movie *True Lies* just popped into my head, and I had to re-enact it."

"Oh boy!"

"Well, one thing led to another, and he was willing to go a little further than the average guy."

"How much further?" I asked.

"We got into some serious kink. I got to have one of my fantasies play out."

"Do I want to know?"

"You may not. I'll tell you if you do. But it was a one-time thing. I scratched an itch and satisfied my curiosity."

"Okay, what was the fantasy?"

"Triple penetration," she said with a straight face.

"Triple ... tri—triple penetration? You mean three penises?"

"Yup. I'd heard about it and was curious about it," she said matter-of-factly.

"Three guys?" I was shocked.

"No, one guy and two dildos," she said.

I had nothing else to say. So I just stood there silent. I couldn't conceive of how this was done. Or why my friend would want to try it.

"Was it fun?" I finally asked.

"Yes, and no," she said. "Yes, it was fun to experiment, to break taboos, it was fun to push my own boundaries, it was fun to go out of my comfort zone too. But it hurt quite a bit, even though the pain was a pleasurable pain, if you know what I mean."

I did know what she meant. That exquisite pain that you forget, not unlike the pain of birth for many women.

"Would you do it again?" I asked.

"Maybe, but I would not use dildos," she said. "I think that's what hurts. They are too rigid. It was okay for a double but not a triple."

My own mind was going now. Double penetration? Two penises, one in each hole? Hmm, now color me intrigued.

"Can you work with him? Andrews?" I asked.

"Of course, I have no intention of being with him again. It was a single hook-up for fun."

"My last question: does Rick know?" I asked.

"No. Not yet. I plan on telling him soon. I didn't mean to not tell him, but we all may be working together, so I want to clear the air before that."

"Good, secret hook-ups break things."

"I agree," she said.

We walked back down to Gwen and Andrews' office. Lora left and I turned back to Andrews and Gwen.

Andrews was staring at Gwen again and nodding his agreement too.

"Andrews, what news do you have for me?"

"Um, yeah," he mumbled, tearing his eyes away from Gwen's face. "The investigations we did into the two builders indicates both are in good standing with the Builder's Association, neither have any liens or legal issues, and neither have ties to organized crime. I would say these are good people to work with."

"That's good to hear!" I said.

"I'm going to work with Lora to work out the security issues for the ball itself. She has some venues that she wants to show me to assess. Considering we're talking about a lot of money, we need to have the best security we can."

"Thanks, Andrews, I'm confident you'll do just that. Anything else for me?"

"Not at this time," he answered. Andrews left to go find Lora's office.

"He's a good-looking man," breathed out Gwen.

"I hadn't noticed," I said. Which was not true. I had. "He's single too."

"I don't date," she said too quickly.

"But you do hook-ups, no?" I asked.

She looked at me then and grinned. That was the first time I'd seen her smile. She was pretty when she smiled. Gwen was usually so surly looking.

"Why don't we all meet for drinks tonight while you're still in town? I know of a great little place that isn't usually too busy," I suggested.

"I'd like that," said Gwen.

"I'll ask Lora to come too." I returned to my office and picked up my phone to call everyone.

Lora and Andrews came knocking on my door at that moment.

"Oh, speak of the queen. Good timing, you two. We're going out for drinks after work. Want to join?" I asked.

"Yes," was the answer from both of them.

"Falon, I have an idea," said Lora. "Why don't we get Rick and his restaurant to come cater the event? Big-time winners of a prestigious restaurateur award coming up from Atlanta to cater the event of the year? I think it would draw a lot of thick wallets."

"That's a smashing idea! Do it! Tell them the fee is no object," I added.

"Perhaps we can link their launch with the Gala in some way."

"There is a good cross-promotional opportunity there, for sure," I said. "Can you add that to your plate?"

"Yeah, I think I can handle that," said Lora.

There were so many good things falling into place, it was difficult not to get giddy with optimism. But I knew I had to keep a lid on my excitement. There was still a long way to go before the night of the ball.

Right now I had to make the news and social media aware of our project. That meant I needed a press release. So I sat down to work on that. Starting was tough.

"Project Tiny House—A Home For Everyone Gala & Dinner" was a mouthful.

How about "Tiny House Gala—A Home for Everyone?" That was a little better. We needed to make it the event of the year to be at!

My phone rang.

"Project Tiny House, this is Falon. How can I help you?"

"Falon Robertson, your voice sounds good to my ears!" said the caller.

"Rick? Is that you?" I cried. "It has been so long! How are you doing?"

"We are doing wonderfully. Very, very busy with building the new restaurant. Lora called me a few minutes ago and was telling me that you needed some caterers for the Gala you're planning," he said.

"Yes, Mark and I have started a foundation to try to solve homelessness. It's called Project Tiny House. We will make an announcement soon to launch the pilot project here in Montreal in October. We're having a Gala and dinner to raise money on October 27th. Actually, I'm hoping to shame some of the other billionaires and millionaires into giving over some serious coin to put toward their own projects in their own cities. We've announced that we will match their donations up to a total of a hundred $100 million."

"Wow!" said Rick. "Well, count us in! Not only will we happily cater this for you, but we will be making a donation that night too. If it can go toward a project in Atlanta, wonderful. If not, I know you'll make sure it gets into the right hands."

"Rick, you guys are wonderful. I am looking forward to seeing the new restaurant!"

"How many courses do you want? Do you have a specific type of menu in mind?" ask Rick.

"Lora is handling all those details, so you can work that out with her. But I would love a very expensive meal with dessert at midnight."

"Sounds good," said Rick. "I'll coordinate with her."

"I'm so excited!" I screeched.

"Easy, Falon, don't blow a blood vessel yet!" he teased.

"I know, it's just I've never done anything like this before with this much money on the line," I said. "It's scary and exciting."

Getting off the phone with Rick, I was almost panting. Beyond the business of the conversation, my brain, flashed memories of almost having sex with him.

27 - Coming Clean

— Lora

Telling the truth is not difficult. Admitting you did something that may be construed as wrong is.

It was Rick's turn in Montreal this week. He was staying with me like always. Our life was good. It felt right being with him. Mundane things felt good. I loved waking up every morning. Going to bed with him was exciting too. Our lovemaking was always epic, even if it was fairly conventional.

He even got along with my kids. They adored him. Especially the two younger ones, because he tirelessly gave them piggyback rides. My oldest was more wary but thought that was more about protecting me than not liking Rick.

The time had come for me to come clean to him, about my past, about the tryst with Andrews, and about my lifestyle. I had to lay it all on the table for him to judge before we went any further. I waited for a weekend when the kids' father had them. I decided an old fashioned seduction was called for. I cooked him a special dinner, laid the table with candles and linen, and wore his favorite emerald green dress.

When he got home and saw me, he looked a little like a cartoon character as his eyes bugged out. I giggled and walked over to give him a hug.

He wrapped his arms around me like he had so many times before, and I knew that he loved me. I could feel it in every fiber of his being.

I loved him too, and it was time to make this commitment to him.

I broke the hug and took his hands in mine and led him to a chair and I sat on the couch.

"I need to tell you something," I started.

"Is this a confession about past experiences?" he asked.

"A little, yes."

"No need."

"Yes, I need to. I love you so much, that before we go any further I need to come clean. You need to know the dark parts of me too. I need you to judge me, and hopefully our love will be enough to let you forgive me. I'd like it if you let me tell the whole story before interrupting or reacting."

"You have my word," he said to me. He looked scared, like I was going to break up with him.

With his consent to begin, I told him about my past, what I used to do for a living. I was an exotic dancer. I wasn't ashamed of that. I made good money, and I didn't take side deals, but there is a terrible reputation about dancers. Most of us were just girls trying to make a decent living.

Next, I told him about my promiscuity, and that I enjoyed sex immensely, and had many partners. I was always careful and was tested for STDs regularly. I also told him that since meeting him, I had basically given up sex with other men, except one time.

He looked at me with that statement with one eyebrow raised in question. He didn't say anything, though. He kept his word.

Then I told him about my kinky side. How I'd relished in trying out new things, and not always one-on-one. His face got a bit pale but he didn't say anything. At some of my comments, I could swear desire briefly flashed in his eyes as he thought of me doing those things.

I told him I had fantasies, most of which I wanted to experience with him, because he was the very best partner I'd ever had, and as an expression of the deep love I felt for him. To explore each other's bodies without qualm, and to experience things beyond our boundaries together meant a lot to me.

He cleared his throat a little at that statement. I could see him squirm a bit and cross his legs to hide an arousal too. Well, at least he wasn't angry yet.

Now the worst part. Telling him about my hook-up with Andrews.

"Last June, when all hell broke loose, Falon and Mark were on the run, and she had been assaulted, I ended up in a hotel room with Andrews. I was extremely stressed, scared for Falon and myself, and over tired. Historically, my method to relieve stress has always been sex. I'd find a hook-up and bang my brains out.

"I went and had a shower, and because I was horny as hell I kept thinking of relieving myself. I did some in the shower, but it didn't really help too much. When I came out of the shower, there was Andrews, sitting in a chair in shadow. The first thing that jumped into my head was the movie *True Lies*. Suddenly, I was acting out that scene in the hotel room.

"One thing led to the inevitable, and we ended up having sex. Not just sex, but kinky sex. He did things for me from my fantasies that I had wanted to try, but never had the opportunity.

"It was a one-time hook-up that scratched an itch. There was no emotion involved and no feelings to hurt, except perhaps yours," I concluded. Then I fell silent and waited.

And waited.

Finally, he spoke. Hesitantly at first.

"The first thing to go through my mind as you sat me down was that you wanted to break up with me."

He paused and swallowed. "That thought drove a stake through my heart. I know I wouldn't be able to live without you."

Again he paused.

"As you told me about your past, I started to relax and listen. I irrationally got pissed off when you told me about your promiscuity. I have no right to be angry about what has happened before us. I told myself to stop being stupid. I was with other women before you. This is no different.

"When you got into the part about kinky desires, well ... that had a different effect on me. I had already had those thoughts after the anal sex we had. That was a mind-blowing experience, by the way. I had wanted to try with someone, but I didn't know how to ask for something like that. My mind was aroused about the possibilities with you. Well, not just my mind was aroused," he added with a grin.

Swallowing, he continued: "Hearing about Andrews was tough. I nearly gave in to the anger. But again, I told myself that it wasn't love, it was an itch, and besides we hadn't committed to each other yet. I mean, in my heart, I'm committed, but I know you hadn't.

"My brain blanked for a minute when you stopped. The truth of it shocked me and it took a while to bring myself back into focus. Your past, even your recent past, doesn't matter to me. It doesn't matter more than you. It doesn't matter more than being with you."

Rick got up from the chair and came and sat on the couch beside me. Taking my hands in his, he looked me in the eyes.

"Lora, we have just made a commitment to each other. I love you, with every fiber of my being. You are my one. I can no more not forgive you than not love you. If you would let me share these fantasies, I would try to fulfill them for you. I would do anything to make you happy."

Tears were streaming down my face. What a man! He'd heard what I had told him, and it hasn't changed anything. *Oh my Goddess, please let me spend eternity with this remarkable being. Let me be worthy.*

I swallowed and gulped and croaked out something I didn't understand. So I just kissed him. Passionately, deeply with everything I had.

He broke the kiss; his fangs were extended and his eyes were glowing with passion. His pants were pretty tight too.

"Now, about this fantasy you did with Andrews..." he said.

A grin spread across my face.

"Do you want to try?" I asked.

"Well, tell me about it first, please."

"It's triple penetration," I said.

"So we tried a double, right? Me and a toy. That was new for me, and remarkably stimulating. What's triple penetration?"

"Three penises. I used two dildos," I said.

"I understand two, so where was the third?"

"Two in my vagina."

"Did you enjoy it?" he asked,

"Not as much as I thought I would. But the dildos give a different sensation. I would rather have two penises. If I were to try again."

"Hmm, a second man. He would take your ass and I would take your vagina. Would we be face-to-face?"

"Yes," I grinned. "In that scenario, you and I would be face to face, and the extra would be standing behind me."

"I could do that," he said. "But we would need the right person."

"Someone close who doesn't mind sharing," I suggested.

"Yes, but also someone who knows what we are. This will get very steamy, and we men will become extremely aroused," he said. "Remember, our arousal gets very aggressive too."

"Do you think Mark and Falon would be interested?" I asked.

"We'd have to ask," he said. "How do we do three?"

"Andrews knows about us," I said, hesitating. "There is another thing to consider."

"What's that?"

"You guys are all very well endowed," I said.

"That would add to the act I would suppose," suggested Rick.

"Let's wait until after this Gala is over before we bring this up with anyone, okay?"

"Okay, good idea," he said. "But I'll need practice."

Rick took me in his arms and held me close. We completely forgot about dinner. We were too busy feasting on each other.

28 - Brewing Trouble

— Derek

Derek was sitting in the hotel room reading some reports that had come in from the branch in Atlanta. The television was running for background noise. It was a small room, because Derek didn't like spending money on things that weren't necessary. One bed was as good as the next. *Why pay $300 when a $99 room will do?* Of course, the $99 room was smelly and not so clean, but he didn't really care. Not caring went along with being a righteous warrior.

Then the news came on and the first item grabbed Derek's attention.

"Billionaire Mark Chisholm and his wife, Falon, have announced a Gala night to raise money for homelessness and a new project they've launched called Project Tiny House. We go now to the project's offices to speak to Falon Robertson," said the news anchor.

"Hi there, I'm Betty Channer, here with Falon Robertson. Falon, you and Mark Chisholm are recent newlyweds, are you not?"

"Yes, Betty, we are. We tied the knot in a private ceremony in Oregon a few months ago. But I'm really excited to let you know about our new initiative."

"Tell me about it," said Betty.

"Project Tiny House is our initiative to end homelessness. We're rolling out the pilot project here in Montreal, and if successful we hope to set up a project in every major city. We've been very fortunate in our business dealings, and it's time to give back to the communities that helped us succeed."

"What is the Gala about?" asked Betty.

"The Gala is the kick-off. We're inviting other successful entrepreneurs, businesspeople, and corporations to come to our Gala, have some fun, and make a donation. Our foundation, Project Tiny House, will match each donation, up to a total of $100 million. We recognize that in order to make a dent in this problem, we need to throw some serious money at it. We want it to succeed. We want everyone to have a home. Everyone deserves a home. A home for everyone."

"You certainly are passionate about this," said Betty. "Will you be sending out invitations or is this an open event for the general public?"

"We will be sending out invitations, but there will be a limited number of seats available on the night of the Gala. People who have not been invited, but who want to participate can make a donation and get a ticket. The ticket price is the donation for individuals," said Falon.

"I hear there is exciting news about the catering company," said Betty.

"Yes, a very good friend of ours who owns an award-winning restaurant in Atlanta, Georgia, and is opening a second restaurant here in Montreal. They will be catering the dinner. The food that night is sure to be spectacular!"

"What is the restaurant's name?"

"The restaurant is called Escalata—owned jointly by Chefs Justin Madera and Ricardo Benal. They are building Escalata II in Old Montreal, to be opened at the end of this year."

"Do you have any other plans solidified?" asked Betty.

"No, but as we do, you'll be the first to know!"

"Excellent!" said Betty. "This is sure to be the event of the year for Montrealers. Save the date in your calendar! August 27th. The venue will be announced soon."

Derek got up and shut off the TV.

They were planning a Gala—a very public Gala, that would have cameras and the media there. "Perfect!" said Derek out loud. All he had to do now was find out where it was and they could plan the takedown of those "vampires" once and for all.

The wind was swinging his way for a change. He could now start laying his trap for them. First, he had to call a meeting of his order members and let them know what was happening. Then he had to plan the attack, exactly when, where, and how. They were not going to slip out of his hands again!

29 - Party Preparations

— Falon

I stepped down from the platform they had me standing on for the interview and took off the mic clipped to my blouse. The lights for the television crew were terribly hot and bright. It felt like I was melting. Gregory showed up that instant with a cold can of iced tea.

"Oh, bless you, Gregory!" I took the can and put it at the back of my neck under my hair.

"Falon, the reporter had some follow-up questions. Do you want me to handle them?" asked Gregory.

"Would you please? If there is one that you don't have an answer for, let me know. And thanks!"

Escaping into my office, I closed the door for a minute of quiet. I had no idea that doing this would put me in the limelight so much. It worried me that Mark's family would get angry with all the publicity. So far no, so maybe I shouldn't worry until there was a problem.

Lora knocked on my door.

"Come in."

"Hey, Falon, I've got confirmation on our venue. The Windsor Ballrooms have been booked from 1:00 p.m. on August 27th to 10:00 a.m. August 28th. The event starts at 6:00 p.m., so that gives us five hours for setup, and if we close the event by 3:00 a.m., seven hours for take down. We have two rooms: Peacock Alley for cocktails at 6:00, and then the Windsor Ballroom for dinner and dancing at 7:00 p.m.," said Lora. "They will serve breakfast in the Peacock Alley at 7:00 a.m. for those who have booked a room at the hotel."

"Yeah," I said delightedly. "It's so nice to get the place you want."

"Well, it certainly helps that I was booking this for Mark, and that we are throwing a lot of money around. They were originally partially booked. But they chose to reschedule the other party so that they would get a big fat paycheck from us."

"Whatever works."

"Let's update the media with a news release. I'll get Gregory on it. Now that we have the venue nailed down, Andrews can work out a detailed plan for securing the money and the hall. I don't really want cash on hand, but people will bring cash to feel good. We may collect donations from the general public if we put a collection box outside the door."

"Uh, can I speak to you for a minute? It's personal," she asked.

"Of course. Shut the door."

"I talked to Rick and we're all squared away," she said.

"Oh, that is wonderful. Did he take it badly?" I asked.

"No, in fact he was more than intrigued. He suggested we do our own group or foursome."

My thoughts skipped a second. *What?*

"Did you say foursome? As in four people having sex together?" I asked.

"Yes, I did. Actually I said group too," she grinned. "Does it shock you?"

"Not really, it sort of made my vagina squeeze a bit. Is that a good thing?" I asked. "How does a group have sex together? Wait, isn't that an orgy?"

"Yup, that's an orgy. It's not that different from us having hot tub sex with two guys together. Initially, you pair off, then form three, then if people are willing, others join in. It's a fantasy of mine. If you're willing, we would need males from the same species…"

"Hmm, that's right," I thought. "So you would have both Rick and Mark fuck you? What am I doing?"

"You're getting oral sex from one of them," she said. "And then if you want, they can both fuck you while I get oral sex."

I couldn't help it, I got all wet with just the thought of this. Not something I'd ever contemplated. I was a pretty conventional girl sexually, but Lora was a wild ride. Maybe it would be fun to try once, if Mark was willing.

"How many people exactly? Is there a third man? What is he doing?" I asked.

"Well, he typically is with the second girl, and sometimes joins in on the three to make it a four," explained Lora.

Orgy? Orgy! Wow, sex with three guys at once, how do you do that? *My God, do I want to try this?* It might trigger Mark's jealousy and possessiveness. And mine too. *I'm not convinced it's something I am into.*

"I can't see how this works, so I'll just have to take your word for it. Bottom line, while I've never contemplated being a member of an orgy, my body apparently likes the idea. I have found that I am much lustier since the turn."

"I tell you what, ask Mark if he's willing. If he is, I'll set it up," said Lora.

She left me sitting there with my brain going a hundred miles an hour. *What was I doing?* I needed to clear my mind. Okay, Gregory could follow up with the media and prepare the new release. Then Mark called and asked me if I wanted to meet him for dinner. Perfect! This struck me as a good opportunity to do some more team building.

So I notified the team that we were going out to meet Mark at our favorite restaurant. I got mostly appreciative confirmations, but Lora didn't answer. *Huh.*

I got there first and told the hostess that we would be nine people. She brought me to the back of the restaurant to a large table. Mark and Gwen arrived next, and I was happy to see her light up when Andrews came in right behind her with Grisham and Parsons. Next to arrive was Gregory, and he came bearing a lot of papers.

"Sorry, Falon, but I need final decisions on a bunch of things," he said.

"Okay, let's go through them quickly."

He whipped through the stack, and we got it all done and signatures on the ones he needed. He then took the pile back to his car and locked it in the trunk. He returned with Lora and Rick.

"Look who I found wandering like a lost puppy outside," said Lora with a smirk.

"Rick, come sit down. Join the war meeting!" I yelled.

"War meeting?"

"Don't worry, love, she says things like that. We just ignore her," chuckled Lora.

"Hey!" I said.

Everyone was seated and Mark ordered a bottle of champagne.

The server got everyone a glass and I stood to make a toast.

"Everyone, I thank you all from the bottom of my heart that you are embracing this cause with me, that you are working so hard to help me help others and bring about positive change. I salute you, my dear friends."

I took a sip and then the tears started falling down my face. I couldn't believe how lucky I was to have such a great group of friends—people willing to work so hard for me.

Mark stood up and made a toast too.

"I'd like to second that, plus add that never before has our family tried to do something like this. I'm proud that we are now looking forward to making this a yearly event. Let's end homelessness!"

"Hear, hear!" was voiced by everyone.

Sitting there, watching all the faces before me, I realized I had played matchmaker again. Gwen and Andrews were talking head-to-head, as were Lora and Rick. Gregory was eyeing Parsons, but I didn't know if they were both gay or not. The only odd one out was Grisham. I'd have to do something about that.

Time passed quickly with all the things we had to do. It seemed like we never had enough time. It was now three weeks before the Gala.

All the arrangements were made, the invitations went out a week ago—some of the RSVPs were already back. We were getting a good response. Most importantly, Mark's extremely wealthy contacts and business associates were all buying into the event. Three hundred invitations had gone out and been accepted. Another one hundred tickets for the cocktail party only were available to purchase in advance, and they were selling out too.

Andrews had asked me for a meeting, and I wondered what it was about, because he usually just dropped in.

Mark came in through my office door with Andrews and they sat down.

"What's up, gentlemen?" I asked. "Please don't tell me bad news."

"I've got some bad news," started Andrews.

"Damn. Things were going too well. What happened?" I asked.

"We've discovered an attack plan from Derek's Order. They are planning on attacking you two during the Gala."

"Huh. Now that we know about it, can we thwart it?" I asked.

"I don't know yet. It could be difficult. What I may be able to do is disrupt the plans so he knows we're on to him."

"What are they planning on doing?" asked Mark.

"What we've uncovered is this: they are going to infiltrate the Gala through the catering team. They have replaced a number of the servers with their own people. We had to use an agency for the servers, so we don't know the people personally. That left a hole in the security that I couldn't fill. Knowing this, I've asked the agency for photos and bios of all the staff assigned to us. We can pay attention and hopefully undermine their people."

"Anything else?"

"With their people in place, they are then going to attempt to take hostages and threaten to blow up the Gala if you don't come forward and reveal yourself as an Immortal," explained Andrews. "The whole scheme is supposed to undermine you and expose who you really are."

"If the family gets wind of this, it won't be good," I said nervously.

"This is a very different tactic from what the Fraternal Order usually does," said Mark. "They don't go in for big gestures and reveals. They usually want to keep things on the down low, just like us."

"You're right. Remember, Derek is nuts. He's got some vendetta against you. Can you think of a reason?" said Andrews. "Wait, this could be an opportunity."

"What do you mean?" I asked.

"Well, what if my organization were to seek out the Fraternal Order and let them know that one of their own is going after people who are not vampires."

"Would that entail letting them know about us as a species?" asked Mark.

"I don't think so. I'll have to think about it. Let me work on this idea. As a security company, I may have some leverage I can use. Perhaps we can get the Fraternal Order to deal with Derek for us."

30 - Switzerland

— Andrews

Sometimes when you see an opportunity, you have to jump on it. That's the idea Andrews had when he was speaking to Mark and Falon about Derek's plan. The opportunity existed to get the "big guns" to take out the imposter. Trouble was, he only had two weeks to make it happen.

Was that enough time to make contact with the Fraternal Order and let them know they had a renegade member who had gone off the deep end? The bigger question was how to do that without giving away the Olde Ones' existence?

They already had enough information and evidence to prove that Staung was about to expose the Fraternal Order in the most public way possible. Would that be enough?

Andrews was on his way to Geneva. That is where the headquarters of the Fraternal Order were supposed to be located. All he had to do was make contact with them and they were likely to reach out to him. He had to be careful so he wouldn't be captured.

Grisham was with him for this trip. Parsons was left at home to run the security they had designed for the Gala and to keep an eye on Staung and his minions. If there was a problem, Parsons was authorized to take the Chisholms to ground without any hesitation.

Sitting on a café patio in Geneva, Grisham and Andrews went over their plan to attract the Fraternal Order's attention. It would involve pretending to be chased by a vampire and banging on their door coincidentally, seeking help. The Fraternal Order's HQ was a mansion in Troinex, Geneva, Switzerland.

They learned through back channels that there was a bookstore in town that you could go in and ask for a specific edition of Bram Stoker's *Dracula*. This was a clue to the shopkeeper that you were looking for the Fraternal Order.

Currently, they were across the street from the shop, waiting for the business day to end. A few minutes before closing time, the two men walked across the street and entered the bookstore.

Grisham walked up to the shopkeeper. She was a stout, older woman in her sixties, wearing an apron over a light blue dress.

"*Sprichst du Englisch?*" asked Grisham. *Do you speak English?*

"Ya, I do," said the shopkeeper. "What can I do for you?"

"I'm looking for the second edition of Bram Stoker's *Dracula* in hardcover. It's for a friend," said Grisham.

"Oh, one moment and I'll see if we have one in our rare book section in the back," replied the shopkeeper.

The shopkeeper went into the back of the store and down a narrow set of stairs. They heard some banging around as if boxes were being moved around. It was taking a while, so they weren't sure if the noise was a cover or he was actually looking for a book, which meant that their intel was wrong and that wasn't what to ask for.

Some fifteen minutes later the shopkeeper came back upstairs carrying a book.

"Here you go, young man," said the shopkeeper. "That will be 120 Euros."

Grisham glanced at Andrews and he shrugged his shoulders.

"Could I have this wrapped and delivered to my friend? She is staying at the Auberge de Saviese, room 205. It's a birthday gift," asked Grisham.

"*Certainement, monsieur,*" replied the shopkeeper.

"Is there an extra charge for this service?"

"No."

Grisham handed over his credit card and made the purchase. The two men left the shop wondering if their ruse had worked.

"Okay, what now, boss?" asked Grisham.

"That sort of went unexpectedly easily, didn't it?" Andrews remarked. "Lets go over to the café to have a cup and watch the store. Perhaps the shopkeeper will leave and we can follow."

It didn't take long. They'd barely received their coffees when they saw the shopkeeper leave and lock up. Interestingly, she walked up the street. Andrews and Grisham threw down some money for the coffees and started following her on the opposite side of the street. Only one followed at once, while the other stopped and looked in a window. They stayed in touch using concealed radio 'comms'.

The shopkeeper had walked almost twelve blocks before she stopped at a butcher shop and went in. Andrews had been the one on her tail at that point, so he stopped and waited while Grisham continued down the street and around a corner to wait.

When the shopkeeper exited the butcher shop, she wasn't holding any packages, which might mean she had been delivering a message and not shopping.

"Shopkeeper is on the move again, pick her up in a few seconds," said Andrews into the comm.

"Got her, will continue on her route," responded Grisham.

Andrews went into the butcher shop. When he got inside, he was surprised. There was a counter, but no meat was on display.

"I'm sorry, is this not a butcher shop?" asked Andrews.

"Ya, it is. What can I get you?" asked a man behind the counter.

"I'm new here, so I don't know how things are done yet," apologized Andrews. "How do we order meat?"

"Just tell me what you want, I will prepare it in the back," said the butcher.

"Okay, I need some help please. I think my friend is in trouble with a…"—dropping his voice to a whisper—"…vampire," said Andrews.

For a minute, the butcher just stared at him. Then he burst out laughing.

"Oh, you Americans! Such comedians!" said the butcher.

"I'm a Canadian, eh," said Andrews. "So you cannot help me with that?"

"I only serve cow and pig here," mused the butcher, still chuckling.

"Okay, thanks for that."

Andrews got back out onto the street and briskly started walking the same direction as the shopkeeper.

"Grisham, any developments?"

"Nope, still following. We're about six blocks from the butcher."

"Wow, that little woman moves fast," said Andrews.

"Yes, and she picked up speed after the butcher. I'm almost running to keep her in view right now."

"Let's abort and grab a taxi back to the auberge," said Andrews.

"Roger."

By the time Andrews caught up to Grisham, he had a taxi pulling up to the curb. Fifteen minutes later, they were back at the auberge and entering their room. Grisham was in and Andrews was about to close the door when a very big guy pushed his way inside with another in tow.

Knocking over Andrews, Grisham drew his weapon and yelled at them to stop. The first big guy jumped over Andrews and leapt at Grisham, gun and all, and grabbed his wrist. Grisham got a shot off but missed because the assailant had managed to hit his hand off the axis.

The second guy had Andrews in a full nelson hold so he couldn't move, while the first guy turned Grisham's gun on him and ordered him to sit the hell down. Andrews glanced down at the fist holding him and saw the tattoo of the Fraternal Order: the three blades. So they had made contact.

"Which one of you asked for *Dracula*?" asked Big Guy #1.

"I did," answered Grisham.

"Why?"

"Because we needed to make contact with the Fraternal Order," answered Andrews.

"Okay, you've made contact. What do you want with us?" asked Big Guy #2.

"We have a situation in Montreal, Canada, that we think you should know about. It concerns the safety and secrecy of your organization," answered Andrews.

"Go on."

"A man named Derek Staung is currently in Montreal. He is planning on a very big, very public, attack on a very wealthy, prominent businessman named Mark Chisholm and his wife at a major charity Gala where there will be lots of media and lots of very important people, giving away lots of money."

"Who is Derek Staung, and why should the Fraternal Order care?"

"Well, at least you aren't denying your own existence," said Andrews. "But you sure need to do a better job on gathering intel. Anyway, Derek Staung is running a heretical splinter chapter of the Order out of New Orleans, Louisiana, without the education, knowledge, or honor of your brotherhood. We have also uncovered that he's become rather unstable. He is recruiting impressionable young men who wanna be heroes to flesh out his 'club,' plus psycho punks who just want to 'kill vamps like on TV' to his aid. He's also convinced six or seven others in order to defect to his way of thinking."

"The problem is that Staung wants *a public* display of unmasking and then killing vamps, so that he can look like a Big Man. This Gala will be about as public as it gets, with TV, radio, and newspaper photographers in attendance when he does it. They will catch everything that happens on camera. Everything.

We are familiar with the good work your Order does to protect humanity from the shadows, and Derek's blatant self-promotion will jeopardize your work."

"Give me your coordinates," said Big Guy #1. "I will bring this to the council and we will decide if we take action or not. Good day."

"Will you let us know?" asked Grisham.

"No. You will know when we take action or not. If we decide he is, in fact, a heretic or just a dangerous imbecile, we will take action."

With that, they left the hotel room, tossing Andrews' and Grisham's weapons back to them on the way out the door.

"Well, I don't know if that was a success or not," mumbled Andrews as he nursed a bruised shoulder. "Certainly doesn't leave me confident that they'll intervene on our behalf, does it?"

"No. So we better get back home, fast. The Gala is only a few days away."

They caught the next flight back to Montreal, where Andrews brought Mark up to date. He let him know that they had made contact but received no assurances they would do anything.

To that end, Andrews planned to hire four more bodyguards to shadow the Chisholms all day, and require Mark to wear Kevlar under his shirt. He also insisted that Falon's dress had Kevlar stitched into the front, but since it was a strapless and backless dress, she wouldn't be well-protected.

31 - Gwen

— Andrews

Andrews was sitting in the office when the phone rang.

"Andrews speaking," he answered.

"Hello there, it's Gwen speaking."

"Oh, um, hello there, Gwen. What can I do for you?" he stumbled over his tongue.

An image of the woman flooded his mind. He remembered meeting her the first time and what had happened to his body. Andrews prided himself on being very reserved and level-headed. He didn't lose his mind over a pretty woman, not even a sexy knockout. Not even when Lora seduced him had he lost control of his emotions. This woman, though—this woman did something to his libido that sent it completely swerving around the corner.

I haven't become tongue-tied around a woman since I was fifteen, for God's sake. Get it together, Andrews! Maybe it's because her eyes see right into my very soul and I want to get lost in them? Nah, Andrews, snap out of it. You're a player, you don't get involved. Love 'em and leave 'em, that's you. Smarten up!

"Andrews, I never got your first name," Gwen started. "I wanted to invite you out for a drink, and maybe dinner."

"Um, thank you. Did you have a security matter you needed to discuss?" he asked. "My first name is Robert, by the way."

"I like that, Robert. May I call you Robert instead? It's more personal."

"Of course, if you like," answered Andrews.

"I don't have a security issue, I just want to have some alone time with you," she said.

This beauty wants to be alone with me? It's Mark's sister. She's an immortal. What does she want with a human like me? Am I an entree on her menu? Am I even an appetizer?

"Uh, that would be fine," Andrews stammered. "When did you want to get together? I have some time tomorrow afternoon, if you like."

"How about right now?" she asked.

"I'm not doing anything, I'm just writing up reports. So yes, I can make some time for you. Would you like to come to my office?" he asked.

"I'm already here."

A knock sounded on his door right before it opened to reveal Gwen standing there in the light of the hallway.

God, she's beautiful. That blond hair and those electric blue eyes—they are my kryptonite. As Billy Joel says, "Blonde over blue." Whoa! Okay Andrews, keep it in your pants unless she otherwise commands!

He was dumbstruck for a few moments. It took him at least to the count of ten before his brain reengaged with his body.

"Please, come on in, please!" Andrews said, putting down the phone.

Gwen walked in with a swish of her hips. A tall woman, her eyes were nearly level with Andrews'. As he walked around to the front of his desk, he pulled out a chair for her to sit, but she glanced around, saw the couch and sat there instead. Patting the seat beside her, she put her bag on the floor, and undid her coat.

Andrews watched her sit on the couch and his mind started racing. *What is she doing? Oh Geez, she's taking off her coat ... and she is not wearing anything under it. What is this, a fantasy movie? Or is it dinner time – and I'm the Special of the Day?*

Andrews sucked in his breath as he saw the top of her breasts through the opening of her coat. He watched her smile secretly when she heard his reaction. Gwen then undid more of her coat, performing a slow strip tease to tantalize him.

She pulled the edges of her coat away from her body, revealing that she was not wearing anything underneath. Her areolas were large and pronounced, and her nipples were already scintillated and erect. She just needed his touch.

Andrews was transfixed as her breasts came into complete view. They looked like the breasts of a twenty-something, even though he knew she was much older. They were full and round and oh-so-squeezable. As her coat dropped to the couch, she revealed that she was entirely naked. For the second time in six months, his jeans suddenly became uncomfortably tight as his erection sprang up.

I've got to start wearing boxers! he thought. *What am I supposed to do with this?*

"You seem a little perplexed," Gwen said softly. "Did I misread you earlier?"

"Um, no, ma'am, you did not," he stammered again. "I just didn't expect you would act."

"I act when I feel the need to," she said softly. She stood up and let the coat slip off onto the couch. That left her standing there in the moonlight coming in from the window. Her skin glowed like it was quicksilver and her eyes were glowing too. She stepped over to Andrews and put her hand down his pants and grasped his hard cock.

"I want to fuck you," Gwen said without preamble. "Now."

She unzipped his pants and pushed them off his hips.

"I like that you wear minimal clothing," she said.

Andrews started undoing the buttons of his shirt, but she grabbed his shirt and ripped it off him, popping all the buttons not yet undone. She stood there and let her eyes rove salaciously across his body. Then she let her hands touch everything, everywhere. She took his cock again and pushed it between her legs and squeezed it.

Taking his head in her hands, she crushed his mouth with hers and probed him with her tongue. As he gave back, he felt a small prick on his tongue. He didn't think anything of it until he felt the euphoria. His brain suddenly flew so high he could barely think. His cock was getting harder by the moment, and was now leaking in anticipation of getting action. At that moment, he decided to stop being a post and actually participate in this seduction.

Andrews grabbed her ass with his hands, turned around and landed her on the desk. Taking her head in his hands, he kissed her hard, demanding her entire mouth. She gave back everything she had until they were both gasping for breath. Breaking the kiss, he cleared the desk with a sweep of his hand, grabbed her hands and shoved her down on her back.

A long, pleased groan came from deep in her throat, so low in tone it almost sounded like a growl. She raised her arms above her head and splayed her legs, giving him access.

Instead of going for the obvious right away, Andrews knelt between her legs and pulled her ass to the edge of the desk. Now, he could play with her pussy. Using the fingers of one hand, he slipped them between her petals and opened her up. Using his lips only, he sucked her clit into his mouth and kept sucking on it until she groaned. Flicking his tongue over the extremely sensitive nub, he excited it until it swelled up and erect. Then he gently took it between his teeth and pulled. Gwen was squirming with arousal and begging him to take her.

Andrews stood up and slipped two fingers inside her vagina, and watched as she sighed and moaned with pleasure. But that wasn't enough, she wanted more, so he added a finger, and curled them around until he could touch that erogenous spot inside. Working that spot, he drove her to almost frothing at the mouth; she was secreting juice like a lemonade stand. He bent down and licked it up like it was ice cream.

"I want more," she yelled.

"No!" he said, suddenly seizing control. "Not yet." She groaned in frustration.

Andrews continued to work her vagina with one hand, cupping one of her breasts with the other. It was perfectly formed and creamy white. He sucked on her nipple. It showed its appreciation by standing up and getting hard. He sucked hard on the breast until his mouth was full. Gwen was groaning from his touch and grabbing her other breast and applying her own pinches.

He changed breasts, nipping and licking, then blowing on it to make it cold. It reacted by stiffening more. Pushing both breasts together, he pushed his face between them and inhaled her scent.

As he was bent over her and playing with her breasts and vagina, Gwen had taken hold of his cock, applying pressure to his head, squeezing and rubbing it. She was playing her fingers up and down its length. It was now very happy and wriggling in her fingers.

Suddenly Gwen tugged urgently on his cock. That caused him to stop what he was doing and pay attention to her. She jumped off the desk and led him to the couch by his cock. She sat down and took him in her mouth and sucked on him hard. There was a sharp pain, but more of the high happened too, and he almost ejaculated in her mouth. He never did that unless the lady wanted it like that. But his brain was not attached at the moment, so he couldn't ask her.

When Andrews looked down at what she was doing to his cock, he saw her fangs, and it was all he could do to hold on to his orgasm. Gwen sucked hard on and took him completely into her mouth. Not something mere mortals could do. His erection was thick and long, and most women could only manage a third of his length at best.

"You have excellent control for a human," she said once she removed him from her mouth.

"I generally ask the lady beforehand if she wants to drink," he explained. "Not everyone enjoys cum in their mouth."

"Take me," she commanded. "Now!"

Andrews threw her down on the couch on her chest, pulled her ass up in the air, and plunged himself into her in one stroke. After he was impaled, he stood still for a few moments.

"Oh my God, I'm sorry! I don't know what came over me," he said, ashamed of his brutality.

"Andrews, I commanded you, you had no choice but to comply. Now, fuck me hard, please?" she asked.

"Your wish is my command, my lady." He proceeded to pound into her as far as he could, bottoming out with each thrust. His balls whacked her pussy each time. She was making enough noise for three as she squealed in delight and excitement. He took her hard as she asked, and when he came, he was deep inside her.

"Robert, you can reach completely inside me. How wonderful," Gwen purred. "It's nice to have a full-sized male for a change."

Their sexcapades were momentous. With a touch, she brought Andrews up several times, and he gave her a dozen orgasms. She wanted it every way possible, and he gave it to her.

At the end of the night, the sun was coming up, Andrews was exhausted, and very sore.

"Oh my God, my balls are sore!" he groaned as he lay on the floor. They had enjoyed orgasms on the couch, on the floor, up against the wall, on his desk, in the chair, and finally, her on top on the floor.

Gwen, on the other hand, looked fresh, like she could go again several more times. She looked down at him indulgently.

"You're a good human. I've never had one that could keep up with me and still satisfy me after half a dozen shots. I think I'll keep you."

Spluttering, Andrews coughed and cleared his throat.

"Thank you?" he said. "I don't know if I want to be kept, though."

Gwen smiled. She knelt down on the floor beside him and grasped his hand. Lifting it to her mouth palm up, she bit into the heel of his hand.

"Ow! Oh! Oh my, what is that?" he squeaked as his eyes rolled back in his head with pleasure. "Gwen, what are you doing to me?"

"That is the benefit of being with one of my kind. You will have unspeakably good sex and a climax like no other," she answered. "Oh, that's a little bit addictive, though."

Andrews felt his body go through an orgasm without sex. How was that possible? He felt his cock harden and explode all without any touch, and the high was unbelievably, impossibly intense.

This could be very addictive, he agreed. He looked up at her and realized that he didn't care. He wanted this woman.

"Robert, I'll tell you what. I want you to have free will. You will come to me on your own, I will not command it. But you are very satisfying, and I want to share this—" waving her hands down her body—"with you, often. So take a few days and give me your decision after this Gala is over."

With that, Gwen was suddenly, inexplicably dressed. She put her shoes on and let herself out the door, closing it quietly behind her.

Andrews lay on the floor, so satiated and spent that he could barely move. Every muscle in his body seemed like he was lying in a warm ocean, floating and completely relaxed. He didn't want to get up. He wasn't sure if he even could if he wanted to.

So this is what the women mean when they say boneless ... huh!

There was a knock on the door. Andrews couldn't move. Maybe they'd go away.

Another knock on his door came with someone saying, "Andrews, are you in there?"

Falon. Good God, she cannot see me like this!

"Just a minute, Falon!" he shouted. "I'll be there in a second."

He weakly got to his feet and tugged on his jeans before the door handle twisted and she entered.

"Was I interrupting something?" she asked, noting the half-dressed man in front of her. She could smell the sex in the air—it was thick. Clearly, he had been having it with someone, but no one was there at the moment.

"N-n-n-no, no interruption," Andrews stammered. "What can I do for you?"

32 - Final Details

— Derek

Gala Day had arrived, and Derek Staung was concealed in the hall's staging area, waiting for the guests to arrive. Once again, he reviewed his plan of attack.

It was perfect, undeniably perfect.

Derek's people were in place. They would do as he told them when the time came.

They all had their specific jobs. For instance, Derek had replaced six of the original waiters with people he had chosen. This wait staff would help 'serve' the Chisholms at the head table with the justice they so richly deserved

He had one replacement working at the bar. This acolyte would add a narcotic to the cocktails at the pre-dinner cocktail party. He would make sure guests were sufficiently drugged at dinnertime so that they would be unable to respond to the assault when it occurred, but still conscious and able to see everything that would befall the Chisholms!

Some of the kitchen staff were also compromised. He had people there washing dishes who would lock the doors and ensure no one could leave the building once dinner started.

The trap was set, baited, and ready to spring.

Waiting for the action was excruciating, and Derek wasn't a patient man. There was still an hour or two before this Gala got started. So he monitored the situation from the safety of the staging area so he could keep an eye on everything. And as he waited, Derek played out the plan yet one more time in his head, marveling at his own brilliance.

The best part of his plan was that his six personal Order agents Derek had concealed in the room were poised to take control of the head table at his command. When he gave them the Go sign, they would launch special crossbow bolts through the black hearts of the drugged Chisholm and his vampire bride and the other people sitting at the head table. Meanwhile, if the archers missed their targets, there was a concealed team of wait staff ready with wooden stakes, as backup, that could take down the Chisholms.

Yes, his plan was perfect. He had thought of everything.

Only after his enemies had been rendered utterly helpless, Derek would march up triumphantly to the table and remove these demons' heads himself with a shining sword! He would then hold their severed heads aloft while declaring that he, Derek Staung, had executed the vampires living in plain sight!

The assault would take all of one minute if everyone did their jobs correctly, and there was no real danger to himself since the Olde Ones would be defenceless by the time he arrived at their table. And then, then the glorious magnificence of Detek's heroism would be captured on video for the entire world to see!

.

The announcement for everyone to take their seats in the ballroom startled Derek out of his reverie. He grinned to himself wickedly. *Showtime!*

33 - Final Details

What Derek didn't know was that Andrews' people were also in place, and they had been preparing to strike while he sat idly dreaming of personal glory.

In fact, Andrews' people had already identified each one of Derek's substitutes in the wait staff and were ready to take them out of commission. They also knew who else been compromised. This included the bartender who was drugging the drinks. They manhandled him off the floor discreetly while dumping the drugged drinks down the sink. Andrews knew that Derek had planned some sort of targeted hit, and considering he believed Derek would play out the "vampire" scenario for his assassins, he was expecting a wooden weapon, possibly a stake or some other Hollywood vampire cliche like a crossbow. However, Andrews also knew that Derek knew that only a catastrophic injury to the heart or head would kill an immortal. So Andrews also expected him and someone to show up with a katana for some head chopping.

As for crowd suppression? Archers were a favorite of the Fraternal Order. Because Staung fancied himself to be a 'true knight' of the Order, Andrews expected archers to play a part in the attack. This meant his team had to find where the archers had positioned themselves and take them out with extreme prejudice. But the plan he was most worried about was the decapitations of Mark and Falon. Andrews could not let Staung succeed. So, drawing on his military experience, he decided to make life harder for Staung's team by changing things up at the last minute.

"Mark, I need to make some last-minute changes to the head table," said Andrews when Mark picked up his phone.

"Tell Falon. I'm not the one in charge," said Mark.

"Got it." Andrews called Falon next.

"Falon, I need to make some last-minute changes to the head table," said Andrews when she picked up her phone.

"Oh, could you please tell Gregory? He's been handling all that for me."

"Got it," Andrews said. "Third time's the charm, I hope."

"Gregory, it's Andrews. Are you doing the seating?"

"Yes, that's my baby. What's up?"

"I need to make some changes," said Andrews.

"Who to where?"

"No it's an addition, and a new table," answered Andrews. "I need to add two bodyguards and their dates to the head table. Which means there will be four more bodies. I need the bodyguards sitting beside Falon and Mark."

"Oh, that's no problem. What are their names?"

"Geoffrey Parsons and his plus one, and the other bodyguard is James Grisham. His plus one is Jennifer Grisham."

"Got it," said Gregory. "Anything else to change?"

"Not that I can think of now, but I will let you know."

34 - The Gala

— Falon

It was the day of the Gala! I was so excited! It had been a blistering last three weeks making subtle changes to deal with the attack plans that Andrews uncovered. But we were there. Everything was ready, all the food was made. The Windsor was gorgeous, and the wine was chilled. We were finally able to get dressed.

The guests are coming. Eeek!

"Hun, could you please do my tie?" asked Mark.

"Of course," I said as I fixed his bow tie. God, he was handsome in his tuxedo. He had a new one made in the current fashion by Ralph Lauren. The tux fit him absolutely perfectly. *I could just eat him up right now!*

"You are beautiful tonight, love," he murmured into my ear. "I love that red dress on you. It hugs all your curves perfectly. And those shoes! Wow!"

"Well, you're pretty gorgeous yourself. I can see I'll be beating the ladies off you all night. Thank you, Mark," I said.

"You were right, this dress is perfect. I feel so feminine and pretty in this dress."

The dress I had was from Versace, a strapless gown in a clingy red stretchy fabric. It defied gravity by clinging to my breasts in spite of the fact that the plunging neckline dove down to my navel. The back had a deep V almost down to my butt, that was criss-crossed with laces at the bottom of the V.

There was a beautiful train that draped from the bottom of the V in the back and flowed to the floor. The dress hugged my curves beautifully, and fell in a straight line to the floor from just under my butt. Needless to say, there was a slit up the front to mid thigh to enable me to walk. The gown was accented with a long pair of red gloves to mid bicep.

The shoes were black stilettos adorned with ruby rhinestones. They had straps wrapping around my foot and ankle.

"Just one thing is missing," he said slyly. He walked into his closet and came out with a flat box. "Here, I got this out of storage for you. It's a family heirloom. All the women in my family have worn it for special occasions. It's called Aphrodite's Rose."

I opened the box to find a huge ruby pendant cut into a rose and surrounded by diamonds. It had to be the size of a silver dollar!

"Oh, Mark, this is exquisite! Put it on for me?"

I watched in the mirror as he put it around my neck and fastened it and added a kiss to seal the deal. The pendant perfectly nestled just above the top of my cleavage. Then Mark gave me another box, which contained the earrings to match. Beautiful drops of ruby with a cluster of diamonds.

I felt like a queen with these jewels on.

"Ready?" he asked. "Oh! I forgot one thing." He ran back to his closet and pulled out another box. This one was obviously for rings.

I opened the box, and inside was the largest diamond ring I had ever seen. It had smaller rubies all around it, set in platinum. The matching wedding band was simple in comparison, just a plain platinum band.

"The diamond is a VS1 five carat oval cut with rubies."

"Oh my God, Mark, this is way too much!"

"No, it's not. And we're married, so you need a wedding ring. And I cannot get you a wedding ring without the engagement ring. Who do you think I am?" he teased.

"My, it's absolutely beautiful. I love it." I honestly didn't know what to say. He placed the rings on my hand and kissed them in place.

"Now we're ready!" he said. He offered me his arm and I took it, draping the hand with the large rock over the arm so it was plainly visible to everyone.

Andrews was there to escort us to the limo. He did a double take when he saw the ring.

"Well, I hadn't expected that tonight. That's another thing to watch for—someone trying to steal those jewels. You look gorgeous, Falon!"

"Thank you, Andrews. I promise I'll be careful."

"Here's your ride to the Windsor Ballroom."

Driving up to the building, I saw they had the red carpet out for the dignitaries who were coming. They had spotlights on the building to show off the building-high posters draped down the sides of the doors. They looked spectacular. There were huge sprays of flowers all along the red carpet and up the steps. To the side of the red carpet, there were cordons blocking the sidewalk from the building to the curb, and there were already people lining up on one side.

"Wow, this feels like Oscar night!" I said.

"A little," answered Mark. "Keep close to me, okay?"

The limo dropped us off at the end of the red carpet and doormen came to open the door for both Mark and I.

As we walked up the carpet, there were camera flashes going off everywhere as people were taking our picture. We walked inside for a minute to see how things looked. Gregory met me at the door.

"Falon, Mark, I'm glad you're both here," said Gregory.

"Is there a problem?"

"Oh no! I'm just glad you're here. It's one less thing to worry about."

"Where do you want us first?"

"I'm going to station you right over here to greet folks coming in. They'll go through a security check first, then their invite will be verified before they will be let into the first room. You'll be greeting them between security and the inside door."

"Sounds good. Is everything under control?" I asked. "Should I ask that?"

"Yes, everything is under control. Lora has done an unspeakably good job of organizing this." He smiled, because I knew he had done at least half the work himself.

"Well, good job, Gregory. I'm so very proud of what you have accomplished with Lora's help."

He glowed a little.

We had a chance to look around a bit on our way to our station. Inside, the place was absolutely beautiful. Mark checked that there were cameras covering every angle of the door inside and out, as well as along the hallways. Security was well covered. He smiled when he saw what a great job Andrews and his guys had done.

Our first job tonight was to greet everyone as they came in. Some of Mark's colleagues and business associates were attending and we wanted to make sure they were greeted. When we got to our spot, I saw that Gregory had thoughtfully placed two stools for us to sit on.

Before dinner, we were scheduled to make a speech about our project, what it meant to us, and what we hoped to accomplish. You know, tug on their heartstrings and get them to donate lots of money. We'd also tell them we'd match their donations up to a hundred million dollars, so if the night went well we should raise two hundred million dollars for this project. Then we would invite everyone for dinner. The rest of the night was whatever would happen. We had a great DJ lined up, and Rick's restaurant had brought their mixologist as well to create a cocktail just for this event.

Standing by the front doors but inside the hall, we had three bodyguards watching over us. We didn't expect any trouble now, but it was still a little nerve-racking. Most of the guests who'd RSVP'd had started to arrive. As they walked up the carpet, they got their photos taken. There were some large names coming. Most from the business world, but there were a few celebrities and sports stars too. Just before us, one of the bodyguards standing behind us told us who they were so we could greet them properly and invite them inside to have a cocktail.

As the invitees filed in, I noticed that the crowd of people gathering on the sidewalk was getting larger. They were hoping to get tickets to the cocktail party when they went on sale. We had originally said that we would leave one hundred places for the general public to have access to the cocktail party with a donation of $100. However, the invitations we sent out were all confirmed.

"Ah, Mark, Falon," said Andrews. "I just wanted you to know that we have a full complement of guests. There is no room to sell additional seats. Shall I go announce that?"

"Yes, it will disappoint people, but perhaps they'll make a donation anyway."

Andrews went outside to the waiting crowd and announced that there was no room left.

"Folks," explained Andrews, "we are very sorry that we cannot have you, but the city has a limit to the number of people we can have in Peacock Hall. You can always leave your donation with the ticket office to my left."

A number of people decided to leave a donation and then left.

Every one of our three hundred seats were filled either by invitation. The fact that we had too many people wanting to purchase tickets at the door signified how many people wanted to help with this initiative. It gave me a swelling of pride in my heart.

Everyone was dressed to the nines. So much money had showed up, I was staggered by the display. Mark had some powerful friends, and most of them came from out of town too. I hadn't tallied the donations yet, but Gregory was keeping track of that. He was updating the electronic display of the donations in the ballroom. He'd set up this enormous monitor that displayed a thermometer with our goal of $200,000,000 at the top. As money was donated, the image filled up, giving a nice visual on the total.

It was almost 7:00, and that meant we would be bringing everyone in for dinner. The plan was that I announce dinner and ask everyone to make their pledge and then find their seats at the tables. I was nervous. There was a security concern that Andrews told me was taken care of, but it was still nerve-racking. Gregory gave me the signal. Walking up to the podium at the end of Peacock Hall, I faced the crowd.

"Ladies and gentlemen, if I could have your attention for a moment please," I started off traditionally.

The room fell quiet as everyone turned to look at me.

"First, I would like to express our deepest thanks to you for coming tonight to help us launch this initiative. It's an issue dear to my heart, and I am excited to get started."

Polite applause broke out for a moment or two.

"Second, wow! You all look marvelous! I've never seen so many designers in one room in my life!

The audience laughed gently.

"We'll be taking our seats in the ballroom for dinner momentarily. Could I please ask you to make your pledge or donation now if you haven't, and then move into the ballroom to find your seats. There are hosts waiting to show you to your table. For security reasons, please have your invitation available for them to verify."

There was a slow-moving stampede as the guests made their way to the one of the four doors to the ballroom next door. Some were going to the tables where the pledging was being made, but for the most part it seemed people were eager to get the dinner started. Andrews had changed out three of the wait staff at the last minute with people he had chosen because he wasn't sure about them.

It only took about twenty minutes to get everyone seated. Not bad! I took my place at the podium again, this time in the ballroom where the DJ was set up.

"Ladies and gentlemen, welcome to our first-ever Gala night for Project Tiny House. We plan on making this a yearly event, and hope to spread this initiative to all major cities."

"As you are all aware, homelessness can happen to anyone. Even a successful family can experience one too many emergencies and lose everything. It takes hardly anything at all to tip the scales sometimes. Homelessness now affects more people in the middle-income bracket than ever before. Once in a situation where you are homeless, whether you're living out of your vehicle or on the streets, you cannot receive social assistance, you cannot receive mail, you cannot get medical attention, and it's difficult to find a job. So the downward spiral continues. The saddest thing is today this is happening to families with children, not just individuals.

"We want to arrest that spiral. By giving a homeless family or person a place to call home, they suddenly become eligible for all that aid. They can get mail, then can find a job. Once they have a job, they start building a life again. They won't need the tiny home for long, and once they are on their own again, that tiny home will go to another.

"We will put an end to homelessness! We just have to work together. We have selected a team of builders and designers to create five tiny home designs from sustainable materials. Each tiny home will have everything a person needs to have a complete home. And each tiny home will have its own address.

"Part of our team will be working with Social Services to identify and locate people in need, to help them get off the streets and out of their cars. If they need medical attention, that will now be possible too, because they will be in a monitored neighborhood. Medical staff including a physician, a nurse, and a psychologist will make regular visits to monitor the health of all who live there. Not everyone will be able to leave their tiny home, but those who can will leave stronger and able to live on their own.

"Tonight is about getting people with money—that's you—to help us get this started. Mark and I have pledged to match everyone's donation to a total of one hundred million dollars."

There were lots of murmurs from the audience when I said that.

"Giving us the potential of seeing two hundred million dollars donated tonight! So dig deep, people!"

"Your wait staff is starting to bring out the first course, so I'll stop talking now and let you enjoy your dinner. Please feel free to get up and dance whenever you want. Our DJ will be spinning tunes for us all night. If you haven't made a donation yet, you can do so all night long. Our pledge desks will remain open for you."

"*Bon appetit!*"

The guests were giving me applause and I blushed in embarrassment. When I got to our table, Mark was there and so was Andrews, Grisham and his wife, and Parsons. They were joining us at the table.

"Nice speech," said Jennifer, Grisham's wife.

"Thanks," I said. "I kind of winged it."

"That was off the top of your head?" she asked.

"Not really. I had some cue cards in front of me on the podium, but I didn't pick them up so people wouldn't see them."

"Clever," Jennifer said. "I'll have to remember that trick."

Mark pulled out my chair and helped me to sit down with my tight dress then sat himself. No sooner were we all sitting than a waiter came to pour wine and water for us all. My throat was dry, so I reached for the water immediately. Andrews stopped my hand.

"Don't yet," he said. "I need to test the water."

He dipped a strip of paper into it and held it below the table. Watching it, he expected something that didn't happen.

"Okay, you're good on the water," he said.

I picked up my glass and took a long drink. Half finished, I set my glass back down, and the waiter filled the glass immediately. Andrews tested the water again, confirming it was still safe.

I noticed that Grisham and Parsons were doing the same thing to all the glasses. Were we concerned about poison tonight?

Gregory went up to the podium and rang a goblet to get people's attention.

"Ladies and gentlemen, my name is Gregory and I'm your emcee for the evening. I want to tell you where the donations are right now. Drumroll please, Mr. DJ!"

A rolling drumroll started and everyone looked toward the monitor. The tally line on the bar was climbing slowly: eleven million, twenty-two million, thirty-seven million, then stopped with a loud cymbal clap.

"Folks, we've received pledges so far in the amount of thirty-seven million dollars! Together with the Chisholm's matching donation, that brings us to seventy-four million dollars total. Wow, thank you so much. Watch the monitor for updates."

At the end of the first course, it was up to forty-two million, and then it jumped when people got up and added their donations. Gregory came over to our table to let me know that walk-ins and street donations totalled another two point three million so far.

Gregory made another top-up to the graphic between the entree and dessert. We were up to eighty-nine million dollars. Almost at our target! Mark asked me to dance, so we got up and spun around the floor for a few minutes. Then we started to visit the tables and speak to the invited guests. We were hoping to catch those who hadn't pledged yet. Then we could shame them into it—in a friendly way. By the time we got back to our table, dessert was served, and we could sit down. Andrews suddenly looked very nervous.

"What's up, Andrews?"

"My Spidey Sense has gone off."

He was carefully scanning the ballroom—every corner. Parsons left the table and started walking the perimeter, as did Grisham.

Jennifer stayed with us. She was in the security firm too. I had noticed a gun carefully concealed under her dress, and a knife strapped to her thigh.

Andrews got up from the table and started walking between the tables. He made his way to a column beside the wall. The walls were curtained, and the columns were like Greek decorations, so someone could hide behind them. He got to one column and stood up against it and looked back toward our table. He noted that there was a direct line of sight. He vanished behind the column the next second and I watched as the curtains moved.

When I heard a sharp yell, I was startled. Andrews appeared in front of the column again and nodded once.

"Jennifer, what does that mean?" I asked. "The nod."

"It means he's taken one man down," she answered.

"How many are there?" I asked.

"We think there are six in the ballroom, six on the wait staff, one in the kitchen, and another on the bar service. We can take care of the bar, kitchen, and the wait staff easily. It's the six in here that are hidden that we have to focus on."

I scanned the room again and spotted Grisham and Parsons doing similar things—vanishing behind the columns and reappearing. When they had all nodded, Jennifer stood behind us and next to the stage.

"Okay, we've neutralized three of them," said Jennifer.

"Do we know where Derek is?"

"No, they don't know where he is and he's the big problem," answered Mark.

Back in his latest hiding spot in the kitchen, Derek was frantically trying to reach his people. He had been listening to the comms as one by one their radios went dead. He had to get a visual on what was happening. *Where are my waiters? Where are my archers? What is going on?*

To find out, Derek decided to take a chance and exit the kitchen through the door that accessed the balconies of the ballroom. They weren't using them for this Gala, so he had recommended them to his team of three sharpshooting crossbowmen, to use them to fire the bolts. As soon as he got up there, he knew there was a big problem. None of his sharpshooters were upstairs.

Crouching on the first balcony, Derek could see the head table and one of the backup positions for the archers. Where are they? It was a column about forty feet from the head table draped with curtains from ceiling to floor. The facility kept extra chairs and supplies stacked inside these columns. He was looking frantically for his henchmen when he spotted Andrews exit the curtains. Staying out of sight, Derek keyed his radio once more.

"Two, this is One. Come in."

"Come in Two, over."

"Three, are you there?"

"Four, this is One. Over."

None of them were answering. So they were all compromised. Well, he would do this by himself. Running back into the kitchen, he frantically looked around for a knife.

I'm going to get those God-damned vamps if it's the last thing I do! They will no longer walk this earth and poison innocent people. The world will know who we are and will worship us! thought Derek.

Finding a large chef's knife sitting on the counter, he picked it up and walked briskly through the kitchen. On another counter at the meat station sat a large raw roast of some kind with a bone. He ran over to it, swinging the blade wildly to test it, and slammed it down on the meat. The blade cut cleanly through the whole roast and embedded itself in the wooden counter underneath.

The exhilarating force of the collision sent ringing vibrations through the knife and into Derek's hand and arm, locking it in place. He couldn't move his arm at all. All his fingers had gone numb.

Where are my people? What's happened to my plan?

Out of the corner of his eye, Derek caught the movement of something in a reflection on a pot hanging to his left. When he turned around to look at what it was, the only thing he saw was the flash of the gleaming sword blade that liberated his head from his body.

As Derek's head departed from his neck, his eyes registered a tattoo on the hand that held the sword: the Fraternal Order.

"Brother? What are you doing here?

As the electricity died in Derek's brain, his head bounced across the kitchen floor and then spun to rest against a shiny cooler door. The last sound he ever heard was a single word contemptuously spat out by the assassin: "Traitor."

Andrews was making his way back to the head table when he glanced down one of the hallways leading to the kitchen. There, moving very swiftly, were three people, wrapped in shadows, carrying a body bag. They were gone in a second. When he sat down, the others had also returned.

"Situation has been neutralized," reported Andrews.

"All threats have been eliminated and removed," said the others. "The danger has passed."

"Well, now we can truly enjoy tonight!" said Mark. "I've never been a fan of party crashers."

"That was almost anti-climatic," said Falon.

"I prefer that to what could have happened," said Andrews.

Epilogue

The balance of the night went without a single problem. The food was spectacular, the music was festive, and the alcohol flowed. As the wee hours of the night passed, guests started leaving, but not before making sure they had made a donation. Many came and thanked us for initiating this charity.

Mark and I were touched with the outpouring of love from our city. The mayor of Montreal was seated at table two, in honor of his position. He came up to us at the end of the night to thank us.

"Mr. and Mrs. Chisholm, on behalf of the staff at City Hall, I would personally like to thank you for your extraordinary work. Your Gala is a tremendous success. I look forward to working with you on this initiative.

"Thank you, Mr. Mayor. It's our city now too. When I married Falon, I adopted Montreal. We will solve this problem and then we'll take on another," said Mark.

The two men shook hands and then the mayor escorted his wife out of the building.

"Did he make a donation?" I asked.

"Yes, according to the tables, the mayor and his wife personally donated $10,000," said Gregory.

"Oh, Gregory, I didn't see you there!" I said, spinning around.

"Did you have a good night?" asked Mark.

"I did. I got to eat. I got to dance. I met someone interesting," said Gregory.

"Do tell!"

"Not yet," he said. "I don't want to jinx it."

"But seriously, Gregory, did you have a good night? Surely you weren't working all night—please tell me you didn't work all night."

"No, I didn't work all night. Once dinner was served, I sat down with the office staff at table five and ate with them. I got up periodically to check on things, but mostly I partied with them all night."

"Oh good! Because you earned this night too," I said.

Once all the guests had left, it was around 1:30 a.m. I gathered all our friends and people who worked so hard to accomplish this night.

"Friends, on behalf of Mark and myself, I want to thank you for all the immensely hard work everyone did in these past eight weeks or so. You made this night an amazing success.

"To let you know, we raised $213,563,678 dollars tonight!" Gregory shouted out.

There was an eruption of cheering that went on for five minutes as everyone celebrated the success.

"With that money, we are going to make a difference!" I shouted. "I have a little something for all of you. If you pass by our table before you leave so I can thank you in person, you can pick it up."

"Again, thank you, everyone!"

Mark helped me down from the stage and we went back to our table. There was a large rolling cart there with about three dozen packages on it. As our friends and workers came to see us, we gave out gifts and hugs.

We finished our gift-giving, and Mark took my hand and looked at me with a huge smile on his face.

"You are something else," he said to me. "I'm so proud of you! Look at what you've accomplished!"

"Thank you, love," I said. Hugging him, I said, "I couldn't have done it without you."

Excerpt from Book 5

IMMORTAL HUNT

1—After the Ball

The charity gala was done, and it was a resounding success. It was truly epic!

After working together so closely for the past three months on the gala, Falon's crew had grown very close. The threat to their lives by Derek Staung had them all strung out. Now that he and his organization had been neutralized, there was a collective feeling among the crew of, "Whew, we dodged that bullet."

This feeling of profound relief was expressed in their group hug at the end of the evening. When Justin and Rick could finally leave the kitchen and join them, the party level went up a few notches. The crew had a blast dancing until every last gala guest was gone at 1:30 am.

They were all there: Greggory, Andrews, Grisham, Parsons and his wife, Rick, Justin, Mark and Falon, as well as Gwen and

Lora—all on the floor in a circle dancing up a storm. Each of them took turns doing their thing in the middle and showing off.

The venue staff were busy cleaning up and putting everything away. They were finished by 3:30 a.m. By that time, the crew had dispersed some, with a few couples going off in corners to do more intimate kinds of celebrating.

Falon and Mark were feeling drained from the fun and stress of doing the gala, but more from the fact that they had lived with an assassin hunting them for the past few months.

"Hey, everyone," called Falon. "Why don't we blow this pop stand and go back to our place? We have some munchies and a good bar and lots of space for crashing."

Murmurs of consent from Gwen and Andrews, as well as from Rick and Lora. Justin begged off saying he had to be back at the construction site by 10:00, and, interestingly, Greggory took off with him. Andrews' staff also decided to go home. So the six of those who remained got into the limo and went back to Mark and Falon's.

"I'm so glad we all got through this night," said Falon. "It was really scary waiting to see if we would stop Derek."

"I agree," said Mark. "It was tense for a while."

"Andrews, thank you to your team for an excellent job at protecting us all," said Gwen. "I really don't want to lose my head."

There was nervous laughter.

"Yeah, that was a little too close for comfort," said Mark.

"You know that we didn't take out Derek," said Andrews. "It was the Order who did the dirty work. I saw them carrying out a body when I was heading to the head table to protect you."

"Wow, that means reaching out to them worked," said Mark.

"Yes, it seems to have. I just don't know if that put us on their radar, though."

"Mmmm, yes, I see what you mean," said Mark. They were silent for a minute or so, all contemplating what might happen if the Order came after them.

"Everyone, let's take hands," said Lora. "Now repeat after me: We survived! We are here! We will love!"

They grasped each others' hands, and repeated what she said.

"Oh, come on, people, say it with feeling!"

They all put more energy into it this time.

"Not good enough," said Lora.

"We survived! We are here! We will love!" they all screamed together.

"That's better. We will protect each other," said Lora. She got tingles down her back as they all screamed the chant together. There was something about the six of them that drew some sort of power, or created some sort of power. She couldn't place her finger on it. But being a witch, she surely felt it. It lifted the hairs on the back of her neck. "Now kiss the person on your left."

Since they were sitting in a circle in the back of the limo, Falon turned to her left and kissed Mark. Lora turned to her left and kissed Andrews. Gwen reached across and kissed Rick.

"That was nice," said Lora. "You're a good kisser, Andrews."

"So is Rick," said Gwen.

Once the limo stopped, they piled out and went into the townhouse. Rick took Lora's hand and pulled her into a hug.

"Hey, gorgeous, get comfortable with me?" he asked.

"I think so," Lora said. "Let me go to the bathroom and be right back." Lora went into the main floor powder room and took off her jewels and shoes, then took off the bra that was pinching her boobs, and the underwear that was crawling up her crack. Stuffing it all in her bag, she let down her hair and put the pins in the bag too.

"That feels better," Lora said to her reflection. Fluffing her tresses, she went out to find Rick, who had taken up the corner of one of the sofas. He had removed the jacket and vest of his tux, removed the tie and rolled up his sleeves. He'd also opened a few buttons on his shirt.

"Damn, you look good, Rick!" said Lora. "I'll just have to eat you up." Climbing onto his lap, she proceeded to kiss him ardently.

Andrews was watching with amusement. He glanced at Gwen, who was smiling like a cat with a mouse in her mouth.

"I'll be right back too," she told Andrews in a lowered voice. "Find us a sofa."

Andrews, tingling all over, shucked his clothes like Rick, and sat opposite them on another sofa. Gwen came out a few minutes later, also liberated of undergarments, and sat down beside him.

"Let's see what we have here," she teased as she undid his buttons and kissed his body down the opening to his belt.

Falon was sitting in Mark's lap, her legs swung up and over the arm of the chair while he was liberally applying kisses. He was also making good use of the slit in her dress with one of his hands. The small moans escaping her throat were turning him on even more.

"Falon, you are so sexy right now," he whispered into her ear.

"So are you," she said as she undid his tie and threw it on the floor. Next, she started to undo his shirt, reaching inside for a nipple and tweaking it with her finger.

Mark responded by inserting his finger behind her thong and caressing her mound ever so gently.

"The others are suitably engaged, they won't even notice us," he murmured into her ear.

"I don't care if they do," Falon said. "In fact, I hope they do!" She kicked off her shoes and hiked up her dress so she could straddle him. He pulled her forward so he could take a nipple that was escaping and suck on it not so gently.

The scent of pheromones and sex in the room became elevated as the three couples got more involved in what they were doing. So did the energy in the room. With four immortals aroused, the power in the room became palpable. It wasn't long before they were all emitting moans and sighs.

"Hon, there is not enough room in this chair," complained Mark. "Let me move the chair and table out of the way."

He slid the chair back and moved the table clear of the room, then brought the cushions back. They sat down on the cushions where the chair had been. Falon then straddled Mark with her dress basically gathered around her hips. She was working on removing his shirt, as he had already taken off the jacket and vest.

"That's a good idea," said Lora. She got up and pulled Rick to a standing position, then grabbed all the cushions off the sofa and piled them up on the floor. Rick then stretched out on the floor using the cushions to lean on. Lora stretched out with him.

Sensing this infusion of power again, Lora asked into the quiet, "So would anyone be interested in having sex together?" A couple of people shifted. Lora wasn't sure whether it was discomfort or something else. She scanned the group: all the immortals' eyes were glowing with power, arousal, and interest, even Falon's.

"No one is into a little kink?" she asked again. "We could start slow, by swapping partners."

"I don't know if I want anyone else," said Mark.

"Oh, that's because you've already done it," said Gwen. Falon looked at Mark questioningly.

"Yes, I've participated in such things," he said.

"I haven't," said Falon. "But I'm willing to experiment."

"Who would you have gone with?" asked Gwen.

"Mark takes me, you take Rick, and Falon gets Andrews," said Lora.

Everyone thought about that while looking at each other—and in particular their new potential partner.

"We can make it a game," said Lora.

"How so?" Asked Andrews.

"The girl chooses the kink, the boy sets the method," said Gwen. "For example, I choose to be submissive." Her eyes were starting to glow as she imagined the play.

"And I choose to be the dominant," said Rick. His eyes were glowing ever so slightly.

"Okay, I choose multiple penetration," said Lora.

"Then I'll choose the toys," said Mark.

"Well, what would you like?" Andrews asked Falon. "I'm experienced in all kinds of kink."

"Hmm, I'll choose submission too," she said.

"I will choose master then," said Andrews.

"Now what?" asked Falon.

Rick got up and went to Gwen and looked down on her. She rolled her eyes downward and immediately went into a submissive position. "On your knees, Gwen," he said.

She sank to her knees. "What's your safe word, Gwen?"

"Clock."

He took his tie and tied her wrists behind her back. He walked around her and spanked her ass. The sound of skin on skin resonated in the room. Gwen cried out and then moaned as her body enjoyed the spanking. Rick alternated between spanking and caressing.

"Were you naughty?" he asked.

"I was very naughty. Punish me."

Rick slapped the other cheek, then gently brushed his fingers across her skin, giving her gooseflesh and taking the sting out of the slap. Each slap made her moan as he caressed it. Her arousal was building, releasing pheromones that fed the others too, not just Rick. He had a cockstand that needed attention.

Moving in front of her, he pushed his cock into her face. She opened her mouth and searched for it with her tongue. As he pushed himself in her mouth, she scraped her teeth across his skin. When she sealed her lips around his shaft and started sucking, he almost lost it.

He took her head and held it as he gently moved in and out of her mouth. She was biting down and giving him little shocks of venom. He was about to lose control, so he pulled out suddenly. She whimpered at the loss of her toy. Rick untied her hands in the back and retied them in the front. With the extra mobility, she took hold of his cock and pumped him hard, then drew him into her mouth deeply, purring deep in her throat, and bit his penis. He instinctively started pumping deeper, and as his arousal grew she took him deeper so that when he came he was nearly completely buried down her throat. She grabbed his balls as he ejaculated, gently squeezing them, making him gasp, and cry out.

Rick pulled out and knelt on the floor beside Gwen, undoing all the ties. Gwen glanced at the others.

"Falon, come here and sit," demanded Andrews as he walked to another cushion. Andrews handed Falon a blindfold and told her to put it on. Then he told her to lie down on her stomach. He raised her arms above her head and tied them together with his tie.

"We don't proceed without a safe word," he whispered in her ear.

"How about 'cookie?'" said Falon.

"That will work."

Standing behind her, he pushed her dress over her hips, exposing her ass.

Andrews spanked Falon on her ass and her breath caught in surprise. He kissed away the sting and slapped the other side, again making her gasp, and kissing away the hurt.

Falon was getting aroused in spite of herself. When Andrews took two fingers and played with her vagina, her body responded by getting very wet. He used her own plentiful juices to lube two fingers and pushed them into her anus. This time, the surprise and the pain made her cry out again. But that was quickly overtaken by him penetrating her vagina. She groaned deeply as she felt his fingers and his cock push deep inside.

Andrews nodded and thrust even harder into Falon, making her cry out again. Then he pulled out and was hovering at her opening, not going in. Falon squirmed. She started to speak, but

Andrews spanked her for talking, then pulled away from her entirely.

"You are not allowed to move," he told her. "No matter what you hear."

Falon whimpered quietly, her body so hungry to be fucked hard it ached. But she held her tongue and stayed like that, face on the floor, ass high in the air.

Lora had sidled up to Mark when Falon left, removed her dress and pressed her body up against Mark's, grinding. Mark's eyes started glowing like the other immortals, and his body responded. She showed him several dildos, and he chose one that was as large as himself. She presented her ass to him and he started to stimulate her, getting her wet.

Lora was wiggling her pussy in front of Mark. He took hold of her hips and buried his nose in her scent, kissing and licking, making her even more excited. He used some fingers in her vagina to bring her close to climax, and stopped before she got too far. He then took one of his fingers, licked it, and inserted it into her anus. Lora squealed with delight and wiggled even more. Moving his finger, he stretched her anus and applied the lube that she handed him. When she was suitably slick, he started inserting the dildo.

Mark was watching Lora's ass as he pushed the dildo in. Her hips were bucking and she was very excited. Getting up on his knees, he rubbed his cock in her opening and pushed inside her vagina. Lora immediately started keening and moaning, her body pushing back on him to get him deeper inside. She handed him another dildo and started pumping her hips against him. For a minute Mark wondered what to do with it. He glanced at Rick for explanation.

Rick was watching Mark. When he saw Lora give him a second dildo, he knew the answer to Mark's question. He went over to them and told Mark she wanted two in one hole. Mark looked surprised.

"Are you secure in your masculinity?" Rick asked Mark.

"I think I am."

"Let's try something, then," he said. "Lora, do you want the two of us?"

"Oh my God, yes!" she cried. "Separate from me, Mark, just a moment."

He pulled away and Lora turned around and straddled Rick, taking him deep into her vagina. Then she bent over flattening herself against his body, exposing her ass.

Mark looked at them, and asked, "Now what?"

Use a dildo in my ass, and join Rick in my vagina," she said matter-of-factly.

Mark lubed the dildo and inserted it in her ass carefully. Rick and she were groaning with the sensations. Then he lubed his own cock and started to push into her vagina. *Oh fuck it was tight!* Rick gasped loudly as he felt Mark join him. The sensations were wild. Lora was humming with pleasure. Mark kept pushing. He could feel Rick next to him, moving, and it stimulated his cock too.

By the time he had most of his cock inside, all three were gasping with the pain and pleasure of it—in particular Lora, because they were well-endowed cocks.

The guys synchronized their rhythms and thrust together to the maximum. Mark pushed in deeper and Rick indicated he was close to climax because the sensation of the two penises rubbing each other was nearly too much to bear. The men stopped what they were doing for a moment.

Lora couldn't take that. She was moaning between them and couldn't stay still. Her hips kept moving in rhythm on them both, delighted in the fullness, her breath taken away.

As Lora moved herself on the two cocks, Mark's vision started to blur from the arousal. The pressure from her very tight vagina and feeling of Rick next to him inside her was making his head swim.

Gwen was watching this, very aroused. She was watching Andrews and Falon and decided to join their duo to make it a trio too. Picking up a double-ended dildo from the toys, she walked over to Andrews where he was bent over Falon. Gwen lubed up one end and plunged it into Andrews' ass and watched as he yelped and then moaned.

"Ah God, it's been a while—keep going," he said, in a voice thick with arousal. Gwen put the other end into herself and smashed them together. As Andrews was fucking Falon, she was fucking him and getting fucked herself. A win-win-win.

Gwen circled her own clit with her fingers. All three of them were linked as their arousal climbed together. Close to their climax, their hearts all synchronized as they crested the wave as one. Gwen reached across Andrews and placed her hand in Falon's mouth, encouraging her to bite down. She then sank her teeth into Andrews' shoulder, and then Falon's. The venom pushed them to euphoria as they finished.

Lora's threesome came to a blinding climax at the same time. Mark bit Lora, then Andrews. Their hearts had synchronized like the other trio, and all three were screaming and moaning until they collapsed in a heap.

The two trios slumped on the floor in one heap of entangled bodies. Eventually, they all came back to consciousness.

Falon was first. She panicked when she couldn't see, but then remembered she was blindfolded. Her hands were still bound and there was a body on top of her. Gwen became conscious next, and pulled away from Andrews, removing the dildo. She untied Falon and removed her blindfold. Andrews had separated from Falon, sprawled with his head on her stomach. He was still slightly hard.

Falon looked at Gwen and smiled. She felt very close to her now. When she realized it was Andrews who had penetrated her, she got a sizzle inside. She had wanted to fuck him. When Andrews opened his eyes, the first thing he saw was Falon's pussy. His cock stood up immediately. He remembered what Gwen had done to him, and that brought back memories of the experimenting he had done in college with his roommate. It had been enjoyable, but nothing like what it was with Gwen.

Rick, Lora, and Mark were entangled in an interesting way. As Andrews looked at them, he realized that Rick had shared Lora with Mark. They both had penetrated her.

Mark was on top, so he straightened up and disengaged his cock from Lora. When he did, Rick also came out, so she had a small river of semen coming out of her. Mark went to find a towel. Lora was lying on top of Rick, and she wasn't awake yet.

Rick woke up when Mark pulled out. The sensation triggered another hard-on, and his now hard cock pushed up against Lora. Mark returned with hot water, towels, and cloths for them all to clean up. Lora woke up just as Rick took the dildo out of her ass.

Mark realized that Falon was with Andrews and Gwen. He felt a jealous surge rise up in his gut and he didn't know why. There was really no reason. He decided he was going to let that go once and for all. They had all survived a life-threatening event and had all just shared in life-affirming sex games with each other. *Let's leave the possessiveness outside.*

By some unheard yet agreed-upon signal, they gathered all the cushions together and then cuddled in one pile, intertwined and in contact, hands on breasts, on cocks, on asses, touching intimately and completely comfortable with it.

A breakthrough seemed to have happened.

As day broke and sunshine filtered in through the curtains, they were yawning and stretching, still in contact with each other. They looked like a puppy pile.

Gwen broke the silence.

"Well, that was fun!" she said.

All of them burst into laughter.

"That was truly remarkable," answered Mark.

"I had fun," said Lora.

"You started it," said Gwen.

"I finished it," said Andrews.

"You certainly did, my wonderful human," said Gwen. "Which is something I want to correct."

"Are you going to ask for permission from the family council?" asked Mark.

"No, because you were put through hell when you did," said Gwen. "I'm not going to."

"Get permission," he said. "It's easier in the long run."

"Fine," said Gwen. "I will."

"Wow, what a ride!" said Rick, waking up. "How's everyone feeling?"

"I'm surprisingly not sore," said Lora.

"Neither am I," said Falon. "We have to make Andrews an immortal."

"Can we make Lora one too?" asked Rick.

"Oh! That would be interesting, an immortal witch," said Lora.

"Well, we could have our own ceremony," said Mark. Gwen grinned and glanced at Falon.

"Can we participate again?" she asked.

"In the ceremony?" asked Gwen.

"Ya, why not?" asked Falon. "It's just another excuse to have heart-stopping sex with my guy." She looked over at Mark and their eyes connected, like they had so many years ago in that bar. The heat coming off them was palpable to the other immortals.

"Okay, you two, enough of that," Gwen chided them.

"I want to be able to bite my lover too," said Lora.

"Gwen, do you realize that we've gone from lonely immortal singles to creating our own close group of immortal friends?" said Mark. "What a small miracle." He was looking at Falon when he said that.

"I feel blessed," said Gwen.

"So do I," said Rick. "I never believed I would find community and love by other beings like myself."

"We are a community," said Falon.

"Indeed," said Andrews and Lora.

"Who's making breakfast? I'm starved!" cried Lora.

What's Next

Book 5 - Immortal Hunt.

Our six immortals have an expedition to Cuba and the Caribbean, looking for their ancestors and more immortals. They find more than they bargained for.

Magic, time travel, and lots of hot steamy scenes to keep the pace fast, fun, and interesting.

There may be a pirate or two as well.

About The Author

Linda Ashton Trott

Ms Trott, a native of Montreal, Canada, currently lives in the nation's capital with her husband of twenty-four years, their four cats, and eight Japanese Koi.

When not writing, Ms Trott can be found in their backyard relaxing by the pond or editing her husband's stories.

Ms Trott has always had an interest in all things supernatural, the occult, UFOs, aliens, and the paranormal. It seemed natural to combine one or more of these elements into a unique universe in which to tell interesting stories.

These are not children's stories. "It's funny, I never sat down with the intention of writing Adult books," Linda once said. "But here they are. I wanted to express physical love honestly without cutesy acronyms and vague names."

These stories contain explicit language and hot, steamy sex scenes that will leave you panting.

Books In This Series

The Immortal Stories Series

The Immortals are a race of beings that came to Earth many tens of thousands of years ago. Their stories stretch across time and have become woven into the history of humans. Their society is hidden from humans even though they live among them. Forbidden from developing romantic liaisons with humans, some break the rules and form close bonds and get married. But this always comes with consequences.

1 - Immortal Desire

One immortal and one human.

As Zisis's world collides with Falon's, she is left to cope and deal with the blowback. Their love affair is erotic, passionate, and stirs the soul, but it is ill-fated. This is a story of romance, heartbreak, hardship, and survival. The sex is hot and steamy, the highs euphoric, and the lows devastating.

2 - Immortal Fulfillment

What a twist! What has Mark done?

After a nasty life twist has her rethinking a relationship with her Texan, Falon needs to decide which direction to go. Is she back to square one? Certainly not! Between hurricanes, hot tub invites, and road trips with hot, sexy guys, there is plenty of action and adventure.

3 - Immortal Peril

The Family is NOT happy!

Lora meets Rick, a talented dessert chef in an up-and-coming restaurant in Atlanta, Georgia, while visiting her best friend, Falon, who is on contract work there. Lora and Rick hit it off in ways she can't believe—one hot weekend in Miami and she can't get him out of her mind. So, when invited to Atlanta again, this time by Rick, she doesn't hesitate!

When Mark disappears without a trace, Falon is left to find out what happened.

4 - Immortal Victory

Out of the fire and into the frying pan!

Falon gets out of one problem only to find herself in danger again. An ancient enemy is targeting the immortals and will stop at nothing to eliminate them. Dodging assassins and traps, Falon decides to end homelessness, one person at a time.

Her BFF Lora discovers that true love sex generates magical energy while she looks for her ancestors.

Gwen finds a partner in Andrews.

5 - Immortal Hunt

Having just survived a coordinated attack from an ancient enemy, the immortals rejoice and celebrate their success. Attention turns toward locating their ancestors when a news item catches Lora's attention and gives her a very important clue to finding them. The immortals are off on a great adventure to distant places. Pirates, witches, time travel, spooky castles, and volcanic caves are some of the encounters happening this time. Don't miss out on the adventure!

6 - Immortal Nexus

New is old, and old is new

Surely, saving a coven of witches from a pocket dimension would be a highlight in life. But it's not. The immortals return home to everyday life; family, moving, school, raising teens, and of course, spicy lovemaking.

We meet a new character with a deep past. And when a new couple moves in across the street, Falon notices some familiar characteristics. She makes it her mission to meet the new neighbors.

Family matters are front and center in this story. The close-knit group of immortals is becoming a family, and some stories need sharing like Andrews' tale of being hired by aliens.

Justin and Rick finally open the new restaurant. It was a New Year's Eve celebration with a bang!

7 - Immortal Generation — Coming 2023

Short Stories

First Contact: An Immortal Origin Story

The Immortal's Origin Story started 33,000 years ago, when they arrived on Earth. *First Contact* follows the story of how the immortals meet the first humans and what happens when they interact and live together.

Praise for the Series

What are readers saying about this new series?

"Yet again I've got an ARC for this author and I've got to say that these books just get better and better. I loved this one [Book 6] and it is my favourite so far out of the series. There is now so many new people with there own stories that I don't think it will get boring any time soon. My favourite couple were Falon and Mark but I have quickly fallen in love with Margaret and Abeo and I didn't see the twist and turns right at the end. Brilliant book by a brilliant author."

... Sam ***** Amazon

"Linda Ashton Trott has a real gift for crafting intricate sex scenes that are highly charged and also entirely believable. She really brings you into the bedroom in a joyful way. The will-they-or-won't-they story keeps you wondering, right up to the plot twist at the end, which sets readers up for Book 2."

... Amy **** Amazon

"Ohhhhh! This book was good! Hot hot scenes with enough of a story in between to keep you hooked. We all need to become Leopard Ladies! Nice quick read. Can't wait to read book 2 of the series!"

... Josée **** Goodreads

"Brilliant book loved the storyline and I couldn't put it down once I started. I loved the characters and got really absorbed in to their lives and feelings.

all I can say is Wow I loved every part of it (#3). I'm really sad that the book ended the way it did as I wanted to carry on reading and finding out what was going to happen. I love this series and all the characters. Hopefully there should be another one."

... Sam ***** Amazon

"Picking up where the first book ended, this installment of the series was the heroine's journey of self-discovery in order to make the right decisions for her, something I really enjoyed!

This book was sexy, fun and the character development was great! Ioved how the heroine slowly took back control of her life and found empowerment in her spontaneity."

...Nikita **** Goodreads

"wow! amazing, fast paced and enthralling new world! Wonderful characters that charmed me from the beginning. Honestly this was a wonderfully perfect read to help me escape from the world for a bit.

Amazing (#3). I love this world and it's characters. Great storyline and well written. This series has been amazing to read. Definitely need to pick them up."

*... Naomi ***** Amazon*

"Yet again I'm absolutely totally blown away by this book (#4). I love the characters and the story line. Linda has written a fantastic book with steamy scenes that I didn't think were possible but brilliant. I loved the fact that we're now starting to see smaller named characters have a bigger role. It's very well written and can't wait to read more of the series."

*...Sam ***** Amazon*

Being an Indie Author

I've chosen to publish independently. This means I don't have the big machine of a traditional publishing company behind me. Reviews are very important on Amazon because they determine how visible you are in the marketplace. That makes your review, and every other review I receive, the most important tool in my marketing toolbox. If you've enjoyed reading this book, please consider spending a few minutes leaving me a review on Amazon. It doesn't have to be long.

Thank you!

See my website at www.lindaashtontrott.com to join the mailing list. You will not be inundated with mail, I promise! It will let you know when the latest book is released and if there are freebies.

Visit my Amazon author's page at
https://www.amazon.com/~/e/B09TG29J19